The
New
Girl

The New Girl

Harriet Walker

HODDER &
STOUGHTON

First published in Great Britain in 2020 by Hodder & Stoughton
An Hachette UK company

1

Copyright © Harriet Walker 2020

A CIP catalogue record for this title is available from the British Library

Hardback ISBN 9781529304008
Trade Paperback ISBN 9781529304022
eBook ISBN 9781529304015

Typeset by Hewer Text UK Ltd, Edinburgh
Printed and bound in Great Britain by Clays Ltd, Elcograf S.p.A.

Hodder & Stoughton policy is to use papers that are natural, renewable
and recyclable products and made from wood grown in sustainable
forests. The logging and manufacturing processes are expected to
conform to the environmental regulations of the country of origin.

Hodder & Stoughton Ltd
Carmelite House
50 Victoria Embankment
London EC4Y 0DZ

www.hodder.co.uk

For Moomy and Pops, who got me here
because they got themselves so far

The
New
Girl

It looked like she had fallen from the sky.

She was lying on the floor in front of them all, a small puddle of black ink blooming next to her head.

The drum and thud of footfalls died as shoes slowed and stopped, then began to arrange themselves around her. The busy swish of people passing quieted to a few mere shuffles and gasps. Even those subsided within seconds, like coughs at a recital. The chatter of a hundred mouths stopped, as if they had been gagged.

Beyond her – beyond the scene and heedless of the shocked pause it demanded of the onlookers – the world continued. Raindrops broke on the windows; a bird sang in imitation of a mobile phone. In the distance, a door slammed somewhere – the wind must have closed it, because all human activity was, for now, on hiatus for this frozen moment. For her.

Above the body stood two young women, a tableau in symmetry of dumbstruck horror: hands clamped to mouths, eyes roving wildly around the hall – looking everywhere, enquiring urgently of everyone – except in one direction.

The women would not look at each other.

They would never ask each other that question.

The farther the black ink travelled along the pistachio lino-leum, the paler and less viscous it became, and the more it began to look like what it really was: blood.

PART ONE

I

Margot Jones

I first felt the baby move the day Winnie's son was born. Born, and died an hour later.

I had just stepped from the shower and wrapped a towel around my torso when, deep within, there came a faint throb of activity. A not-quite-roll but a barrelling sensation nonetheless, like cresting a dip in the road. A single kick of a swimming stroke, a fillip, a half-pipe completed in utero: the quickening.

It made me gasp, and feel faintly nauseous at the idea of something living inside me. Blame science fiction. Once, this moment spoke of the miracle of life, of the Divine Countenance smiling on the humble and the highborn alike, but these days, every pregnant woman's reference point is an alien escaping a man's chest cavity in a spray of gore.

I smiled then, as the goosebumps on my arms subsided. Later, I would remember my brief shiver of disgust and feel ashamed.

In those same minutes, Winnie's boy was hurtling through hospital corridors in a tiny plastic cot, traces of his mother's blood still clinging to his purplish limbs. By the time I saw the blur of messages and medical terms on my phone from my oldest friend – his heart had slowed, then rallied – and replied to them in a tumble of horror and relief, it had happened.

The next said, simply, *He's dead.*

I called, but there was no answer. It didn't cross my mind then that I might never speak to my best friend again, but the hollowing sensation that replaced the earlier sprightliness in my gut seemed to presage it – that this awful, awful thing might be the first in twenty years we wouldn't be able to face together. Once the well-wishers disperse and the casserole dishes have been returned, once time goes on and the seasons continue to change, mourning a child is a lonely business.

I left a voicemail and, after I hung up, couldn't remember a word of what I had said. I sent a text: 'I'm so sorry, I love you, I'm here when you need me.'

I have to get to work. I was due back in the office today after almost a month away at the shows. When I'd started out as an assistant and general dogsbody, I only went to fashion week in London, and even then on the sort of ticket that promised, at best, a standing spot at the back of a draughty hall or warehouse. From there, I'd had to crane my neck for a glimpse of the otherworldly creations below the models' chins.

In those days, I remembered designers' collections for the soundtrack and the hairstyles rather than the clothes – those I looked at online afterwards. As I climbed the career rungs, I realised why so many fashion editors were obsessed with shoes: you could only see them once you'd secured your spot on the front row.

This season, I had been to New York, Paris, and Milan too, as I'd done twice a year for the past decade. Except this time, I carried my little swimmer with me, sat cocooning it on hard benches and plush brocade chairs, ushered him or her (we wouldn't find out which, Nick didn't want to) beyond the velvet ropes and black-clad doormen at designer parties and luxury store openings, clinking champagne coupes without drinking from them.

I laughed at my extra passenger when I thought about how impossible it was to smuggle in a plus-one at these events – especially one who was quite so intent on locating and polishing off whatever elegantly minuscule amuse-bouche happened to be offered on silver platters by waiters who looked like they'd been hewn from marble.

But I was back in London now and had to get to the office. They were choosing my maternity cover today. The person who would take over the job I'd spent ten hard years working for. The prospect of handing it over had seemed appalling, until now. All I could think of now was the little life that had failed to launch just a few miles away.

Winnie and I had been together just that weekend, chatting and giggling. Planning the months we would spend, loosed from our desks and free to roam in daylight hours, with each other and our tiny companions. A new coffee place with regulation bare brickwork and lightbulbs hanging on industrial cable had opened a few minutes' walk down the road from my and Nick's house, and Winnie's bus stopped right outside it.

Winnie knew she was having a boy, had asked the sonographer to let her know as soon as he could tell. She wanted to be able to plan for him and to name him, she said, when I teased her about being a control freak. He had been Jack since twenty weeks.

I had gone to the loo in Winnie's home – I seemed to spend most of my time sitting on one now, squeezing out a few drops every half an hour even though my bladder felt constantly full – and marvelled at the rows of tiny white bodysuits hanging up to dry in my friend's bathroom. Then again at the slatted wooden cot made up with bright white sheets, the changing table stocked with nappies, cotton wool, various lotions that even I had never heard of despite having to write about obscure and esoteric-sounding beauty products every so often at work.

Winnie had always been more maternal than me, calmer, more patient, and more instinctive. Kinder, too. She would be such a natural mother that I was grateful for the five months between her due date and mine – five months of expert nurturing that I'd be able to crib from Winnie just as I had my best friend's science notes at school.

I sat on the bus to the office, chest tight at the thought of all that prep, all the folding, stacking, straightening, the lining up of things just so for when Jack finally arrived; eyes stinging at the prospect of Winnie and her husband, Charles, going home to a house so loaded with anticipation it had practically hummed last weekend. I had a vision of their redbrick terrace itself sagging with grief when two, rather than three, reentered it that evening.

They had seemed so ready to be parents – vibrating with potential, sparkling with nervous excitement. As Winnie had nested so thoroughly, Charles had been tying up loose ends at work. His plan was to be at home with them both for the first six weeks of Jack's life.

'We'll probably end up killing each other,' Winnie had laughed last Sunday. 'Being under each other's feet for so long.'

I doubted either of them would even raise their voice to the other in that time. They never did.

There was not a note of disharmony between them, as Charles went back and forth from the kitchen, bringing us mugs of tea, fetching the various baby props that Winnie called out for in her show-and-tell for me of what they had amassed ahead of the birth. He'd been as enthusiastic as she was, as pregnant with the father that he would become as she was full of baby.

More than just another protective husband, Charles reminded me of those dogs that refuse to budge from their pregnant owner's side. He couldn't do enough for Winnie; he was devoted to her. He had learned foot massage from YouTube. When the time came for them to say goodbye to me, he stood next to her on the front step with his arm protectively around her as they waved me off.

The next scene should have been his opening the door to me to introduce his brand-new son. Not this.

I usually read the news on my phone on my journey into work, but today my eyes absorbed no sense of the words in front of them. As the double-decker made its way through the smog-hazy streets of southeast London, I tried to reconcile the Jack we had all been waiting for, and all the potential he represented, with this dead baby, cried and keened over instead of cuddled and cooed at, still now where he had squirmed under the tight skin of Winnie's belly only days ago.

It was as though I had woken in a parallel universe, showered and dressed in one and boarded the number 40 to this bizarre new destination. Back in the real world, Jack was surely freshly delivered this morning, warm and snuffly in his mother's arms – arms that, as my most adored friend and loyal champion, Winnie had pressed around me so many times, too.

But my own baby had now moved in this alternate reality. It had asserted its presence, its existence, its claim on me and on the world. And it was the most real – the most alive – thing I had ever felt.

The candidates were lined up along one wall by the time I arrived at the office, their glossy heads bent over the screens in their hands as they sat beneath a supersized plastic rendering of the magazine's logo: HAUTE. It was one of Moff's favourite tricks, the placing of the hopeful under this rather literal beacon.

I knew my boss well enough to realise she art-directed almost every aspect of her life. A newshound first and foremost, Moff saw stories everywhere: shoots, page layouts, and headlines were her daily bread. Two women vying with each other for the rare chance to work at one of the country's most successful fashion magazines – if only for the time that I was on maternity leave – was precisely the sort of real-life scoop that its editor in chief, Emily Moffatt, thrived on. I wouldn't have put it past her to commission the one not chosen to write about the experience for the next issue.

I hurried past them without looking too closely, grateful that my pregnant stomach wasn't obvious just yet, that I still appeared much like the two sleek, well-dressed women who had come to jostle for my position. Though not among the hungriest-looking portion of the fashion industry, I am tall and fairly slim, and I knew with healthy cynicism that this would be a valuable asset for the power play to come during this morning's interviews. *Not waddling and irrelevant just yet, thanks very much.*

As much as Moff was looking for a stand-in as quick and efficient a writer as her current fashion editor, I was all too aware that my boss would also have a beady eye on how each candidate might look on camera and on the cover, how each might carry off the eye-wateringly expensive designer clothes that hung as higgledy-piggledy and as tightly packed as charity shop donations in the fashion cupboard down the hall.

When I'd arrived as an intern all those years ago, I had been ushered into that cupboard by Moff's PA and instructed to 'give it a bit of a tidy'.

There was a lot about working at *Haute* that didn't quite live up to *The Devil Wears Prada* paradigm I had arrived with fresh in my mind, aged twenty-two, a month after I'd seen it in the cinema. The freezing-cold office loos that the male bike couriers dropping off logoed garment bags would sneak into to read their tabloids between jobs; the greasy smell of bacon rolls wafting in from Spiros's café on the landing; the blokes from upstairs who worked on *Goal!* and scratched themselves in the lifts; and the mice that regularly appeared beneath the wheels of my office chair to eat the box of cereal I left on my desk.

But it was the state of its fashion cupboard that was the greatest point of divergence from that industry fairy tale. I remembered a time when my eyes, like everyone else's, had lit up at the prospect of seeing inside it. I had expected – *as everyone had after that bloody movie* – something like a pristine designer boutique, with bottom-lit shelves and discreet house music, shoes and bags in neat rows along each wall as if ready to purchase.

My disappointment at the sight that had greeted me instead was so strong it bordered on disgust. The size of a bathroom – a small one at that – with shelves lining each wall from floor to ceiling and four clothes rails standing in rows in the middle, its floor was waist-deep, from the door to the window on the far wall, with stiff, luxurious carrier bags from the sort of boutiques that I had, at that point, only ever read about.

Out of them spilled satin stilettos in rich jewel colours, crocodile handbags studded with rose-gold rivets and spikes, printed silk blouses, frothy tulle skirts, leather, denim, shiny lamé, and sparkling sequins. All sent in for the editors and stylists to pick from, to photograph on the hottest models for their pages, to try on and write about, to hype, to hero-worship, to shout about, and to shill – and for the assistants, supposedly, to send back once they were finished with them.

I had never seen such beautiful things close up, had certainly never touched anything like them, never before tried such things on (until the door had been closed on me), but neither had I witnessed such nonchalance towards things that cost triple my monthly salary or more. I had been careful of my belongings from a young age, neat and rigorous, and respectful of an object's worth – not to mention its price. I realised then the gulf between me and the women beyond the door. For them beauty and money were equally disposable, because they had an infinite supply of each.

I liked to think that Moff had hired me for my sparkling prose, my witty repartee, and a writing style that sang from the page – all of which the boss had indeed come to appreciate in her fashion editor – but I knew in my heart that I'd got the job for transforming that cupboard from a yard sale into a lending library.

I had taken a deep breath to steady myself, then cleared the floor of its glamorous debris, lining up the smaller items on shelves initialled according to which editor had requested them and when they'd arrived, and the clothing on hangers ordered by their designer names and the season's trends. Every so often a single shoe or earring would rise like flotsam and jetsam to the top of the pile, and I'd set it aside in the hope of making it once again part of a pair.

I uncovered things that the team had long since assumed were lost and had been charged the full price for by the labels' furious PRs – a fur coat that went straight to Moff's corner office, which she had worn on a semiregular basis every winter since; a diamond hairslide that Trina, the beauty editor, had clipped in on her wedding day; a bias-cut silk sheath dress that Laura, the then-fashion editor, packed for the shows every season, with a theatrical wink directed at me but done for the rest of the office's benefit.

'Many thanks, Miss Jones! Fashion's most fabulous cleaning lady!' she'd trill.

That had stung a bit. My beginnings admittedly were more ordinary than those of the rest of the women in the office, many of whom came less from family homes than from dynastic seats, but I'd hardly grown up on the breadline. Still, my Northern accent and the fact I'd caught Moff's eye for clearing up after them was too delightful a Cinderella narrative not to stick.

I blushed and shrugged: among my finds was a crumpled gabardine trench coat of the sort I liked to imagine Jackie O throwing on over a black sweater and cigarette pants, something for which I would have had to save for several years to buy from the label, and that would have caused me severe angst had I ever had to part with quite so much money for it in a shop.

It was mine, they told me, for the amazing job I'd done for them – little expecting that, ten years on, I'd still be in the office. Still wearing that trench occasionally, in fact, only now more senior than all of them.

I still hadn't heard from Winnie by the time the first interview was scheduled to start. I found I couldn't put the tragedy from my mind without another vision of the little cotton hats I'd bought for Jack, the ridiculously small socks we'd both been laughing at on Sunday, the plastic bath propped up beside the sink, floating into my head.

I could hardly believe I hadn't cried yet – thanks to the pregnant hormonal fug I existed in, I'd found myself welling up regularly at TV ads for donkey sanctuaries and life insurance in recent weeks. Instead I felt my friend's grief as a dull physical ache, in my throat, my heart, my shaking hands, and my stomach, where all fluttering had given way to a sadness as still and as heavy as a boulder. *Perhaps there is an unhappiness beyond tears that is just pain.*

I couldn't tell Moff: I wouldn't know how to say it and she wouldn't know how to hear it. It'd sound like something out of a schmaltzy TV programme. *That's the only place you hear about children dying. Children die every day and we just pretend it doesn't happen.* I didn't want to risk bursting into tears in front of my boss: Moff wasn't good with emotions. She'd be shocked and standoffish, and then she would almost certainly send me home. The last thing I wanted was to be alone today.

So I hung my coat up behind my desk and smoothed the oversized shirt I had on underneath with a pair of indigo jeans. *Not in maternity-wear yet!* I rummaged in my stiff leather handbag (pregnancy notes, prenatal vitamins, water bottle, makeup bag) for the black leather pochette that contained my phone, security pass, and notebook, and headed into the glass-walled meeting room next door to Moff's office.

The two women who had applied to cover my job knew me already. They recognised me from my byline photo, an unflatteringly cropped headshot that I loathed and that accompanied most of my articles, right next to my name along the top. They knew me from my seat at the shows, where elaborately calligraphed cards are placed on cushions or at intentionally narrow-hipped intervals on white benches to signify whose bottom goes where. While attendees scan for their own names along the length of the catwalk, they take in the rest as they go, either to drop ambitiously into conversation later on or so they can take merciless aim at that person's perceived failings in the privacy of their own clique.

I had told Moff I had a vague idea of who the two newcomers were, too. In truth, I knew exactly. I had put the same effort into researching my potential replacements as I would into finding my baby's carer once I was ready to come back. This job might not have been performing backflips in my stomach, but it was just as much a part of me. Full-on, often stressful, sometimes infuriating, but fun and fast-paced: I loved it. Only the most capable pair of hands would do.

A woman capable of following Moff's orders, and equally capable of fucking off again in a year's time.

The first, whom I knew from the society pages, was married to a tinned-food company heir worth millions. I saw Moff's interest pique at the sheer wealth this woman exuded, at her perfect hair caught back in a ponytail that hung down over one shoulder, her glowing skin and buffed nude nails, the pterodactyl-wing elbows that come from consuming just enough calories to function. Her doll-like frame was clad in perfectly fitting black trousers, a simple turtleneck, and a pair of loafers that almost every editor was on the waiting list for.

My blood ran cold at the prospect of this woman's occupying my desk; I had always been uncomfortable around people this rich and this polished. I knew I was being touchy and insecure (Winnie always upbraided me for it, wagging a finger and tutting: 'not attractive!') but this woman was everything I wasn't, and if she ended up doing my job, Moff might realise how much its original incumbent was lacking in. The confidence that comes with a certain type of education, the presence that gloss and beauty can bestow, the easy chitchat born of an innate knowledge that other people will want to listen. *Absolutely not.*

While Moff tittered at the woman's anecdotes and enquired about other horsey people they had in common, I worked out my strategy. I suspected that someone who didn't strictly need the money the role came with was likely to flinch at the devotion that Moff required of all her staffers. I threw her a few examples of late nights in the office to finish the pages ahead of print deadlines, of writing breaking news on my phone in the street in the rain, of filing a story within minutes to make sure *Haute*'s was the very first online.

The woman's deep-set dark eyes widened on either side of her aristocratic nose. *Too easy!* She'd politely retract her interest by email on her way home in a cab.

'And so now we have . . .' Moff looked at the next résumé, once the first interviewee had swished from the meeting room and the second taken a seat on the other side of the red Perspex table. 'Margot?'

'Oh no,' a warm voice corrected her as its owner slid her arms from the sleeves of a well-cut dark blazer. 'It says that on my résumé, but I've never been a Margot – too formal and fusty for me.' The woman beamed, all telephone-box red lips and tumbling dark curls.

'I'm Maggie.'

2

Maggie Beecher

She almost *died* when she realised what she'd said. Formal!
Fusty! Only about the woman's actual name – the name her
eyes had danced over for years every time she read an issue of
Haute, and the name on the masthead inside that hers might
well have replaced. She guessed it wouldn't now. *Christ,
Maggie, what an idiot move.*

She was always being told, usually by men on building
sites or in pubs, that she had a big mouth – with bright red
lipstick on, it was one of her best features – but it had never
felt big enough to get both feet in it at the same time. Until
now. What could she say? She was terrible when she was
nervous.

And she was *really* nervous about this interview. These jobs
don't come up very often – why would they? It's a pretty plush
deal, being fashion editor of a glossy magazine.

You sit there writing about nice things, while the people
who make the nice things send them to you, so you can see
exactly how nice they are. You travel a lot – to fashion week,
sure, but also to interview beautiful, glamorous people in
beautiful, exotic locations, and sometimes simply because a
brand who wants to get on your good side has enough money
to take you there.

Let's just say it was a job she could definitely see herself
doing, at least for a year or so until Margot Jones wanted it
back. Maggie would be more than happy to keep Margot's
seat warm for her.

To the fashion editor's credit, she was nice about it. As Maggie was trying to disguise the full-body cringe her mistake had triggered, Margot smiled and threw her a lifeline.

'Maggie, hi! I never knew you were a Margot, there's always more of us than I realise. How are you?'

What Maggie was tempted to say, by way of an apology, was that the woman opposite her was a total Margot, every inch an M-a-r-g-o-t, in the way she was so, so not. She had never lived up to her elegant name: she was short and busty, a bit crass, and prone to excruciating social gaffes.

The other Margot was tall and willowy – tidy – with long, straight blond hair and very clear, pale skin. She looked immaculate, as always, even though she was probably feeling ropy as fuck underneath it all. How pregnant was she anyway? She couldn't be that far along. Maggie was more bloated than she was, especially when she'd got her arms stuck in the sleeves of the blazer she'd borrowed from her flatmate, Cath.

But Maggie didn't say any of that. She said: 'Yeah, I'm good, thanks.'

Maggie saw the lights go out behind Emily Moffatt's eyes at that point – before, they'd been twinkling merrily at her mistake and Margot's potential irritation – and cursed her usual curse for not being sparkier or more interesting. But Margot seemed to have faith in her.

They'd first met years ago, on the sort of press trip that brands didn't tend to do that often anymore: expensive, excessive, and thoroughly unnecessary. Some niche vodka company whisked a bunch of journos off to Iceland for three days, put them up in a razzy hotel, chauffeured them to the hot springs in a fleet of black Mercedes, laid on a helicopter tour of the geysers, and wined and dined them all in edgy Reykjavík restaurants. Maggie had wangled a spot by promising to write about it for the food and drink column in the local paper; Margot was there because she was fashion editor at *Haute,* and that's the sort of person who needs to know about your niche vodka if you want it to become less niche, in certain circles at least.

It was an odd group. Maggie's heart had sunk slightly when they'd all met up at the gate before the flight and the majority were middle-aged men who covered the consumer beat for the big newspapers. Middle-aged men and this incredibly glamorous blond woman in a black leather biker jacket, grey jeans, and ankle boots who looked as dismayed with her fellow travellers as Maggie was. They might have been thrown together by circumstance, but they bonded after that. The men used the trip to behave like bachelors and drink as though they were childless; the two women entertained themselves by watching them at it.

'Makes me almost glad to be terminally single,' Maggie said to Margot on the first night as they sat with their backs to the subway-tiled wall in a cocktail bar that styled itself as a sort of hipster laboratory and served drinks in conical flasks and test tubes. Endearingly European not to realise that there was nothing remotely cool about that concept.

'I'd rather be on my own forever than married to him,' she continued as one of the group chased a pixieish Icelandic woman across a dance floor pulsating with people half his age.

Perhaps that was a bit strong, but Maggie was feeling bitter at the time. Her last serious relationship had been nearly six years ago, and she was a couple of months off her thirtieth birthday. She'd gone on some dates since then, had a couple of few-month things, but still nothing long-term. The difference now was that she was finally okay with being by herself. She quite enjoyed it most of the time.

'Safer to have a baby hatched in one of these,' Margot had replied, waving the half-empty test tube that she was drinking from. The green liquid sloshed inside.

They laughed then and traded stories about their worst dates: the nose-picker, the drunk, the slightly threatening one (Margot), the one with the full-length leather coat (Maggie).

Maggie got the impression – and she often got it from women her age in a couple – that Margot was trying to convince Maggie that she would always be single at heart. Lots of them believed that deep down they were this happy-go-lucky girl who lived in a crap flat full of shoes and had just accidentally met the one guy who wasn't a shit. Otherwise they'd have been in Maggie's shoes. In her crap flat. It was an attempt at solidarity, she supposed, which, when it comes from somebody more successful than you, is just another version of pity, isn't it?

They had fun together on the trip. They'd meet for breakfast at the hotel and sit together on all the outings. It was like the friendships you develop at Brownie camp or during Freshers Week: functional but intense, warm but temporary. When she got back, Maggie bought herself approximations of all the outfits she'd seen Margot in, only from significantly cheaper shops where the clothes came in plastic bags rather than paper ones. It sounded a bit creepy when she put it like that, but it was Margot's job to persuade everyone else to dress like her, after all. Maggie supposed she might have been a bit embarrassed if the other woman had found out.

She'd seen Margot a few times since then, at launch parties and the occasional dinner thrown by a new label or a fancy stationery brand – or at a distance from her back-row perch at the shows – and they always chatted. When Margot had texted to say she was pregnant and asked whether Maggie would be up for covering her job, she couldn't believe her luck. It wasn't a dead cert that she'd get it, she knew that much, but having Margot's seal of approval had to count in her favour.

As a freelancer, she was never quite stone broke, but it was either feast or famine when it came to commissions, and there was all too often a bit of a lull between them. A salaried job appealed to Maggie: she could relax a bit, maybe make a start on the savings account she'd been lying to her parents about, or the pension she assured them she had opened. And at a magazine like *Haute* – she would have said it was the icing on the cake, but from what she'd seen that morning, Maggie was fairly sure nobody in that office touched the stuff, iced or otherwise.

She had to say, once they'd got over that initial hitch, the interview seemed to go quite well. Maggie was no fashion editor, but she was a journalist through and through: she knew a good story when she saw one, she knew where to look for them, and she was a master in the art of turning a mere thing into a Thing.

Maggie had always been fascinated by what turned a matter of taste into a trend. She'd discovered, early on, that most people just wanted to know about the stuff that somebody else thinks is worth being interested in.

Her enthusiasm seemed to get Emily Moffatt back on her side reasonably quickly, too – once the editor in chief realised she wasn't just a nervous amateur. Emily Moffatt. Maggie had to keep using her full name because she was *Emily Moffatt*. In magazines, there was nobody more impressive or more high-powered. She got a lot of criticism beyond the fashion world – she was a bitch, a tyrant, a bit of a caricature – but everyone Maggie knew who'd worked with her agreed she was a pro. Even the ones who'd shared an office with her for years still spoke of Emily Moffatt in hushed tones.

And there she was, just like her photo from the papers, sitting opposite Maggie, interviewing Maggie. That artfully blow-dried, raven-black do – the sort that looks like it might lift off like Lego hair; a grey Prince of Wales-check trouser suit so sharply tailored you could dice carrots with it; and a face so subtly, so impeccably worked on you'd have had to cut her open and count the rings to find out her age. Interviewing Maggie!

She had felt, rather than seen, the editor looking at her when she entered the room. Emily Moffatt had appraised Maggie from head to toe in one expressionless rake of the eyes, starting with her hair (she'd had it blow-dried professionally that morning, knowing precisely that her frizzy curls wouldn't play ball on such an important occasion) and finishing with the embroidered velvet slippers she'd panic-bought the night before (she remembered Margot wearing something similar when they'd last bumped into each other).

Somewhere in between, Emily Moffatt took in Maggie's borrowed blazer (a far better cut and fabric than anything she could afford); her 'perfect white tee,' as fashion editors called it (as far as she could tell, the perfection stemmed from its costing almost a hundred quid); her black trousers (reliable, smart); and her vital statistics. It felt like that, anyway. Maggie almost wondered whether her prospective boss would tell her she was in the wrong-size bra, like those fitters in posh shops who know whether you're a 34C or D from sight alone.

She'd never reveal how long it had taken her to choose this outfit, but she'd missed the deadline on another article because of it. What do you wear to an interview with somebody who decided six months ago what you should be wearing right now?

From the moment she'd started mixing with them – albeit from a distance – Maggie had always been surprised by how fashion editors dressed in real life. They might have been telling you on those shiny pages that the seventies would be big next season, or that it was all about polka-dot everything, but they were more likely to be in jeans and a sweater, or a white cotton shirt, when you spotted them in the wild. Granted, they'd be the It-jeans du jour and the sweater would always be one million per cent cashmere, but a few larger-than-life types aside, these women were rarely the peacocks you'd expect them to be.

For them, power dressing wasn't a 'look at me' thing. Status came from going unnoticed, from signalling that they were above the fray – it's much harder to stand out subtly than it is in a yellow frou-frou frock and matching heels. They left that sort of look to the social media crowd.

At her most cynical, Maggie firmly believed that fashion editors dressed like this as part of an unspoken competition to show off how beautiful they all were, too. It takes youth, exercise, grooming, and a lot of bone structure (or a bit of help) to look good in very little makeup, a navy sweater, and baggy denim. Obviously, Margot had it nailed. Maggie, on the other hand, looked like the sort of teenage boy who communicates only in grunts if she wasn't wearing a full face of slap and something that pulled her in at the waist. It had taken all her strength not to turn up to the interview in heels.

Her flatmate, Cath, couldn't believe it. 'You're never going in your slippers, Maggie?' she'd called in her broad Irish accent that morning as Maggie tore about, trying to get ready.

If Maggie had had more time before her train, she would have pointed out to her flatmate that, if she were being *truly* fashionable, she'd have been wearing them with a pair of silk pyjama bottoms, too. No, really.

If Emily Moffatt had done a full survey of Maggie as she sat down, then Margot, Maggie observed, was the opposite. The younger woman seemed lost in her own world, icy blue eyes unfocused, a sliver of tooth visible as she chewed her bottom lip, one hand worrying the pen she was holding. She had barely even seemed to register Maggie until she had started talking (oh *God,* that stupid opening gambit again).

In fact, Margot was so zoned out that Maggie wondered whether they were going to pretend they didn't know each other. She'd heard of some maternity covers where the

pregnant woman and applicant had to do that, because the
person in charge wouldn't give anyone suggested by their
employee a fair hearing – they didn't like the idea of the new
person's having been sanctioned by the old, in case they were
left with a duffer or a bore, somebody the mum-to-be deemed
a safe choice.

Of course she'd wondered whether Margot had sought her
out precisely because she didn't think Maggie was a threat.
She'd have been an idiot not to. The answer seemed plain
enough: she was shorter, fatter, less glamorous, and less
successful than her. Little ordinary-looking Maggie to Scandi-
chic Margot. She was exactly who Margot would want doing
her maternity cover. But Maggie liked to think the fashion
editor also believed she was up to the job, and that she'd be a
loyal presence at her desk rather than a snake in the grass.

Margot had been friendly enough once they'd started and
warmed up as things went on. The rest of the interview was
more like a chat than an interrogation; Maggie even managed
a few jokes along the way. As they finished up and Emily
Moffatt told the candidate she'd hear from her PA within a
few days, Margot even flashed her a warm smile. Maggie felt
like the pregnant woman was telling her it had gone well, and
she was so relieved she almost forgot to ask her question.

She'd always been told that asking your own question
during an interview makes you look positive and engaged – as
long as you ask the right one, of course. She had come with
one all prepared.

'What are the chances of remaining a contributor at *Haute*
once Margot is back from her maternity leave?' Maggie said,
directing it towards the magazine's head honcho.

It was then that something odd happened to Margot. One
minute, she'd been checking her phone – that quick email
refresh and catch-up that has become acceptable even when
someone is talking to you. The next, she was pale and

trembling, her lips white against grey, clammy skin in which her eyes stood out, urgent and piercing. Staring at Maggie but also through her, the sinews in her neck taut.

'We'll have to get back to you on that, Maggie,' she said curtly. 'If there isn't anything else . . . ?'

3

Margot

The photo hadn't shown on my screen when it arrived, only the name I had been waiting for – willing – to flash up on it all morning, ever since I had heard the awful news.

Winnie. *How are you, darling? How can you be? How can you continue, now that the future has become the past?*

My hands shook as I opened the message from my friend, and it loaded slowly on my phone. It was big, downloading gradually.

In the photo, Jack was wearing one of his white cotton hats, absurdly large on his head even though they'd been no bigger than Winnie's palm when she'd showed them off on Sunday afternoon. He was in a white all-in-one with feet and sleeves that doubled as gloves, though they hadn't been folded over and his tiny hands protruded from the ends. Long little fingers topped with fingernails that were immaculate despite their impossibly small scale, like a ship in a bottle. I imagined those fingers waving like seaweed in an invisible current as he slept.

Except he wasn't sleeping. The front of the white suit was rumpled and spotted; the hat sat above one final expression. His eyes were closed, his eyelashes dark against the mottled skin, and his lips blue. Tubes wrapped around him, appearing from under one limb and disappearing between the popper fastenings on his suit, snaking out from another side, connecting who-knew-where with who-knew-what, their purpose understood only by the professionals. He lay, limp and awkwardly propped, with a cuddly rabbit at one side.

I felt stupid, frivolous, that it was only once I had noticed the tiny smear of blood on the rabbit's plushy fur that the tears finally came.

I was in the bathroom by then, having left Maggie Beecher in the meeting room and Moff heading back to her corner office. I couldn't even remember what I had said to either of them after I'd opened the text. I sat on the toilet in one of the cubicles and let raw, animal-like groans rip through me.

Was I crying for Jack? I had never known him. Perhaps I was crying for the idea of him. Winnie's twiggy-haired boy, a seven-year-old whose football games had been cancelled and boots never muddied; a young man whose college degree certificate had crumbled to dust, whose wedding day had collapsed like melting celluloid, and whose own children had died this morning too, once his allocated breaths had run out. I thought I was crying for Winnie, who had, somehow, to carry on with today and tomorrow and next week, because time has no respect for tragedy.

Through tears and gasped air, I realised I was sobbing as though I had been wounded, too. I cried out of pure pain and hurt, outraged that life could have done this to someone I loved, bewildered at the violence that had come out from nowhere. I felt the injustice of it like a blade being slowly pressed into flesh: sharp, insistent, accumulating.

If this is how I feel, how must it be for them? I wasn't to know how often I would ask myself that question in the months to come. I wasn't to know either that, although I wouldn't cry for Winnie and Charles again, I would grieve daily. That these hot tears and choking sobs, this labour in a cubicle of the office toilets, had birthed a feeling I would never again be without.

There had been no words with the picture, and no follow-up message. Winnie must not have known what to say. I certainly didn't. As my eyes dried and my breathing moderated, I clicked to reply: 'what a beautiful baby he was. I'm so so sorry.'

I called Nick then, and prepared to collect my things and go home. Work could wait.

I clung to Nick for several minutes without speaking when he got home that evening. He didn't much go in for prolonged physical affection, but he seemed to need the embrace as much as I did.

When we'd first met, five years ago, I had unthinkingly subjected him, my new favourite person, to all the hand-holding, knee-stroking, and back-patting that I, in my extremely tactile family, had grown up with. It wasn't that Nick didn't appreciate the sentiment, he explained, he just wasn't quite sure what to do with it, and sometimes, he confessed, it made him feel itchy. There was, I supposed, something rather needy about it after all, and I now only cornered him for hugs, or showered him with kisses, when I felt I had a good enough excuse.

But the day Winnie's baby died, he sought comfort from me as much as I did from him, bending his six-foot frame around mine, his mussed sandy head resting on top of my blond one, which I laid instinctively on his shoulder even before he had shrugged his coat or his rucksack off. It made my heart beat more slowly, relaxed it from a hard lump in my throat back to its rightful position in my chest. It even stirred the fizzy little presence in my stomach once again, ignorant of all the day's goings-on but aware somehow that Daddy was home.

'Jesus, Margot, how terrible. How absolutely fucking awful.' He sat on our steep wooden stairs and rested his head in his hands briefly. 'Have you spoken to her?'

'No,' I admitted. 'I've called but she hasn't picked up. Sent a few messages, but ...' My voice trailed off, and I looked around for the apple I had been eating, left on the low midcentury coffee table. I usually had food in my hands these days, but today I hadn't felt hungry until just a few minutes before Nick's arrival. When my appetite had returned, it had kicked in with such intensity I had been able to think of little else, barely able to form a sentence.

The apple was also a distraction tactic, something to focus on as I spoke, so that my true feelings – the ones located just behind my grief for the dead baby and his parents – wouldn't show through.

As I answered Nick's question, I felt ever more keenly the growing sense of shame at the fact I still hadn't spoken to my best friend about the unspeakable thing that had happened that morning. I felt it as a judgment on our relationship, on how close we were, on whether Winnie really needed me. *How pathetic to have made Winnie's tragedy all about my feeling rejected. She's probably too distraught to even pick up the phone.* But still, it niggled: *I would have rung her immediately.*

In female friendships, the currency of love doesn't always come with an equal exchange rate. I had often felt I leaned on Winnie and asked her for advice more than my friend required of me. Winnie had always looked out for me, stood up for me, stroked my hair when I was upset, held it back during the drunken teenage years – apart from that one awful term at school, which I didn't like to think about. Sixteen-year-old girls fall out all the time; it was amazing we'd only done so once.

I had always assumed our dynamic was set this way because Winnie was older than I by a couple of months and an only child, but as we'd become adults, I often wondered whether it was because Winnie had resolved to keep me at a distance. Whether the ripples from all those years ago reached further than I had realised.

It wasn't about Nick; Winnie loved him. And it wasn't because we had conflicting views – Winnie and I agreed on everything, from art and politics to the relative merits of new celebrity haircuts or which TV box sets to watch. Winnie was just less demonstrative, I had decided, more levelheaded and less in need of talking down. I couldn't remember the last time my oldest friend had had a crisis; I seemed to average one every couple of months. They were usually fixed by a bottle of red wine and thorough dissection, no matter how trivial, as I sat on Winnie's kilim rug and patted her cat, Clover.

Since we had both become pregnant, our friendship had intensified again. We were like we had been as schoolgirls – BH, as I thought of it: *before Helen* – emailing each other throughout the day from our desks, then messaging all night. This buggy or that one; which vitamins to take; have you read so-and-so's guide to painless labour, and does such a thing even exist?

I was delighted by our renewed closeness. It had ebbed and flowed throughout our twenties as our lives took different turns: Winnie had settled down early with Charles; I had taken longer to find Nick and thus drawn out my days of staying out late and getting up even later.

I had been careful not to say anything to Winnie about this step up in contact, however. I knew my friend well enough to realise that an impassioned declaration would only make her feel awkward. Years ago, I had written my oldest friend a card on her and Charles's wedding day full of emotion and bare-hearted sentiment; Winnie had opened it, read it, and never mentioned it again.

'Ah well,' said Nick, dusting the day from his work trousers and standing to climb the stairs, 'I guess we just have to be there for them when they're ready. No reply to your messages?'

'There was one.' I tried and failed to swallow the lump in my throat, my voice wavering at the memory of the photo. I never wanted to see it again, that little body and the lifeless face, but I knew I was letting Winnie down by only noticing the horror in the image, by focusing on the grotesque instead of the gorgeous little boy beneath.

'Here.' I passed my phone to Nick, whose face paled when he saw it.

'Christ, did she really need to send you this?' he blurted out.

I felt silly admitting I hadn't really stopped to consider the photo. I had spent most of the day looking at it, was unable to clear the image from my mind, but I had failed to see that there was something strange – aggressive almost – about sending a picture of a dead baby to a pregnant woman. Winnie hadn't meant it like that though; she'd sent it because the two of us were so close. *So close she won't answer the phone when I call.*

'She's my best friend, Nick,' I replied dully. 'We share everything.'

'Poor Winnie,' he murmured, then pulled me to him once again and kissed the top of my head. 'Nobody deserves this. How will they ever recover?'

That night I dreamed of incubators and ventilators, of life-support systems and trolleys, cots and deathbeds. Sometimes I was prone on them, calling out for help that I knew would never come. Sometimes I was looking down at Winnie, who was dressed not in the standard-issue blue hospital gown but in the green and grey of our school uniform.

Gifted with a Technicolor imagination at the best of times, I had experienced some of the most vivid dreams of my life since I had become pregnant. I travelled the world several times over between putting the light out and the pips of my alarm clock, each journey more real and more immersive than the last.

The week I found out about our baby, I had dreamed a long and involved conversation about it with my grandmother, who had died nearly a decade ago. When I passed the twelve-week mark and began to tell people my news, my psyche pressed 'play' on a scene of me breastfeeding a blond and pinkly cherubic baby girl on my and Nick's bed, light streaming through the shutters on the windows. I had almost been disappointed to wake.

Tonight's dreams were dark, though, and airless. Time after time, I delivered dead babies, dressed tiny corpses, tried to feed them only to realise they had no mouths. I woke, parched but damp with sweat and with tears, and made my way to the bathroom – *again* – wondering whether Winnie was sleeping, whether Winnie could sleep or ever would again. They must have given her something to help, they must have. *If only I could speak to her.*

When morning finally came, bringing with it a weekend of grey skies and parent-to-be chores, Nick woke to find my side of the bed empty. I had cleaned the house from top to bottom, gone for a walk, bought breakfast things, and read the paper on the iPad. He congratulated me on a day well spent. No need for him to know that, in those dark hours, I had also given up hope that my own child would survive birth or, in the unlikely event that it did, live much beyond the age of five.

We had the first session of our parenting classes a week later. I had coaxed Nick into doing them with the promise of like-minded new fathers no doubt keen to spend their parental leave and childcare hours as a group in the pub. This was only a slight exaggeration of what I wanted to do with my own.

A fortnight ago, I had been excited at the prospect of meeting women who lived in the streets near my own with whom I would huddle together during the delirious tumult of our becoming mothers. But as Nick and I arrived at the instructor's Georgian townhouse and gathered in her dining room, I felt as though I had brought a shadow with me. I saw the other couples laughing, chatting, and exchanging phone numbers, and felt more worldly, and more knowing, for being aware of the truth nobody ever spoke to pregnant women: *there isn't always a happy ending, you know.*

This third generation of humans to be conceived in love and birthed in brightly lit hospitals cannot understand what a place of terror and darkness labour can be. Our ancestors knew only too well: straining for days over a breech baby that would never pass; bleeding out onto rushes for a fortnight, then sweating into stillness even as the child cried hungrily nearby. Now they will scan and check, and measure and recheck, to avoid these things. They will induce and inject and intubate. But every so often the past sneaks in through a fault line, and a modern child dies a historical death.

'Lightning doesn't strike twice,' Nick said as he parked the car. 'I know it's difficult, but our baby is not Winnie's baby, 'Go. These things are very rare.' He reached for my hand, kissed its knuckles, and smiled at me. 'Come on. Let's meet our new drinking buddies.'

They were a disparate bunch, a cross section of the area of South London Nick and I had made our home, from academia and advertising, teachers, bankers, musicians, and other journalists. What united them was the bellies: displayed proudly in stretch jersey, accessorised with bandeaus and bows, and gently caressed throughout by their owners and, more often than not, their partners.

I was not as big as some of the women there, but I immediately felt kinship. Violin-player Sofia, fingers twisting anxiously in her hair; business analyst Adele, who eased her rings off over inflated knuckles and unlaced her sneakers because of her swollen feet; accountant Gemma, whose suit jacket still just about fastened around her middle. They spoke the same patois of bad backs, bleeding gums, night sweats and nausea, a language I had previously only shared with Winnie and assumed nobody else had bothered to master.

There was something cowlike about them all, shifting their weight every so often on the sagging sofa cushions and against the straight-backed chairs. They were all so soft, so benign in their shared heftiness. They were, I realised, the exact opposite of the angular, nervous creatures I spent so much time with at work, whether models or other fashion editors, and I thought briefly of Maggie Beecher, who would – it had been confirmed in an email I had received the previous afternoon from Moff – be stepping into my shoes when the time came.

I had been pleased with the decision – as pleased as I could have felt given what else had happened. Maggie was the perfect solution to my problem. She wasn't the usual entitled and immaculately polished young woman Moff was used to striding into the office – the sort who had a clutch of titles already on her résumé thanks to who her father was or where she'd been to school – but she had more talent than any of them.

Moff liked the glitz and the glamour by proxy that those women brought her, but I knew that what really mattered to my editor was good ideas and a sense of humour. A hard worker, good writer, and even better feminist, Maggie would be so indebted to me for giving her a year in the job that she wouldn't consider screwing me over to keep it. I pictured Maggie's earnest excitement when I'd first mentioned the vacancy to her: that sort of gratitude didn't run out within twelve months.

Faced with my new crowd, and relieved to have a name for the replacement in my old life, I felt more positive than I had for the past seven days. I began to anticipate the little flourishes in my abdomen with excitement, rather than to dread them as harbingers of sadness. What had happened to Winnie was dreadful – cruel and unnecessary – but that wasn't going to be my story.

When my turn came in the group welcome exercise, I smiled and said, 'I'm Margot Jones, I'm nearly eighteen weeks pregnant, and I'm the fashion editor at *Haute* magazine.'

4

Maggie

She didn't think she'd ever been happier than when she answered her phone to Emily Moffatt's offering her the job as Margot's cover. Maggie was in the supermarket when she felt the call vibrating in her coat pocket.

That was one good thing about being single: she could admit that the best moments in life aren't always the ones spent gazing into somebody else's eyes or walking hand in hand along a sandy beach. Sometimes they come from good old hard work and achieving something tangible – like more money, seeing your name in print, and mentally replacing everything in your wardrobe with more expensive versions. She was joking about the last one. Sort of.

'I really liked your style in the interview, Maggie,' Emily Moffatt informed her over the phone in that slightly throaty West Country-posh voice of hers. At first, Maggie thought she meant her outfit and made a mental note to tell Cath that the blazer had done the trick, but then she realised the editor was talking about her attitude.

'You were so enthusiastic, so excitable,' the smooth voice continued in her ear. 'So many people in this job are so jaded. It was enlivening to speak to someone who clearly wasn't worried about being cool.'

Ouch.

It was true, Maggie had never been anything even approaching what the in-crowd would ever term 'cool', but the other woman was wrong about its not bothering her.

She was terrified she'd sit down at Margot's desk and the rest of the office would start laughing at Emily Moffatt's elaborate joke, that a beautiful carbon copy of someone more like Margot would appear and poke her out of the way with a sharp anorexic elbow. Or that she'd show up in Milan and some shiny-haired PR with a clipboard would come and move her to a seat at the back where nobody else would have to look at her.

It wouldn't even need to be that far-fetched: she worried she'd break the chair on her first day, because it'd be the first time an actual bum – as in, one with cheeks as well as bones – had sat on it. Which is why, from now until she started, she'd be going to the gym, mainly eating salads, and knocking back gallons of water a day in a bid to look more like the women who so unnerved her.

That all started tomorrow, of course, because she was going to have a glass of wine right now to celebrate. And maybe another one after that.

'We'll speak again nearer the time, of course, but for now, I'd like you to come up with a few ideas and send them over to me directly,' the editor carried on, firing words at her. 'Let's get you writing for us as soon as possible.'

She started worrying as soon as she hung up the phone.

So you can knock me into shape, Maggie thought. It wasn't just her waist that needed sculpting, it was her words. She was good at constructive criticism though, and once she had written for Emily Moffatt, she could write for anyone. This job was going to be the best thing that had ever happened to Maggie Beecher.

After they spoke, she went home and deleted all the dating apps from her phone: no distractions. She'd been for enough drinks with enough men who weren't quite interested in her to last a lifetime, whereas an opportunity like this only happened so often. She intended to give this job her full attention.

She poured some white wine into the only clean mug in her and Cath's kitchen, sipped it on the sofa, and racked her brains for something she might be able to write for Emily Moffatt. Moff, as they all called her. How would Maggie know when she was allowed to use that nickname too? Perhaps she signed an email with it, and then you knew you were in the club.

It might sound counterintuitive, but the way Maggie hunted for ideas was to see what everybody else had already done – it got the juices flowing in her own head. So as she drank her wine, she flicked through various blogs and news sites on her ancient, slow-functioning laptop. She'd be able to get a new one thanks to this job, and that fizzy, excited feeling returned to her stomach again.

Her mind wandered from what she might bring to *Haute* to the subject of everything Margot had already brought. She typed 'Margot Jones' into the search engine and scrolled through the results. Lots of articles, unsurprisingly, from hot-off-the-press catwalk reports quickly typed even as the models were still leaving the runway to longer, more-in-depth interviews with celebrities and designers that she'd clearly crafted over a few days from her desk.

There was the occasional personal piece, too. She was funny, Margot, and had the all-important ability to laugh at herself. Reading through her counterpart's back catalogue, Maggie felt the fizz settle into something heavier in her stomach. Margot knew this job inside out; how would Maggie ever measure up?

Then she did what she had spent most of her twenties doing, what every psychologist she'd been to see in the years since had told her she mustn't, and what she had eventually started fining herself for, with a little jar of coins that she kept on her bedside table.

She clicked the 'Images' tab and prepared to compare herself ruthlessly and unforgivingly with a woman who made her feel a bit nervous and a bit fat.

She'd always done it; you probably have too. Ex-boyfriend's new girlfriends, current boyfriend's former girlfriends, the friends of those girlfriends, their sisters perhaps, frenemies, frolleagues – whatever you want to call them. She would stare at grainy snapshots of them online until she'd convinced herself that they were prettier, thinner, richer, happier, more clever, and more successful than her. Until she felt like the least important, the loneliest, the ugliest and most boring, most desperate person she knew.

This is where the wonders of modern technology have brought us: to the bathroom scales and the full-length mirror to measure our flaws and obsess over our imperfections. Do you think our grannies pored over sepia photographs of their neighbours and felt like shit? Maggie didn't either.

The human psyche's a fascinating place. There she was, only hours after having been on top of the world, in front of a screen full of photos of the woman she was supposed to be replacing. Her last psychologist would have called it 'self-esteem sabotage'. Maggie took another swig of her wine and began scrolling.

Here was Margot crossing a street in Paris, presumably making her way from one couture show to another, wearing a caramel-coloured sweater, shearling biker jacket, and white jeans. White jeans! Maggie had banned most white items from her wardrobe on the grounds that she drank too much red wine for them to be viable. The fashion editor had the jacket loosely slung over her back without having put her arms in the sleeves, a styling trick Maggie now knew (more research, and more wine) that the fashion industry referred to as 'shoulder-robing'.

There Margot was at a store launch in a grey trouser suit and black turtleneck, the oversized fit of the trousers and jacket conspiring to make her look even slimmer than she really was. Maggie had always wanted to be the sort of woman who could rock up in a suit, but the last time she'd worn one was to her Oxford interview (she didn't get in) and she'd spent the whole day pulling the hems up away from puddles and the crotch seam out of her bum. Trouser suits were made for men, not for women with curves.

In the next picture Maggie found, Margot was posing awkwardly, as though she didn't like having her photograph taken, on some steps. It must have been from quite a while ago, because she had a fringe that had since grown out and her hair was much longer, past her boobs and almost to her waist. Her fluffy grey sweater had deliberately overlong sleeves that covered her hands, her knee-length navy skirt a distinct school-uniform look to it, despite being slit to the thigh. On her feet were black patent Mary Janes with a small kitten heel and her legs were encased to just below the knee in black woollen socks.

Maggie had to do a double take to check Margot wasn't in costume, but there in the caption it said: 'Margot Jones of *Haute* at London Fashion Week.' Behind her was a designer's logo, the show she'd just come out of when the street-style photographer had caught her.

There was always a pack of them at the shows – photographers. They lurked in corners and outside venues during fashion week, hunters dressed in expensive wet-weather gear waiting to set off the *click-click-click* of their digital SLRs at the most deserving outfits they saw. The editors on the front row might have been the ones analysing next season's trends on the catwalk, but the pavement snappers reviewed them right back. Each flash of their cameras was a judgment in their favour, every time a lens was lowered without a picture's being taken a slur on an ensemble no doubt painstakingly put together with precisely this moment in mind.

There was nothing more excruciating than walking up to the door of a show only to see the entire herd of photographers sheathe their cameras as you walked past. Maggie swore some of them did it with a dramatic flourish and a little sigh, just to make you feel even worse about disappointing them. Actually there was something more awful: being asked to step aside so they could get a shot of the person you were with that didn't have you in it spoiling things.

She used to think the key to having your picture taken by them was to trick yourself out in an embarrassment of designer labels – specifically this season's must-have bag or shoes, so that magazines could use pictures of people wearing them on their websites to say, 'Yes, we were right: look at these beautiful people with all the things we told you to buy last issue.' Not that they would have paid for them, though – most editors just borrowed stuff from the fashion cupboard for the shows, as though it was the world's most glamorous branch of Blockbuster Video.

But even in her finery, Maggie had never been one of the ones chased by the photographers, the ones who stopped traffic by posing for the pack in the middle of the road or pretended to talk nonchalantly into their phones while presenting their best angles.

No, what the most photographed had in common wasn't logos and bling, it was high cheekbones, glossy hair, big eyes, pouting lips. Because it was never really about the clothes at all, but about how beautiful you were. How your chromosomes clashed together to make your face; how well your grandparents picked a mate. You could turn up for the pack in a clown suit if you were beautiful and they'd still take your picture.

That's what Maggie thought as she looked at the weird avant-garde schoolgirl getup that Margot had on in this last photo and felt once again the twang of panic at never being able to live up to her. Fashion wasn't at all about clothes, it was about the person wearing them and whether they were found worthy of admiration. And that's when she had an idea that she knew Emily Moffatt would love.

★   ★   ★

Maggie was sitting at the breakfast bar in her and Cath's flat eating avocado on toast for lunch when she saw the name appear on her phone screen. She'd sent the email only a few hours earlier, so the editor must have liked what she saw. Maggie had heard this about Emily Moffatt, that when she got excited about something, she got *really* excited about it – sometimes her enthusiasm ran to several phone calls, texts, and emails a day.

'I love it,' she said when Maggie picked up, skipping the hellos. 'Let's do the shoot next week. I'll put you in touch with Holly, she'll get the clothes ready. Write it up for the Friday after that.'

'Great!' Maggie grinned into the phone. 'That's so kind of you, I'm so excited, I'm really glad you liked the idea!'

'Yes, well,' Emily Moffatt replied, cutting her off in her raptures. 'Next week.'

'Brilliant,' Maggie said, and then: 'thanks so much – Moff.'

There was a moment of hesitation at the end of the line, a faint note somewhere between cough and surprise, and then the phone went dead.

A shoot. For the magazine. She'd be in those pages along-side the models and celebrities and society girls. People would open the issue, as Maggie had been doing for years, and wonder who she was, this glamorous, important person. Perhaps teenagers would study her in there, as she had those pages in her bedroom aged fifteen or so, and decide there and then that this was it: this was the job they wanted, the one they'd set their sights on throughout school and university, the one they'd be so proud to tell their friends and their family about once they got it.

After Maggie had her brainwave the night before, she'd jotted down the bare bones of it in her notepad, finished her wine, and slept on it. Sometimes even good ideas had a tendency to unravel under scrutiny. She wanted to make sure she was offering up something that would work.

The premise was simple: that Maggie was not a fashion editor – yet – but that she'd be expected to become one once she took up the job. How does a civilian step into the most stylish shoes in the world? That was what she intended to write about in her first piece for *Haute*, and if she was being honest, she hoped to find out the answer along the way too.

She suspected that the 'Holly' Moff had suggested would have a lot to do with it. As the magazine's stylist, it was Holly's job to dress everyone who appeared on its pages, taking into account the latest trends and their personal tastes, but mainly according to whatever Moff decreed. Maggie knew Emily Moffatt would want her to look the part in the pictures, but she quailed at the idea of baring her own scruffy self in a magazine more usually populated with unreasonably attractive celebrities.

On the counter, her phone buzzed with a message: 'we'll make you fabulous,' it said, 'plenty of Photoshop.'

Not a woman to spare anybody's feelings, Emily Moffatt.

When the day of the shoot came, Maggie had her hair blow-dried and her nails done and had laid off the bread for a week in the knowledge that everybody looks fatter on camera – especially if they're a bit fat to start with.

'Break a leg, Maggie!' Cath called as she ran out of the flat and into the car they'd sent to pick her up. The driver acted as though she was somebody significant, opening the door for her and pointing out the mineral water he'd left in the leather armrest.

I could get used to this, Maggie thought, and then she remembered the fact that all this glamour, all this opulence, had an end date – when Margot returned – and felt suddenly, momentarily, bereft even though her adventure had barely begun. It would be hard to hand it all back, she realised.

Everyone was so welcoming when she got to the studio that the worried feeling in her stomach dissipated almost immediately. Maggie had a tendency to spin out and had done so en route about it all being a ruse to humiliate her, imagining that the pictures would be so hideous the only use they'd be able to find for them was a feature on how *not* to dress.

It was times like this, when she used all her tactics to subdue the panic rising in her chest, that she most felt the absence of a boyfriend, a deep-voiced, calming influence who'd tell her, with quiet authority and gentle insistence, to shut up and stop acting crazy. Then again, it wasn't like any of the men she'd dated had ever done that – at least, not in a nice way.

Holly turned out to be one of those women who looked like they've strolled straight out of the 1970s: long, straight brown hair and a fringe; high-waisted flares and platform sandals; a soft and well-washed band T-shirt tucked in to emphasise her tiny, willowy waist. Maggie had always wanted to wear clothes like that, but she'd look like she was on her way to a nostalgia event. She made a hasty note in her pad for the piece about how the line between style and costume is blurred for fashion editors.

'I've got a few outfits for you,' Holly began even before Maggie had taken her seat to have her makeup done. The last time she had someone do it for her had been her sister's wedding, when it had felt trowelled on inches thick and cracked every time she smiled. That woman had also been the person who'd done the bouquets; the woman on set today was French, with a closely cropped, curly blond quiff that signified her cool credentials, and Maggie doubted her talents ran to floristry.

'Moff was pretty specific about what she wants – daytime casual, daytime smart, evening casual, and then – my personal favourite – glamorama,' Holly continued, ticking off items on her fingers.

Maggie gulped, and the makeup artist began sponging foundation onto her face. 'Glamorama?'

'Don't worry.' The stylist laughed, displaying perfect little teeth. 'We'll make you look major.'

She was right. The woman who emerged from the camera, wielded by a man so hip and so handsome Maggie could barely speak to him throughout the process, wasn't somebody she'd ever met before. Sleek, sexy, glossy, and expensive-looking without seeming snooty, she exuded confidence from the computer screen and storyboard, even though Maggie had felt ridiculous while posing on the spot, hand on hip, chin tilted upwards, and taking a little step into the frame so that her hair bounced just so as the lights popped.

None of the gaucheness, the awkwardness, or the what-do-I-do-with-my-hands-ness had made it into the final edit: Maggie was the best version of herself, wearing the most fabulous clothes she'd ever laid eyes on. She looked like a fashion editor. She'd certainly spent the day pretending to be one. Perhaps that meant she was one? Back at home on the sofa, admiring her manicured nails and looking through the pictures again on her laptop, she certainly felt like one.

'Can't wait to see you in the office when you start,' Holly said as her assistants packed away the clothes and Maggie peeled off a set of false eyelashes in front of the bulb-framed vanity mirror.

She and the rest of the crew had joked that the new girl was a natural.

'Margot will have to watch out!' Holly called, smiling, as Maggie climbed into her second taxi of the day.

5

Margot

I felt a stab of envy when the copies of the new issue landed in the office and the post boys dealt them out to the women at their desks like cards in a poker game. I had seen the layouts of Maggie's story inside, had edited her words to fit them onto the page and into the *Haute* mould. The trouble was, they hadn't needed much doing to them.

I couldn't deny that Maggie had written a great piece. Funny, engaging, heartfelt, and – *always a bonus* – actually useful, it'd be the one that our readers flicked to first, thanks to the strapline I'd come up with for the cover: HELP! MAKE ME A FASHION EDITOR – NOW! Moff encouraged liberal use of exclamation marks.

I had indeed made Maggie a fashion editor. I'd chosen her because I knew Maggie was clever and capable, reliable, hard-working, and in need of a break. I hadn't thought of my replacement as a charity case, but I was aware my job was valuable, and it had seemed right to offer it to someone who really needed it. *Someone grateful who'd repay the debt with loyalty.* Maggie, subsisting on a few commissions a month, had struck me as talent squandered, potential untapped.

Well, Moff has tapped it now. I opened the magazine onto my desk with its usual satisfying *thunk* and found the page where Maggie's feature began. The first spread was a lineup of several versions of her, each wearing a different, of-the-moment trend and posing as though they were all sitting on a front row next to one another.

Here she wore a classic skirt suit and heels, her shiny dark hair tucked into an elegant chignon at the nape of her neck. There she was in patched jeans and a white shirt tied at the waist, focusing the eye on that hourglass figure of hers. To the right, she half-smiled, knowingly goofish, in this season's most achingly cutting-edge ironic tracksuit and sneakers, a look so immensely unflattering I wouldn't have attempted it even if I hadn't been pregnant. Maggie made it look rather sweet, pretty even.

On the following page, next to Maggie's words, was a picture of her in a skintight emerald-green bandage dress and matching crystal-embellished heels, one hand on hip, red lips and smoky eyes set to smoulder.

I eyed her pillowy cleavage enviously: I had never had much of a décolletage myself, but what little there was had inflated slightly with pregnancy – not, I noticed every morning, into anything thrilling or pneumatic, but into two puffy-looking points that I couldn't even put into a proper bra, according to the lingerie saleswoman I'd seen over the weekend.

'You don't want an underwire pressing on those milk ducts!' the bespectacled fitter had trilled while strapping me ruthlessly into a sensible flesh-coloured specimen that made me want to cry.

The transformation of my underwear drawer (I'd also swapped my usual lace and low-slung knickers for the giant cotton variety in the name of comfort) was yet another way being pregnant made me feel like a stranger in my own skin. Whenever I found myself thinking this way, I wished, for a split second that was more muscle memory than an articulated feeling, that I could speak to Winnie about it.

Winnie had always looked after me, soothed me, and listened to me. The pattern had been set when we were at school together. We had been inseparable: an army of two who could finish each other's sentences and paint the nails on each other's left hands simultaneously.

But in the three months since Jack's death, I had only one other message from my oldest friend, a brief and brittle response to numerous variations on a theme of love and solicitude: 'I'm sorry, I can't right now.'

Can't talk? Can't be my friend? Can't stand me for being pregnant?

I knew from our school days that to crowd Winnie when she'd asked for space was a surefire way to alienate her even more. I'd learned that after what Helen did. I didn't like to think of the time we had fallen out at school – Winnie and I rarely talked of Helen now – but I had learned then that the only way to thaw Winnie when she was in her distant, icy mode was to let her defrost in her own time.

After the messages and my calls had gone unanswered, my voicemails unreturned, I had toyed with simply turning up on Winnie's doorstep – only a half-hour walk from my own, but which felt like miles thanks to the radio silence between us – but I knew Winnie would not thank me for it.

I had even asked Nick to drive me round there, but the windows had been dark and the driveway empty. I hadn't realised I had been dreading seeing my friend, but the relief that washed over me when we turned the car around and went straight home felt almost cleansing. I had been afraid, I admitted later to myself, of Winnie's seeing my growing belly, had worried it would offend her, hadn't known how we would talk around it but not *about* it. It would have even got in the way of a hug – a round, firm reproach to Winnie and a reminder of what she didn't have. It had been so long since I had felt scared of my best friend, I had almost forgotten how intense the power that Winnie had over me was. *Almost.*

Winnie would come to me when she was ready. Until then, I tried to let her know she was loved from a distance.

I had sent flowers, first a bouquet and then a packet of seeds that promised to grow into exactly the sort of bright and blowsy blooms of which Winnie was so fond in her little back garden. I hoped they might help during the darkest days. The task of nurturing the dry pods into abundant life struck me as time-consuming in exactly the right way – something constructive and positive, a way to mark off the months of grief with colour and optimism and beauty. I had hoped my friend would shrug off her remoteness and reach out, the way plants push through hard winter soil towards warm sunlight in spring.

Now the idea seemed trite. I should have sent food, should have offered to clean for them, could have run errands, done chores. I would have willingly scrubbed Winnie's floors, my heavy belly scraping the ground in penitential pose, to assuage the survivor's guilt I felt so keenly almost every moment I was awake. Asleep too, in gory, panic-stricken dreamscapes of hospital monitors and tiny corpses.

Winnie was a constant rhythm in my blood. When I wasn't wondering where my friend was or how she passed her days, a new superstition marked my actions: crossing roads, catching trains, climbing stairs were all done to a soundtrack of silent gratitude that my own baby's heart was still beating. When I felt its kicks, my delight was tempered instantly by sorrow and self-reproach, then dulled by fear. I felt Winnie's disapproval and sense of betrayal every time I let myself forget to be scared.

Some women I and my bump walked past made eye contact and smiled – that's how I knew they too had babies and young children at home. Others ignored me, didn't give up their seats because I failed to penetrate their podcasts and their streaming services, wasn't on their radar. *I was like that. You'll feel bad about it when it's your turn.*

Then there were others, who looked straight through me and set their jaws, who glowered at me or stared at my belly without then looking at my face. The didn'ts, and the couldn'ts, the never-quite-got-round-to-its. The ones who had tried but had their hearts broken in the process. One of them had followed me in the supermarket from aisle to aisle, watching what I picked up and tutting at the bottle of wine I eventually returned to the shelf, embarrassed – and then told me I was having a boy.

'Without a doubt,' the woman said, and laid a liver-spotted hand on my rounded stomach. 'That's a little fella in there.'

I should have been able to shrug it off, like the other comments or conversation directed at my bump rather than to me. My body had never been so appraised by strangers, visually and otherwise, before I was pregnant. But the woman's touch felt like a burn, a curse, and I reeled backwards into the shelves behind me – this unwanted, uninvited caress, whose perpetrator sent my thoughts spiralling into a medieval hysteria over hexes and old women with hairy chins.

I was increasingly paranoid. One day, I sensed someone behind me as I walked along a pavement alone near home. The route from the bus stop to our house took me down several quiet residential streets after I turned off the main road with its sprinkling of shops and pubs. There were well-groomed hedgerows for someone to hide behind, driveways to duck into – and, sure enough, whenever I spun around to confront whoever it was, the noise of whose footsteps came and went in the breeze, they were no longer there. *But they had been.*

Nick sensed this weird, jittery pulse in me. 'You have to relax, 'Go, or it really will affect the baby,' he murmured into my hair at night. Because of my stomach, I now slept on my side, facing away from him, which made me feel even more lonely as the nightmares pressed in. 'Do you need to go and talk to someone about it?'

What would I say? That my best friend wouldn't speak to me, that I was worried she hated me, that I didn't know what

I'd done wrong, that none of this was my fault. I remembered this feeling from the six weeks when Winnie and I hadn't spoken at school. They had been the most difficult of my life.

The scream as she fell. The noise she made as she landed.

No, I didn't want to go and talk to someone, not if it meant revisiting all that again.

'It'd just sound like teenage angst,' I told Nick, switching off my bedside light. 'I'm sure Winnie will be in touch when she's ready. And I've got so much to get through at work before I finish, I won't have a chance to worry.'

But instead I found myself with more and more time on my hands in the office. I was passed over for stories, left off agenda lists, not invited to planning meetings, no longer present in Moff's short and unpredictable attention span. In an industry that thrives on what comes next, I found myself old news.

I looked back at the magazine, at the picture of Maggie in her green silk dress. It was supposed to highlight her taste for feminine clothing, in contrast to most fashion editors, who 'exist only in jeans and navy sweaters.' I had taken exception to this line in particular, because I felt it was a dig at my own style; I had worn little else on the trip to Iceland that Maggie and I had met on. Nick had told me I was being overly sensitive and to forget it. *You try forgetting someone when they're stealing your identity.*

'But Maggie's nothing like you,' he'd reasoned, trying to soothe me, rubbing my shoulders in the way he knew I liked. Right now, that seemed to be working in Maggie's favour: she was a breath of fresh air in the magazine, exotic and interesting.

I felt as though Maggie was trying to sit at my desk before the seat had been vacated, let alone gone cold. In the cosy minutes before my alarm went off, I dreamed that Maggie had come into the office, sat down on my lap, squashing my pregnant stomach and begun typing on my keyboard. I woke from these dreams irritable and suspicious, but that was preferable to the cold sweats and tears of the gruesome visions that plagued me during the infinitely chillier small hours.

I closed the magazine without even looking at the small piece I had in there this month.

It wasn't Maggie's article itself that had lodged in my throat when I first found out about it and stuck there, sharp as a piece of glass. It was the fact that nobody had bothered to tell me it was happening. That one day I had heard Holly and the other juniors discussing Maggie's 'fashion editor shoot' and had to ask them what they were talking about. The humiliation! *The bigger I get, the less they see me; it's not like I'm hard to miss these days.*

Now that I was in my seventh month, my bump sat high and proud, the first thing to enter a room, like the mermaid on the prow of a ship. I dressed around it without dressing for it, avoiding the usual maternity clothes, all drapes and wraps, and instead plumping for larger versions of what I usually wore: shirts, loose tunics, a silk kimono that I wore over a black T-shirt with jeans. Plenty of jeans, but by now the ones that came with a waistband that extended up to my armpits. I loathed them, but they were the most comfortable thing I could remember wearing since I had become a fashion editor.

Maybe Moff would be interested in a piece on that.

I laughed at the thought of my editor commissioning anything that might lower the glam factor in the magazine. I had already caught Moff gazing thoughtfully at my puffy feet during our daily news meetings. I had made the mistake of wearing strappy sandals, and my bloated, water-retaining flesh had strained at the rope fastenings until I'd taken them off. A livid crosshatching of strap marks had been cut into my feet, which I'd hidden under my desk all day after Moff had tittered at them as she stalked past.

Laugh back, so they don't think you're a miserable old cow.

'Hey, Maggie,' I had texted when I'd found out about the shoot. 'The piece sounds fantastic! Can't wait to read!'

Too many exclamation marks. Still, I'd wanted to head off this feeling at the onset. It pressed on me day and night, a righteous indignation at the way, as I faded out of people's consciousness at work, Maggie seemed to appear in ever sharper focus.

They were planning future issues in the office, editions that would thump onto doormats and arrive in newsagents long after my baby had come – *if it doesn't die* – so the news of Maggie's appointment had been made public and she'd been into the office a few times. Her contact details had been given as the phone on my desk, which meant I answered it several times daily to PRs desperate to flog their wares to its incoming occupant. I felt like Maggie's PA, like a secretary to my own life tasked with shutting it down as you would a failing company.

'Aww, thanks! It was all Moff's idea,' Maggie replied promptly to my text. 'Hope I don't look too dreadful in the pics!'

Exclamation marks are the way women circle each other now.

It wasn't until that morning, when the bound stacks of magazines had been brought in on the post trolley and I had heard Moff discussing the piece in the lift with one of the suits from upstairs, that I realised Maggie had lied to me.

'We've got this great piece in this month by a new writer called Maggie Beecher, about how a normal woman becomes a fashion editor,' Moff explained. 'Such a fun idea from her, it looks like she'll be a perfect fit here. She's covering Margot's maternity leave.'

Moff gestured towards my stomach, inside which a dull nausea that was nothing to do with my pregnancy had settled.

Why hadn't Maggie been honest with me? My unease combined with a self-righteous indignation that made tears prick the back of my eyes. The injustice of it! I had become the pregnant-woman cliché: out of the loop, undermined, suspicious, and now, embarrassingly, publicly upset. *Precisely what I brought Maggie in to avoid, thanks a bunch.*

I cried when I told Nick about it later that evening. 'I look like an idiot, like I don't know what's going on in the office, and I can't even ask about it or suggest they might have let me know, because then I'll look like a paranoid preggo control freak.'

'Which you are.' He grinned and reached out a hand to stroke mine.

'Which I am,' I admitted through my tears, 'but only because they've made me. I'm really pissed off with Maggie about this.'

'Don't be,' Nick reasoned. 'She shouldn't have lied, 'Go, but maybe she felt weird about the idea, in case it looked like she was muscling in. Moff should have told you – but maybe she forgot?'

He was right, but the fact of Maggie's fib pricked at me for the rest of the evening. She had every right to be ambitious about the role she was taking on; why be coy? I doubted it was a deliberate strategy to unnerve me, or to deceive, although the less charitable part of my brain tried to drag me down that path. I weighed my hormones in the balance and wondered whether I was overreacting; Nick didn't seem at all bothered about his own graphic design work being farmed out to others during his paternity leave.

That's because it's three weeks, and there are only two of them in the company. There's no question that he'll come straight back to his job. And society hasn't taught him to mistrust other men since birth.

Not for the first time, I rued working in an industry that numbered mostly women among its employees. *Women and gay men.* It was a cohort that, during the boozy, child-free years, made for such camaraderie and fun, untainted by sexual competition or alpha male bores, but that conspired, consciously or not, to shut out what many of them referred to as 'the breeders' in later years.

Winnie had always rolled her eyes at the bitchiness of some of my colleagues. She was quick-witted but not sharp-tongued. *She would have been a lioness over this though.* I imagined my friend listing the reasons why, yes, Maggie had indeed let me down, but why it also didn't really matter in the long run.

The idea calmed me, but I was saddened by the fact it wasn't real. I picked up my phone and flicked to Facebook. As its familiar blue and white format loaded on the screen, comforting and subconsciously stress-inducing in equal measure, I felt the usual guilt for not having closed down my account on it when Nick had his. I never posted anything personal, but I could discern its effect on my mood after my rare log-ins: vaguely dissatisfied with myself, irked with the people on there. *Facebook breeds contempt.*

Recently I had found myself thinking less of people who used it all the time. Maggie Beecher, I noticed after accepting her friend request last week, was surprisingly prolific. I scrolled past updates from former colleagues and my hairdresser. *It's all people I don't know anymore and people I never really knew in the first place. Or it's people I know too well for this to be the way we stay in touch.*

Halfway down my feed was a photo of Winnie. It was the first activity of hers I'd seen since Jack's death. She sat, the central pillar in a row of five women whose arms were all linked or draped over one another's shoulders. I recognised Winnie's mother, her aunt, and two other friends from university. They all wore black mourning clothes, but their smiles warmed the image, their grief transformed to strength, support for the woman in their midst who needed it most.

Winnie herself was bright-eyed but hollow-cheeked, her pregnancy pudge gone to reveal her jawline once more. She

looked younger and older at the same time; the fingers clutching the stems of a bunch of pink pansies – were they from the
seeds I bought her? – seemed thin, red, and worn, but her skin
was glowing and clear.

I realised that whenever I had 'seen' my friend in my mind's
eye these past three months, I had imagined her pale and
hunched, dark smudges under her eyes and hair unkempt, her
grief visible as a physical impairment. *Like some kind of tragic
heroine.* She looked here like a woman you'd queue behind in
the corner shop and never suspect what she'd been through.

'Happy to have my nearest and dearest with me to remember Jack today,' read the caption underneath. 'We will never
forget him, or how our friends have helped us through these
last months.'

A wake. Or a memorial service, at least. Winnie and Charles
must have delayed it until they could face socialising again. A
private ceremony when it happened and then a reentry into
the world with a remembrance of Jack's brief life, to celebrate
the very fact of him. I knew Winnie well enough – had seen
her in the aftermath of trauma before – to know that she
wouldn't have wanted to be around people when it was still
fresh and tender.

Nick and I had had no word of it, no invite. As I frantically
searched my email inbox, my junk mail folder, the hall table
where the cleaner left our post, a breathless feeling stole over
me – a seconds-long throb that I felt beyond my own body
but also to the core of it. *Winnie didn't let me know about it,
because she didn't want me there.*

I was devastated. But my earlier tears of frustration were
gone and my eyes remained dry. Instead I felt something more
like cold fury, a righteous tightening of muscles around my
entire body. My hands moved to my belly, where life rose to
meet them, an elbow perhaps or a bony little bottom. *I have
you.*

'I'm really sorry,' Nick said, frowning, when I showed it to him. 'That's ... well, that's sad. It's sad she didn't feel like seeing us. She must be going through so much.'

He put an arm around me and pulled me closer. I was grateful to him for understanding, for not having to explain that what felt increasingly like a schoolgirl standoff – the classic marshalling of allies in the playground to show who had the upper hand – had made me feel, once again, like a frightened child. Scared that nobody liked me anymore, just like all those years ago.

I tried to silence that insecure child inside: reminded myself whose grief was bigger, less escapable, more final. I tried to pity Winnie instead of resenting her for the snub, the implication that I had done something wrong. *I know it's not about me, really.*

I looked at the photo one more time – I had been clutching my phone so tightly, my hand left a condensation mark on its case – and closed the window before I was tempted to look for any more pictures.

That way madness lies.

6

Maggie

Well. She thought she'd get a few responses after the piece came out – a couple of texts from friends perhaps, a few messages passed on by her mum from some of her pals – but nothing like this. She'd never been so in demand! She felt like the most popular girl at school.

First up, five or six giant bunches of flowers arrived at the office for her from PRs congratulating her on taking over from Margot and saying how much they'd enjoyed reading the article. White roses, green-veined hydrangeas, creamy orchids spattered with pink: fashion flowers. They were the sort of bouquets you see in interiors features in society magazines, from florists known only by their surnames with HQs in Mayfair, flowers that brim plentifully from vases on marble console tables and are refreshed every week. They must have cost more than £150 a pop.

Next, she had a steady stream of messages from people over the first week or so of the magazine's being out in the shops. Her close friends were expecting it, so theirs were mainly to tell Maggie how great she looked (sure!) and how cool it was to see her in there, but she got texts from people she hadn't seen for years – exes, school friends, old drinking buddies – and a slew of 'Look at you!'s on Facebook from people she'd met at parties, men she'd had flings with, the sort of acquaintances you didn't really like at the time but whose lives remained interesting enough to click 'Confirm' when they added you.

She'd posted a couple of images up there, of course, with a link to the piece online. *Haute* might have been a print magazine, but you had to spread the word digitally as well. That was where people saw everything now, and Maggie was a committed self-publicist. Part of the job, really, right? Though she had noticed since friending Margot that the fashion editor was pretty reticent about that side of things. Some people thought they were too cool for social media, but they'd have to come round to it eventually.

She put it up on Twitter too, and watched as her followers retweeted and spread the word. She didn't have a huge number, but the ones she did have were interested in what she wrote. Maggie hadn't yet changed her details on there from freelance writer to *Haute*'s acting fashion editor. She did so now with a little giggle, her heart squeezing tight in her chest with pride, and @-ed the magazine's main account, too.

Then came the admirers. Her phone buzzed around the clock with tweets from people she'd never met before, getting in touch to tell her not only that they loved the piece but how good they thought she looked in the pictures, too. Sure, it was a little bit creepy, but the attention was quite flattering and nobody said anything too . . . Besides, the dating ban had been tougher than she expected – having a drink with someone, whether they turned out to be good, bad, ugly, or indifferent, was a basic form of human contact, after all. By giving it up, she'd narrowed her social life by about two-thirds.

Finally came the fashion crowd – a trickle at first, and then a deluge. A couple of editors who'd commissioned her freelance work for other magazines saying welcome and well done. She'd be sitting next to them instead of three rows behind at the shows next season, so it made sense for them to be friendly. Some photographers and stylists wanted to show her their books in case she liked their work enough to commission a shoot for *Haute*.

But it was mainly PRs she heard from – PRs who had seen the piece and realised Maggie Beecher would be a useful contact for getting their brands into the magazine. They wanted to see her for breakfast, lunch, dinner, afternoon tea, and cocktails. She was surprised none of them offered to come and tuck her in at night, too.

They invited her to visit their shops to 'treat herself,' to get her nails done and 'have a natter', for a quick chat and a blow-dry – all on their expense accounts, of course. She took them up on as many of their offers as she could fit in; she could do with a bit of a makeover before she started officially next week. Got to show up looking the part, after all.

Holly in the office had the flowers biked – on an actual motorbike, as if they were a pizza delivery! – home to the flat, where Maggie dug out the few vases she and Cath had and displayed them on their plastic IKEA coffee table, their junk-shop sideboard, the breakfast bar. She'd feel eternally guilty for dividing a particularly elegant bouquet up between several pint glasses that one of them had liberated from the local pub. She was pretty sure that wasn't what Forsyths of Albemarle Street had in mind when they'd arranged those thick stems just so and bound them with silk ribbon.

'Bloody hell, who died?' Cath exclaimed, taking them all in when she got home from work. Beautiful though they were, so many large arrangements in their poky little flat had the effect of making the front room look a bit like a memorial chapel. 'I think I like your new job as much as you do. I could get used to this, now.'

Me too, Cath, oh, me too, Maggie thought. In fact, she'd been wondering whether Margot had ever got used to it all. Whether the outgoing editor had come to expect the lavishness, the pampering, the excessive gratitude, and enough flowers to run a funeral home, or whether she too still whooped with delight when they arrived. Not outwardly, but inwardly

– surely Margot was just as thrilled by it all as Maggie was? Hers had to be the best job in the world.

Maggie didn't think she'd ever get bored of heavy-headed blooms nodding on their stems as a courier handed them over, wondering perhaps who on earth she was to deserve such an offering. Or of opening thick, textured envelopes with her name on them to see gold-edged calligraphed invitations to some of the most exclusive addresses in London. *Her* presence requested, indeed!

What was it Moff had said? 'Jaded.' No, she'd never be jaded with any of this, thank you very much.

Moff. Maggie had to face her again in the morning conference meeting on her first day. After the success of the article and the fact the editor had liked the idea so much, Maggie thought they might have established a bit of a relationship, but Moff greeted the new girl's grin and little wave with a brief tightening of her eyes, as though she were trying to focus on something a very long way away, and kept on talking to the art director.

Maybe she didn't look smart enough, Maggie worried, or maybe she was too smart? She'd had her hair blow-dried the day before after a coffee with someone called Rosie who looked after a brand of folding shoes. Quite a good idea, really – meant you could slip a pair of flats into your handbag for when your heels started to hurt – but not terribly sexy. Maggie tried to imagine Moff's face if she suggested writing a piece on folding shoes, and the vision she came up with made her laugh but also shiver.

She was wearing a new shirtdress that she hadn't been able to resist from a woman who had got in touch to tell Maggie about her boutique, a full-skirted, three-quarter-sleeved floral-print number that buttoned down the front and fell to just below the knee. On her feet, her trusty embroidered slippers again. Given Moff's reaction, Maggie wondered whether she should have worn heels with it after all.

Maggie was making her way out of the corner office and back to the desk that Margot had shown her to that morning, head down and eyes ahead, when she heard her name. 'Maggie,' Moff said at conversational volume, barely audible over the chairs scraping and chitchat, 'can you stay, please?'

She turned to face her new boss as the others filed out and carefully closed the door on the last of them. She could feel her heartbeat in her temples; her mouth was dry and her note-book completely empty of any interesting ideas. There were a few scraps whizzing round her head that she could try to fudge into something if that was the reason Moff had—

'I don't mean to be authoritarian,' the editor continued, tapping one long brown-lacquered fingernail on her desk, 'but what you called me on the phone.'

Oh God, had she not hung up properly? What had she said? What had Moff heard? *Oh Christ, Maggie, that great big bloody mouth of yours!*

'I'm aware that out there' – Moff gestured to the office beyond her frosted windows – 'the girls call me Moff.' She pursed her lips. 'But did you really think they called me it to *my face?*'

Maggie felt a mortified blush creeping up from the bottom of her earlobes, quickly spreading across her cheeks and her chest. Her palms turned clammy. Of course they didn't call Emily Moffatt – Emily Moffatt with her chauffeur, her designer handbags, her seven-inch heels, and her famously chilly demeanor – 'Moff' to her face. Of course they didn't! Maggie could have died. 'I'm so s—'

The editor was laughing. Not great belly-shaking chuckles, admittedly, but a genteel shaking of the shoulders and a husky rumbling noise in her throat. 'Don't be,' Moff said once she had caught her breath. 'If your piece hadn't been so good, I might have been more annoyed. But I liked it. I like *you*. Don't do it again.'

Her attention was on her phone once more, her face fierce and focused as usual. Maggie had been dismissed.

The new girl ran-walked back to her desk, which was next to Margot's until the old fashion editor left and the new one could sit in her spot, almost crippled with embarrassment but crying with laughter, and bursting with a sort of pride that she'd managed to thaw the ice-queen editor enough to make her giggle.

Margot glanced up at her quizzically as Maggie threw herself into her chair, which skittered away on its wheels under her weight and made her laugh harder. She regaled the other woman with what had just happened, making a stricken face at the error she'd made and then one of total shock at the fact Moff had laughed it off.

As Margot hung on the words, her expressions followed suit: interest, confusion, and then total horror at the reveal. But the two women diverged after that: when Maggie's anecdote ended on a smile, Margot still looked distinctly annoyed.

'Hey, it's okay!' Maggie reassured her. 'She didn't mind! She thought it was funny!'

'Haha, yes, you said.' Margot relaxed her features and turned back to her screen, where Maggie briefly glimpsed Facebook's blue insignia before she minimised the tab. 'Phew!'

She isn't worried about me messing up, Maggie realised suddenly. *She's annoyed to hear that I didn't.* It had only been a matter of seconds before Margot had laughed along with her, but it was just enough time to let slip that she was . . . *jealous.* Maggie hadn't expected that. She had thought her predecessor was cool as a cucumber about her. And she found the fact that she had clearly got under that perfect, glowing skin surprisingly satisfying.

She had been intrigued to see Margot Jones in her natural habitat, as it were, in the *Haute* office. She'd had such a quiet charisma when Maggie first met her, and a subtle, if self-conscious, steeliness to her the times she'd seen Margot after that, that Maggie had half expected the girls on the desk to hero-worship her. After all, Margot was their editor – she was beautiful, successful, and currently such a picture of healthy, pregnant bounty she was practically a Renaissance nymph. She was what they all wanted to be, wasn't she?

But instead, to Maggie's fascination, Margot seemed a solitary figure at work, appeared to have neither allies nor enemies. The day Maggie was in, people sort of left Margot to it, and she seemed shy with the few staffers she did talk to. Perhaps it was to do with winding down before she went on maternity leave; she hadn't seemed like the nervous sort at all when they had been in Iceland together. Thoughtful perhaps, but not withdrawn, not interior.

They had arranged to see one of the PRs who'd sent Maggie flowers that afternoon. It was marked in their diaries as a handover meeting but wasn't anything formal, Margot explained. Penny was a friend – they'd known each other for years, so it was simply an opportunity to set her and Maggie up together over a few drinks. Fine by Maggie; they left their desks at five and borrowed Moff's driver, James, to drop them at the bar while she was in a meeting.

It occurred to Maggie en route that a lot of working in fashion involved pretending you were a celebrity, or a minor royal perhaps, and other people's behaving correspondingly. Who ends up drinking in the Wolseley at five-fifteen on a Tuesday unless they have money to burn and no job?

That was the thing, though – nobody had as much money as they liked to make out, and all the A-list behaviour Maggie had witnessed was funded by expense accounts. That was why everybody went a bit overboard with the pomposity and the grandeur, the cultivated patrician attitude of taking everything for granted, the 'this old thing' mentality. Because, as far as

Maggie could tell, to act excited – to imply all this was worth being excited about, that it wasn't the sort of thing you did every day – was to out yourself as grateful, not cool, (whisper it) poor. In fashion, poor was the worst thing you could be.

Maggie had only ever been to the Wolseley once, for her mum's fiftieth, but she could see from Margot's quiet confidence in negotiating a better-situated table and subsequent beeline to the loos that she was a regular. Maggie could also see, from the deference of the waiters and the approving looks Margot got from the clientele as she navigated her silk-clad bump between their tables, that the fashion editor belonged here. Maggie wondered whether she ever would.

Margot walked through the high-ceilinged room without noticing it. From her perch on the leather banquette, her replacement gazed at the veined marble, Doric columns, and black lacquer, at the cheekbones, the blow-dries, the Chanel jackets, and the face-lifts, like a country bumpkin. Slightly self-consciously, Maggie raised her phone and took a picture of herself with the vast golden bar in the background and what she thought was a 'little old me?' expression.

She tweeted the picture and hastily put her phone away as a tanned and very lithe woman slid into the booth next to her.

'Maggie!' she said throatily. 'I'm Penny. Let's get some drinks, shall we?'

She flicked her hair extensions over one shoulder, signalled the waiter, and ordered a bottle of champagne before Maggie had even said hello back.

Now that she was home and sobering up, Maggie could see why Margot had got a bit annoyed. She and Penny had tried to include the pregnant woman, but she wasn't drinking and they really were. It had turned into a bit of a session, actually. Plus, Margot wasn't single, and she and Penny *really* were.

It wasn't often that Maggie met someone who'd been on the market for as long as she had, but Penny had a failed marriage and about a thousand comically awful dates under her belt, and was only too happy to share every detail. The two of them had got on like a house on fire. Maggie had told her about the dating ban, and Penny had made her promise to come on a night out with her instead. She said they'd get all kitted out by her most fabulous brands and hit the town. At that point, Penny had ordered another bottle.

Margot was a little quiet, but she laughed along for the most part. She did that thing where she pretended she was still single at heart, too. Even less convincing now that she had something the size of a watermelon under her dress, Maggie thought.

No, it wasn't the single stuff that got to Margot, Maggie decided, it was the pregnant stuff. It started off innocently enough – they had been asking her how it felt to have something living inside you. Must be pretty weird when it moves, Maggie had volunteered, a bit *Invasion of the Body Snatchers?*

Margot had laughed at that. 'At first, definitely. Actually I felt a bit sick the first time' – she looked a bit sheepish then – 'but then you get used to it. I can tell whether it's sleeping or awake. Sometimes it gets hiccups.'

Again, sobering up and with a bit of distance, Maggie realised now they should have acted like this was something cute. But a few glasses down, it sounded to both Penny and her like something really quite unnerving.

'Urgh!' Maggie said. 'Bad enough when you can't get rid of your own hiccups!'

'Just like when you get a drunk sitting behind you on the night bus!' screeched Penny.

'Same tendency to burps and sick when it gets here too!' They collapsed into lurid giggles. Not quite the usual reverence accorded to pregnant women, but they were so pleased with their jokes, it didn't strike them as inconsiderate.

Margot gave a thin little smile and said something about getting back. As she heaved herself up off the banquette,

Penny got up to go to the loo, and Maggie saw Margot take in the PR's waspish waist in her tight-fitting black dress. She noticed the same slightly grumpy look that had flitted across Margot's features with her earlier.

After Margot had gone and as Maggie waited for Penny to return, she checked her phone. More Twitter replies to the selfie she had posted earlier.

Maggie_B @itsmaggiebetches: Feeling pretty fashionable at the Wolseley this evening

Jenna Smith @hiheelshun replying to @itsmaggiebetches: Ooh jels! Enjoy

Amy Carroll @acl replying to @itsmaggiebetches: You've got to check out the loos – sooo fancy

Mark Stanley @markie replying to @itsmaggiebetches: This new job suits you!

Fashion Bot @fashionbot replying to @itsmaggiebetches: Click here for designer fashion deals

Cocktail Guy @sexpest89 replying to @itsmaggiebetches: Nice tits

Helen Knows @HelenKnows replying to @itsmaggiebetches: Have they finally got rid of @hautemargot? Good riddance! You seem much more interesting

Oops.

7

Margot

Someone had followed me again when I left the bar. As I walked to my taxi, I heard the same insistent footsteps I did every evening on my walk home, this time right behind me in the quiet side street – gaining on me as if their owner would walk right up the back of my legs.

I was bracing myself to turn when a drunken man, short-sleeved and shivering in the cool night, elbowed past to climb into the cab in front of me.

The driver dismissed him with a lazy wave of his hand. 'She's up the duff, mate, sod off,' he said, and I felt a rush of gratitude to him simply for being on my side.

In the back of the taxi, I zoomed in on the tiny profile picture on my screen. It showed a woman I didn't recognise in over-sized joke sunglasses that obscured most of her face, holding a can of beer in a garden. Who did she think she was? And what on earth would she care about who's fashion editor at *Haute*?

It ate away at me all night, the indignation I'd felt earlier at being ignored, patronised, teased, and essentially driven away by Maggie and Penny paling into insignificance. I could just about understand Winnie's distancing herself after what had happened, even though I resented the anxiety and guilt with which it had tinged my own pregnancy. I understood, though it still hurt, why Winnie wouldn't have wanted me and my bump in the background as she said goodbye to her son.

But this Twitter troll was just vicious, unnecessary. Why me? Why so pointed? Winnie and I had had so many conversations around her kitchen table about how difficult it would be to hand over control of the careers we'd created to somebody else, about the territorial impulse that made us want whoever that might be to fail on a grand scale, about managing our worse instincts so we wouldn't be consumed with bitterness during the time we were off with our babies.

Winnie knows exactly which buttons to press.

The thought bounced into my head before I could stop it, and it sounded ludicrous even to me.

Helen knows.

But that was impossible.

The rest of the troll's Twitter page was a long list of replies to various women in the media – columnists, TV presenters, most with much higher profiles than mine – all calibrated to worry and to wound. They went back months, since before Winnie had even been pregnant. I had to concede it was highly unlikely that my clever, erudite, and sociable friend would have indulged in such a pastime – or had the time to.

The next morning, I woke to a reply from Maggie's Twitter account:

Maggie_B @itsmaggiebetches replying to @ HelenKnows: No need to be rude – the brilliant @ hautemargot is off to have a baby and I'm just keep-ing her seat warm for a bit.

I was grateful for that much, at least.

It worried me how quickly, how easily, I had begun to suspect that my best friend could have sent the message. In the light of day, it looked so anodyne, so childish. The work of a lumpen loner with her own issues. Reducing achievements and self-esteem in the innocent-looking little white letter box at the top of her feed was this woman's speciality; once she'd seen on Maggie's profile that she was now acting fashion editor, all she would have had to do was Google the previous holder of the title.

I forgot about her the minute I logged into Facebook, as I regularly did now to scan for more updates from Winnie. There weren't many – sometimes as little as a strong-arm emoji – but I liked them and religiously left a row of kisses underneath to show my school friend that I was still there, still ready to shoulder the burden with her. Not, of course, that Winnie could be in any doubt, given I had also kept up a stream of messages and voicemails that went unanswered, too.

Winnie had posted a simple picture, a still life on the secondhand wooden desk that stood in front of the bay window in her study: a triptych of a fountain pen lying on top of a brand-new leather-bound lined notebook, with a rose-gold charm bracelet beside it, its dangling alphabet beads spelling out 'Jack.'

'Charms for Jack, notebook and pen for me to navigate my feelings,' the post read. 'Vital and life-giving presents from Suze and Lydia, the best friends anyone ever had, and the women who kept my heart beating these past months.'

I recognised the names as Winnie's university friends. I had met them a few times, but Winnie kept her social groups pretty separate; she referred to these two as 'the norms' and told me that I wouldn't like them, although they'd always seemed quite fun to me.

Bit fucking petty, isn't it, Win?

I couldn't help the thought, and knew as it lightninged through my mind what sort of person it made me. But that was what it seemed Winnie wanted – for me to be the bad guy. *Again.* For me to make somebody else's grief all about me. *Again.*

I understood that the post was not so much Winnie moving on as Winnie making a point. I knew exactly what Winnie would have made of those presents, before Jack's death at least. 'Lame, with a double L,' we'd joked at school, a favourite phrase in our lexicon of nonsense. It had fallen out of use after Helen came, because it transpired that quite a lot of what Helen liked was lame with a double L. But Winnie hadn't wanted to hear it.

No, what the post really meant was: *you haven't helped me through my darkest days. You weren't there. I didn't want you to be, and I want that to upset you.*

A memory surfaced – of my pleading with Winnie, begging her not to do the thing she knew would change our lives forever – and I pushed it back down again.

It wasn't my fault.

I knew that nearly five months of eerie, loaded silence from Winnie and observing her from the tortured, overanalysable remove that social media provided had made me paranoid and suspicious. The shifting ground at work, the arrival of Maggie, my changing body, lack of sleep, and the great upheaval ahead of me had all played their role, too. I felt my anxiety physically in my clenched forehead, my grinding teeth and rounded shoulders. Tension thrummed in me constantly like tautness along a wire.

These should have been the most exciting weeks of my life, the final ones before the arrival of my first child, and yet they were tainted by the twisted tricks my mind kept playing on me. In my dreams I climbed endless stairs, the tops of which were concealed by clouds. I knew that my baby was at the summit, even though, looking down, I still carried my bump before me. I tripped time and again, my now-bulky body making me clumsy, but I never fell. I sensed rather than saw the people below – *the crowd, the open mouths* – and woke exhausted.

I asked Nick to delete the picture of Jack that Winnie had sent me; it felt like too much of a betrayal to do it myself. I'd found myself staring at it in spare moments, trying to square the wriggling belly with this unmoving little boy, taking in the tininess and the absence of someone whose presence now loomed so large in my own life.

I had been happy not to know who was growing inside me. We wanted the surprise, Nick and I. The ultimate reward for labour, people told me. I hadn't had a preference for boy over girl or vice versa, though my curiosity came sporadically like an intense itch. But as my due date loomed, I found myself desperately hoping for a daughter. A little girl who would be the opposite of Jack. A beginning rather than an end, a light to Winnie's darkness. *If I had a boy, Winnie wouldn't be able to look at him without thinking of how Jack might have been. A girl will be easier for her once we're back in touch again.*

But when the parcel arrived, it seemed less certain that we ever would be. Nick had signed for and half opened it before he'd realised it was for me. I recognised my name in Winnie's hand instantly – how could I not? Winnie had written me postcards from countless holidays, birthday cards for the best part of twenty years. Before Helen, we had written each other letters – and posted them – despite living around the corner from each other's houses; we shared a diary that we took home on alternate nights and passed between each other before class every morning. The irony wasn't lost on me that, as soon as something worth writing about had happened, we'd stopped writing in it.

Winnie's looped script was as familiar to me as my own signature, and the contents of the brown cardboard box brought back memories, too: the little white hats I had bought for Jack before his birth, returned, with no note. One from the set of six – *the one he'd worn in the hospital* – was missing.

There were other things in the parcel, things I had forgotten ever giving my friend. A fancy corkscrew that some PR had sent me years ago. A first edition of her favourite Sylvia Plath I'd found in a bookstore in Paris one season when I'd been over for the shows. A buttery cream leather handbag I'd been given in Milan. A decorative ceramic bowl, now broken into two. Winnie had purged her house of them: they were tokens of a friendship she no longer wanted a part in.

I felt as if someone had struck me. My stomach was heavy with a weight unrelated to the tiny person living in it. It was sickening to have things that had been given in love thrown back at me in reproach. I would rather Winnie had simply thrown them away, but I knew exactly why she hadn't.

She wants me to feel bad, she wants to punish me. As if she hasn't spent years doing that already.

But I understood the catharsis, Winnie's need to lash out. I myself had felt lighter with Jack's photo gone – and all the more guilty for that. I was finally able to get on with the nesting that I had so far delayed and that my body, more than my mind or my increasingly short to-do list at work, urged me to. My arms ached for laundry loads of little bodysuits, pristine in their whiteness but also in their briefness, my hands to fold them when they were dry and arrange them in the chest of drawers we had bought for the nursery. *The box room. Not a nursery yet.*

We had painted it in dark grey with a bluish tone to it, a similar shade to the one I had worn on our wedding day. Nick had tried to make it a moment out of a rom-com montage, flicking paint at me, kissing my cheek, and taking selfies. I had treated it as a chore, not wanting to invest enthusiasm in case my excitement flagged us on the map of the gods as a happy household in need of some tragedy.

'Very chic,' the girls at work had gushed.

'Very Pinterest!' Maggie had said, grinning, her thumb and first finger looped in a 'perfect' gesture.

'It's not very babyish, so we can use it as an office too,' I replied. *If . . .*

In the end, my last day at work couldn't come quickly enough. I was tired of feeling extraneous, so tired of being tired that I couldn't even muster insecurity or resentment anymore, let alone the motivation to hammer out an article or two. I moved like a beast of burden compared to the sprightly little student interns who flitted between the fashion cupboard (still tidy) and the desk wearing ever more complicated and uncomfortable-looking outfits. *I must seem about a hundred years old to them.*

I noticed too that Maggie had a spring in her step. Not man related, I presumed, remembering the dating ban. So it must have had to do with settling into the job. I remembered when I too had found it exhilarating. And I noted with an affection that, uncurbed, bordered on jealous disdain – and suspicion – all of the tweaks my replacement had made to her appearance.

Gone were the pointy, prissy pumps that Maggie used to trip around in – *a bit corporate secretary* – replaced with jolie laide masculine brogues and must-have loafers, luxe sneakers not designed for running in and block-heeled ankle boots. The silhouette remained body skimming – *have to with boobs like that* – but it had lost what I unkindly thought of as its *provincial edge*. Maggie was altogether more polished these days, more elegant, more sure of herself.

Gone was the nervous clutch at the base of her throat whenever she had to speak in morning conference. Gone the habit of starting every sentence with 'Sorry, but . . .' Gone was the girl who wrote for pennies here and there, and – as of today – gone was the other fashion editor, the original one, replaced with somebody far more dynamic.

I tried to be pleased for my replacement – tried to muster enthusiasm for her as she discovered how luxurious life could be in a role like this, wanted to be excited for Maggie as she indulged and treated herself, just as I had in the early days of being a fashion editor. But all I could see was the energy and the ideas that I was lacking; the waist I no longer had; the social life I had willingly let slide; and, already, the popularity of the woman taking over my job in the office.

I could see how eager Maggie and the rest of the team were to get on with things, without my lurking like a spectre nearby. And, as much as that – not to mention this newly cast, shiny-eyed and dewy-skinned, glamorous version of the woman I'd lined up in my job for the next year – made me uneasy, I had finally reached the stage when the little heartbeat within me drowned out even the most anxious, most paranoid of thoughts.

I didn't notice that Maggie wasn't there as they all gathered around my desk to cut the traditional cartoon caterpillar cake that marked special occasions in the *Haute* office, its dopey white-chocolate face always reserved for Moff, who'd sniff it and nibble one corner before discarding it.

The editor in chief held a bottle of prosecco, pouring it out into plastic cups that were passed around the assembled crowd. *I can't believe you let her get away with calling you Moff.* I thought about all the time I had spent with my editor, all those dinners for two in Milan and Paris. Not once had I come close to cracking the cool carapace with which Emily Moffatt shielded herself from prying eyes, even those she liked.

Recently she'd regaled the office with Maggie's blunder, whipping up affectionate laughter for the new girl, who had blushed and basked in the attention. *You'd have strung me up in front of the posh girls. You would have humiliated me, made me the joke, not laughed along like a conspirator.*

Not now. I heard Winnie's sensible admonishment in my head and dragged my embittered thoughts back to the speech my boss was making to the floor.

'How will we do without you, Margot? You've been here so long it feels like you started during *my* early twenties, not yours.' An appreciative titter. 'Thank you for all your hard work so far – God knows it will stand you in good stead for the slog you have ahead of you. Try to remember what a good night's sleep feels like, won't you?'

She filled her plastic cup and held it aloft. 'Let's have three cheers, please, to wish Margot well. I think you'll all agree, she'll make the most wonderful, very organised, very tidy mother. To Margot, even though she isn't drinking. Hip, hip—'

But her hurrah was lost in a ripple of turned heads and murmurs that had started by the door and worked its way inwards like a Mexican wave. Somewhere near its centre, a blond woman was flapping her hands to hush and divert attention back to the toast, but it was too late.

In glossy magazine offices, a new look – however small – is always something of an event, as the women who work there flock to inspect and compliment it. This – a reveal moment worthy of a Hollywood makeover – had generated its own jamboree.

The cut, a blunt, shoulder-length crop replacing long tendrils of curls; the colour, an expensive-looking honey-cara-mel where there had been mahogany before. *She's been to my hairdresser.*

'Maggie, you look fantastic,' said Emily Moffatt, cup still in the air. The rest of the room nodded in agreement.

'Okay, she does look a bit like you,' admitted Nick. He was staring at the selfie Maggie had uploaded on Instagram earlier that afternoon, presumably on her way back to the office. *On her way back to make sure nobody even noticed me leave.*

'A bit!' I was furious. Not only was this a blatant, not to mention successful, attempt to steal the limelight on my last day, it came with similar creepy *Single White Female* overtones that Maggie's having bought the same embroidered slippers had. I had been prepared to overlook a pair of shoes, but an entire image overhaul, timed to coincide with my leaving party, was hardly an accident.

'It isn't a coincidence, no,' my ever-reasonable husband agreed. He rested a warm hand on my bump and snuggled into my neck, leaving a trail of warm kisses there before surfacing again and looking me in the eye. 'But you should be flattered rather than threatened, 'Go. From what you've told me, Maggie's been so nervous about stepping into your shoes, she had to go out and buy them. And a wig to go with them.' He dug his elbow into my ribs and flashed a silly grin.

'Oh, piss off,' I grumbled, still outraged but leaning into his embrace. 'Why do you always have to be so bloody understanding?'

But I knew he was right, and that it was something to let go of rather than stew on. *Bit sad, really.* I wasn't sure whether I'd be more relieved if Maggie did everything so differently from me that the two of us couldn't really be compared, or whether I wanted Maggie to emerge as a pale imitation while I was off. Or whether, really, I just wanted it to go as smoothly as possible, so that I returned to a calm office and a grateful replacement.

I had carefully buried my competitive streak over the years; recently it had been exhumed without my permission. My younger self had been ambitious, driven when I needed to be by status and the urge to climb a hierarchy. As I neared the top, however, I found comparisons with my peers – my rivals – more stressful: less about how I could match them, whether I was working as hard as them, was as successful, and more about whether they might overtake me at some point, whether in fact they'd soon be coming for my job.

I had thought pregnancy would quiet those voices. So it had been a surprise when I felt the sharp insecurities that I thought I had rid myself of after adolescence pricking me again as my due date approached. It felt so ... teenage. *Was my mother consumed by stuff like this when I was little? I thought having a baby would mean I'd finally grow out of giving a damn.*

If anything, the niggles felt more insistent the more I withdrew from work.

I looked through the beribboned wicker basket of goodies I had been given as I left the office, a pampering parcel designed to make the most of the few weeks left before the baby arrived. *Maybe they didn't entirely forget about me.* I had sent a similar package of artfully boxed, gold-lettered potions and thick, fragrant unguents, cadged from the crate beside the beauty editor's desk, to Winnie a few weeks ago – before the other things had been sent back to me – with a card that simply said: 'thinking of you, lots of love.' *Stupid really – Winnie prefers home remedies and lumpy grey soaps that smell like almonds.*

They had all been at the bottom of the box Winnie had returned, a scene of rage daubed in serums and lotion, the jars with their lids twisted off, tubes squeezed out, so that they had coated the other items in the box in a gloopy layer. *Not that I would have kept them otherwise.* I had dumped the whole thing straight into the dust bin, before Nick saw it and knew my secret shame: that I was a friend unfriended. Sometimes I felt as though I had done something very bad indeed; in my more reflective moments, I tried to see Winnie's actions as those of a woman in great pain.

I ran a bath and tipped a vial of purple, lavender-scented oil into it, under the tap's flow, so it frothed. I wanted to mark the milestone I had reached that day: work finished and only a week until my due date. I just wanted someone to wish me good luck, to tell me I'd done well. Before, I would have texted Winnie, but now – *Is this what social media is for? Because nobody has real friends anymore?*

I opened Twitter on my phone and typed in an update:

Margot Jones @hautemargot: last day done! signing off from @hautemagazine for a little while to work on my new side project #hurryupbaby #donthurry-toomuch #wouldlovetowatchsomeboxsetsfirst

A couple of likes flashed up before I'd even put my phone down on the side by the sink. I had a pang, as I had through-out my pregnancy when referring to the fact of it in public, that I might hurt Winnie's feelings, but my school friend was not on Twitter, I reminded myself. I tested the warm bath-water with my hand.

Pulling my hair back into a bun and settling into the tub, I remembered the days when baths could be hot and deep; for pregnant women, they must be tepid and easy to climb out of, in case of fainting or falling. Baths used to be the time I most treasured alone, a moment to savour as I mentally evaluated my week and physically sloughed off its effects.

I had not felt truly alone for months. The baby inside me was the person who chooses to sit in the row behind in an otherwise empty cinema, somebody on a long train journey with whom one keeps making accidental eye contact. I wasn't annoyed by it; there was a comfort to the presence. I had already decided it had a sense of humour, a cheekiness, a delight in comic timing. I allowed myself just that much of an attachment to the little swimmer.

Not truly alone, but the loneliest I had been for years. Isolated at work, excluded by Winnie. Nick was wonderful, as he always was and would be, but even he had a limited atten-tion span for the interminable buzz in my head of speculation and counter-speculation about what the next few months would bring, at home, at work, for me, for the child, for Winnie, and for Maggie. That buzz rose to the level of a din at times, dropped to a faint hum at others, but it was emotional tinnitus, an internal Greek chorus, that left me feeling hostage to myself if I listened for too long.

I was standing in the very spot where I had first felt my baby move, rubbing scented oil into the drumlike stretched skin of my stomach, when a message flashed up on my phone. A camera icon next to Winnie's name. Instantly I was filled with a sense of dread, as though I had been caught doing wrong.

I know what you did.

It wasn't my fault.

The picture was of another picture. A soft-focus professional portrait of Jack lying inside an oak coffin that was lined with pintucked white satin. His womb-scrunched features had relaxed and there was a faint smile on his rosebud lips, his pouchy cheeks neither sallow nor flushed but now the perfect shade of alive. *No blood anymore.* The caul had been cleaned from a dark thatch of hair that was tamed and combed flat against his head. He wore another of his white onesies; his tiny, perfect hands met across his tummy; and the little toy rabbit was tucked under one arm. A companion.

My heart broke again and with it, my waters.

Unbearable pain – that came later. At first, it was a quiet and insistent ache at the bottom of my back, one that increased its clamour over the next few hours until I could only see colours. We went to the hospital twelve hours after that, by which time I felt the agony like a steel girdle being tightened around my hipbones. I welcomed the cool needle and its icy numbness. I lay on a bed for another day, and in a room full of women – and Nick – Lila took her first breath the next morning.

8

Maggie

She saw Margot's picture on Instagram a few hours after it had been posted. 'What a perfect squish!' Maggie wrote underneath the photo – and the baby really was: peachy pink, with a tuft of hair, full cheeks, and clasped hands, her haunches pulled up on each side like a little rabbit, wearing a grey suit dotted with tiny embroidered stars. Trust Margot to dress her baby impeccably.

Maggie texted her on her way back to the office after lunch: 'well done! She's adorable, love the name. Do you feel like a different person?' She wasn't really expecting a reply, if she was honest, and forgot all about it once she arrived back in front of her inbox.

Maggie had a month before the shows started. Four weeks to prepare for what everybody was telling her would be the most intense period of her life. She knew how it sounded when someone in high heels said that fashion week was a gruelling ordeal that most people can't wait to go home from – hardly like performing open heart surgery or working on an oil rig, you'd point out, and you'd be right.

And yet, the times she'd reported from the shows in London before, Maggie had gone home every night feeling like she'd run a marathon in her stilettos, craving white bread and waking the next morning feeling like she'd been hit over the head. Granted, that might have had something to do with the number of champagne flutes she was offered over the course of the day.

The first show started at nine a.m., and if you were on a crappy ticket, you needed to start queuing at eight-fifteen. On a ticket like Margot's you could turn up at five to and swan in. Then there was a show every hour until about eight p.m. In between, you had just enough time to find a loo or maybe grab a sandwich – but never both – and you were expected to write up each collection before the next one started, so the girls running the website could post the reviews before the other magazines had theirs up. So yes: not a matter of life and death, but stressful nevertheless.

She spent that month in a heightened state of extreme busyness, learning the ropes at the magazine and trying to remember everybody's names, tracking down stories and following up on tips that she thought might work for an article, pitching them to Moff and breathing a silent sigh of relief when they seemed to be exactly the sort of thing the editor was looking for. She noted, not without superstition, that it seemed to be going well.

Maggie was enjoying herself. She had always loved writing, the act of wrangling words into sentences that were not only full of interest and information but worked technically, balanced at each end, with as much action as there was description. It never felt like work, and she was always grateful for that. Words came naturally to her; they never let her down. In fact, they were her longest-term relationship.

No, it was the other side of things that she was finding tricky – the fashion side. The very process of getting dressed in the morning had become a political act. At first, Maggie had worried only about whether she'd measure up to Margot, who was always so sleek without looking like she was ever really trying; now her replacement faced the daily headache of whether her outfit would pass muster in the office.

Intentionally or not, the only route into *Haute* was via a corridor that ran from the elevators down past Moff's windows, with the kitchenette on one side and the bulk of the desks on the other, known as 'the runway.' The magazine's staffers stalked along it in a fresh and arresting ensemble every morning as though there were editors taking notes on either side. Which there practically were.

It wasn't done bitchily – although of course comments were made sotto voce if an outfit was deemed not to have worked – more as a celebration of how good everyone looked. Because, to a woman, they all did. Posh and rangy, cool and streetwise, elegant but with attitude – and then Maggie. Where the rest of them prowled along the runway like cheetahs, Maggie scurried or clomped its length with her head down, eyes glued to her phone, though she could feel theirs scanning her from head to toe.

The first time she went for a drink after work with Holly and her assistant, Amma, they teased her for it.

'We work with clothes, Maggie!' they joshed. 'You have to at least try to look like you enjoy wearing them!'

She really was enjoying them – much more than she ever had before. Largely, Maggie suspected, because the clothes she was now wearing were so much nicer – and so much more expensive – than the ones she'd been wearing before. These ones didn't pull on the bits of her that protruded or need readjusting every five minutes. It had taken only a few strides in a pair of Italian leather heels, a few moments of French silk against her skin, the weight of a chunky handbag dripping in yellow metal, to make her realise with an intensity close to shame the inferiority of what she had had before.

A bottle of wine or more later, Holly and Amma had shown her YouTube clips of the one-named catwalk goddesses they worshipped, telling Maggie to pop a hip like Letisha or roll her shoulders back like Darlene, pointing out the way these wonders sashayed past the audience, a fluid march that somehow lingered over each step even as their heels stomped briskly in time to the techno soundtrack of the show.

Maggie put a bit more effort into the runway after that, and began to take pleasure in showing off the new things she bought and tried on daily.

Her new hair helped too, and the fact she'd lost a bit of weight from not going out drinking with men she didn't know every night. Her cheekbones had emerged for the first time since adolescence, and her waist looked more defined. She still couldn't fit into most of the samples that were hanging in the cupboard – nobody could, apart from the hungriest and most wistful-looking of the interns – but she was ordering a full size smaller whenever she chose clothes to try for the stories she was working on.

She couldn't remember the last time she'd had to add a coin to the self-esteem jar on the nightstand, either.

Maggie wasn't too worried about what she was going to pack for the shows. She had been sent enough things to test-drive that the bits she'd bought after she first met Margot had already been cycled out of rotation and offered to Cath, a role reversal her flatmate had been only too happy about. Maggie's closet was a new and shiny place, supplemented with the designer handbags and shoes she'd bought with her newly inflated pay packet. She wasn't ashamed to admit that some evenings after work, she just went home and laid things out on her bed, imagining the Italian marble piazzas and cobbled Parisian streets she'd be wearing them in.

She wondered whether Margot still did this, or whether, for her, getting dressed was something innate. For Maggie, it had become like piano practice – the more she did it, the better she got and the more she enjoyed figuring out the nuances. She stopped avoiding her reflection and instead greeted it like a friend she'd clap on the back and say was looking well.

The week before she flew to New York, Maggie was walking back along the runway from the loos – chin high, shoulders back – when Holly stuck her head out of the fashion cupboard and beckoned her inside. Maggie had her own shelf in there now, MJ changed for MB on a sticky label, where she stored the things that had been sent in for her to write about or that she was borrowing. She'd been amassing things she thought she could take with her to bolster her own clothes, but Holly was one step ahead.

'Take your pick,' the stylist said, draping one long arm over a rail of clothes. 'We can't send you to the front row without the right kit. Need them back afterwards, mind.'

She gestured to a row of silk shirts, embellished bomber jackets, floral dresses, and brightly coloured knitwear. Maggie could have kissed her. They'd struck up a bit of a friendship after a few more nights in the pub – another singleton with evenings to spare, Holly was far more down-to-earth than her intimidatingly cool exterior suggested. They spent an hour in the cupboard, putting together outfits for each day Maggie would be away, a combination of things from the rail and pieces she had already.

Her favourite was a high-waisted pencil skirt in electric blue houndstooth that Holly told her to wear with a cropped, skinny-sleeved black sweater that showed the tiniest sliver of flesh above the waistband. Maggie's instinct was to wear it with heels, but Holly shook her head: 'too Barbie,' she decreed, producing a chunky pair of white running shoes. 'Leg tint – and no socks,' she instructed, as though addressing a small child.

When she got back to her computer, Maggie had several emails waiting, including one from Penny, the PR she'd met with Margot, about one of her designers, Marc Moreau. Maggie desperately wanted to interview him for the magazine. Marc was dark and brooding, the epitome of edgy

Parisian cool. More important, he dressed anyone who was anyone and was famously indiscreet – just the sort of subject Moff got excited about.

Penny's email was short, to the point, suggesting Maggie could do the interview with Marc when she arrived in Paris for fashion week next month. He'd be busy but he always had time for *Haute,* Penny wrote, words that made Maggie's heart sing after years as a freelancer trying to get quotes in doorways or as celebrities climbed into their cars. More than once she had had to chase a subject down corridors shouting her questions at them. The people she interviewed had no idea who she was, and didn't care because she wasn't attached to a prestigious title.

Would Maggie like to pop into Marc's boutique on Old Bond Street, Penny added, to be measured up for a Moreau suit that she could wear at the shows?

Was there any other answer but yes?

After three weeks of shows, front rows, linen tablecloths, and starched pillowcases with her initials on them, Maggie thought she might have got used to playing at being a fashion editor in New York, London, and Milan, but she couldn't believe her eyes when the porter showed her to her hotel room in Paris.

The places she had stayed in for the previous fashion weeks had been perfectly nice – the anonymously comfortable sort of corporate hotel that the less seedy type of businessman stays in to ensure he gets a good night's sleep before his big meeting. The rooms were functional: quite dark, quite square, clean lines, and even cleaner, excruciatingly well-lit bathrooms. More expensive than what you'd stay in if you were on holiday, Maggie thought, but nowhere near as fancy as you'd expect for what they were charging *Haute*'s business account.

No, her suite – *suite!* – at the Royale was on another level entirely. She had nearly shrieked with excitement earlier as the liveried porter carried her battered old suitcase through the door and into a confection of pink silk brocade and gold curlicues. A sitting room overlooking the square, with the Eiffel Tower in the background; a bedroom with the most enormous four-poster she'd ever seen and a multitude of gilt-edged wardrobes; and a marble bathroom where swan-shaped taps had sparkling jewels for eyes. She spent the most fabulous hour of her life unpacking the designer clothes from her case and lining up her shoes. A whole week, living like she was a regular at Versailles.

She thought back to her first night in New York; the beginning of the month already felt like a distant memory. So did the Maggie who had landed there, jangling with nerves and convinced she'd mess up at the first opportunity.

She'd arrived in Manhattan before Moff, who would fly in midweek when the biggest designers held their shows, and had her first evening there to herself. It was still warm, the close of a long, balmy summer that had ended rather more abruptly in London, and she delighted in wearing a loose chiffon shirtdress to a nearby restaurant and eating on the terrace. Maggie was on the best-dressed holiday of her life; she could hardly believe she was being paid for it.

That feeling didn't quite last – she worked like a dog as soon as the first show kicked things off the next day – but her sense of wonder did. She'd wake early in her light-flooded hotel room (about four times the size of her room at the flat) just to luxuriate in the vast shower and enormous breakfast menu. She walked to shows, checking her maps app surreptitiously, so she could pretend she was a local. Maggie didn't know then that nobody walked, because it implied your publication was too poor to provide you with a driver. Theirs turned up with a ridiculously stretched Lincoln Town Car just in time to collect Moff from the airport.

She'd been nervous about spending quite so much time alone with her new boss – all day in the car between shows and then in the evenings, too – so had brushed up on dinner conversation beforehand, but Moff turned out to be in such demand at cocktail galas and five-course meals that she'd push around the plate but not eat that Maggie barely saw her after the sun had gone down.

Her own social calendar was jammed, too, with store openings, cocktails, buffets, and meals all laid on by the labels and their marketing departments, who took every opportunity to show off their wares to the journalists and buyers who had crammed into the city that week. In Milan, she sat under so many beautifully frescoed ceilings and cut-glass chandeliers that she began to crane her neck habitually when she entered every building. She was glad to see the rest of the invitees doing the same, and capturing it on their phone cameras – they weren't too cool to acknowledge the magnificence of their surroundings.

They were too cool to make friends, though. When Maggie had first sat down in what she still thought of as Margot's seat in New York, she didn't yet know what a travelling circus the shows were – somewhere between a trade fair and a school trip. Editors from each country were seated together in blocks and, within those, stratified by rank – so Moff was on the front row, and Maggie sometimes joined her but usually sat directly behind her on the second bench. That setup meant she was adjacent to or a few seats along from exactly the same selection of other editors and writers for the best part of the month.

As soon as she realised that, Maggie began introducing herself to people. And as soon as she did *that*, they went from frosty hauteur to smiles, wisecracks, and 'Hi, Maggie!' from across the room, waving and pointing out her seat next to them. She didn't know whether it was shyness that had stopped them from introducing themselves first or a sense that she should have known who they were without having to ask, but it all melted away as soon as she started chatting and asking them questions. Maggie had thought she was insecure before she took this job, but she had nothing on fashion people.

What with the other journalists she'd met and the PRs who kept inviting her to drinks and dinner, she'd built up a gang over the past few weeks. It was a strange existence on the road, equal parts glamour and drudgery. They'd go to cocktails in the grounds of a private villa one night, the bar surrounded by Poseidon statues and privet hedges sculpted into high heels, then sit and yawn into a plate of pasta the next. Maggie sipped prosecco under a Renaissance colonnade as models strode past in evening gowns at eleven a.m., then returned to the hotel to write her review in her bra and knickers so she didn't crease her dress, while eating salami straight out of the plastic. She was at events with women so rich they travelled with their own hairdressers, but she dried her now-blond curls every morning in the hotel bathroom with something nailed to the wall that looked like a vacuum cleaner attachment.

Just as she got the hang of each city – early mornings in New York, late nights in Milan – it was time to move on. And although she went to the London shows between the two, she felt like she hadn't been home in years. Five-star hotel ballrooms, royal palaces, corporate penthouses: fashion week London wasn't *her* London, even if it was a chance to sleep in her own bed for four nights.

She had twenty-four hours between landing back from Italy and getting on the Eurostar that she spent unpacking, checking proofs of the magazine's next issue, washing her knickers, and packing again. Thank God she had a whole week in Paris before she next had to face that damn suitcase again.

That said, she had barely had time to turn around before she came out that evening to meet Penny and Marc Moreau.

The interview wasn't for a few days, but the PR insisted she introduce them over drinks. Maggie wasn't sure whether it would be a bit gauche to wear her new suit to meet him, but she'd been aching to put it on ever since the courier dropped it off at the flat.

She had never owned anything so beautiful. The structured shoulders of the blazer gave her a swagger that had always eluded her; the slim-cut, gently flared sleeves skimmed her knuckles to give her every movement a languid grace; the single button fastened at her waist's narrowest point. The trousers, made from the same lightweight black wool, made even her stubby little legs go on for miles. She was wearing it with the chunky white sneakers Holly had suggested and allowed herself a smug little smile in the red-velvet-curtained bathroom of the bar they were in as she studied herself in the mirror.

They ate in the garden courtyard of a restaurant that every unfeasibly attractive person in Paris seemed to know about, were waved along to the front of the line and then on to a corner table where everybody could see them. She was one of the Beautiful People now.

Then they had come here, to a private club in a hôtel particulier that sat on top of the hill at Montmartre, canopied tables spread out along a terrace in front of it. Before she rejoined Penny and Marc, and the gaggle of sharp-eyed black-clad assistants they'd both brought with them, she stood and savoured the view, the city lights of the City of Light twinkling away below her. The Eiffel Tower, Les Invalides, La Défense, Sacré Coeur.

She touched her hair, dusted nonexistent fluff from her blazer. She was so content, so lighthearted, she thought she might float off the edge of the balcony. The feeling had been kicking away inside her ever since the lights had come up on her first catwalk show this season and the first model had strutted out. At some point during Milan, she'd stopped thinking of the show tickets as Margot's and claimed them as her own. In Paris, now she finally voiced what she could no longer ignore, breathing it into life over the most stylish city in the world:

'I don't ever want to give this job back.'

9

Margot

Winnie's next message permeated the bubble in which I spent my days like a bucket of icy water to the soul.

My world had narrowed to the set of a soap opera: kitchen, sitting room, bedroom; my days had become a looping, unpredictable meander between the three according to my and the baby's needs. I lost hours feeding Lila on the sofa, gazing at her downy crown, memorising the thick dark eyelashes splayed along the top of her full pink cheeks, and watching the rhythm of her rosebud mouth as it drained the milk from the veined breasts I no longer recognised as my own.

I sat, unoccupied, for longer than I'd known was possible under the snug weight of my sleeping baby, the fingers of one hand stroking the deep, soft hollow at the back of Lila's neck, the others in the grip of a little fist whose strength was astonishingly disproportionate to its size. For the first two weeks I monitored every shallow breath, every tiny puff of warm air, with one knuckle under Lila's nose.

When I woke in the middle of the night to hungry mews coming from the woven basket next to my and Nick's bed, I sat up instinctively, ready to nurse. I had been expecting that quarter-second of incomprehension that so often comes with a sudden change of state – the unthinking, unfettered moment before memory kicks in – but I never forgot the fact of Lila, even during my deepest snatched hours of sleep. *Does Winnie have those briefest moments before she remembers? Or does Jack still live in her cells the way Lila does in mine?*

I marvelled at how my heart could beat in somebody else's body; I felt the bond between us like the string between a pair of plastic cups. For now though, the farthest Lila ever travelled was to Nick's arms before he left in the morning and back again when he came home from work. He was besotted with her, tired and love-worn. The two of us peered, our shoulders shaking with silent giggles, over the edge of the basket as Lila slept, fast asleep yet with the most serious expressions. When she woke us in the night, I was delighted to have a reason to hold her again.

Still, a month in, my chest tightened at the sight of my tiny daughter. My head felt light and my throat constricted each time I saw her; my stomach jittered as though I were meeting a new boyfriend. *Lila is the best date of my life.*

So when the message came, my defences were down. I had thought nothing of posting on Instagram the photo of Lila, asleep in her car seat on the way home from hospital. If there had been any doubt in my mind before the birth about joining that soppy cohort of people who share pictures of their children, the arrival of Lila had convinced me my followers would be only too appreciative of the chance to adore her unalloyed perfectitude. Maggie had posted a nice comment, along with fifty or so others.

I was wearing Lila against my chest in the stretchy bamboo sling when my phone buzzed. This week the baby would only be soothed by laying one plump cheek against my solar plexus in order to better absorb her mother's heartbeat. I swayed my hips as I opened the text.

'Congratulations. You could have warned me before you put that picture up. Please don't contact me again.'

I forgot about the women who leave the hospital with less than they arrived with.

I felt nauseous for days afterwards. Of course I should have warned Winnie; I couldn't believe I had forgotten to tell my friend about Lila's arrival before posting that first picture of her. *Too wrapped up in myself, once again.* Had I forgotten though, or had I subconsciously ducked sending a message because I felt guilty about my own good fortune? Or because I had sensed, after so many months of silence, that there would be hostility there? Either way, I had been cowardly and weak. And I had made Winnie – tragic Winnie, a mother with no child – feel even worse.

I had forgotten too that Winnie could make me feel insecure the way nothing and nobody else could.

But there was a part of me that was annoyed at the notion of Lila as something to be put on guard against, something to be avoided, an unwanted guest at a party. *Warned. Friends don't use words like that about each other's children. It's not like Winnie showed any interest in my pregnancy after . . .* It felt petty to pursue the thought.

But we were no longer friends, Winnie and I. Female relationships are bonds made of love that are coated with loyalty, so that the inevitable resentments and jealousies cannot weather them; when the fealty is gone and the devotion eroded, envy and reproach seep in like water and decay grows.

Once our safe, dozy bubble had been popped, my days with Lila were a space for panic and terror. *I don't deserve her. I don't deserve her and she will be taken from me. I don't know how to look after her. I'll do something wrong, and I'll lose her.*

Lila died before my eyes several times a day, with every car that went past too quickly or too loudly, every step we climbed on which I might trip. I saw my baby's gruesome end in every action and my own body was the weapon – a sharp elbow, a heavy palm, a full, smothering breast.

It wasn't my fault.

I know what you did.

'Very common in new mothers,' the doctor said when I explained my fears on Nick's gentle suggestion. 'What you're actually seeing are the dangers, Margot. It's just your mind warning you. It's normal.'

But every accident, every cry, every small thing I noticed I could have done better, felt like a warning from Winnie – or a threat. Despite the sleepless nights and the assault of life with a newborn, I knew I must not let myself feel tired or emotional or overwrought, let alone frustrated with Lila's wails or her whims, because to do so would be to show ingratitude. *I must always be grateful that my baby lived.* That knowledge left me more exhausted than any number of night feeds.

I spent those intimate moments, with my daughter nuzzling into me for comfort as much as for sustenance, in a rocking chair in the womblike dark of the nursery, so that we didn't disturb Nick. Having nodded off one night – I jerked awake, convinced the inevitable had happened: *you've suffocated her!* – I now took my phone and silently scrolled through each of my social media apps to keep my bleary eyes open while Lila guzzled noisily.

Stalking Maggie hadn't been a deliberate choice – I even used the verb knowingly with Nick, acknowledging my obsessive tendencies with a self-deprecating shrug. It had just sort of happened one night between the hours of three and five, a window in which anybody's sanity is stretched thin if they find themselves awake.

I had found it surprisingly easy, after Lila's birth, to forget all about work, the office, Moff, and the woman currently doing my job. My head was so full of loving panic, my mind so singularly focused on keeping Lila alive, there was little space for anything else. The vocabulary I used to pride myself on had all but abandoned me; I found myself pointing at things I needed Nick to pass me – a pen, a glass of water – simply making noises, because I couldn't remember what to call them.

But in the solitary darkness before dawn, my companion busy slurping, the jealousy flooded back, as I flicked through image after image of Maggie living the high life. *Living* my *life*. *My* old *life*. Maggie trying on clothes in changing rooms, the camera on her phone angled just so to whittle her waist and emphasise her bust. Maggie sitting down to dinner in the latest cool restaurant with the same PRs who used to invite me and had switched allegiance alarmingly quickly. Maggie looking around the showrooms of various exclusive designer labels, snapping a handbag here, a pair of colourful stilettos there.

'Pictures of shoes always do well on social. People always love shoes,' I remembered the digital editor saying time and again. *People are idiots.* I clicked 'like' on Maggie's most recent pair.

Maggie's pictures had thousands of likes, far more than mine ever did. *That's because she's on there all the time. At least I've retained my mystique.* Maggie did seem to assume an interest on the part of her followers in things that bordered on mundane: shots of her dinner, her makeup bag, even her laundry hung out to dry. My keen editorial eye scanned for rogue socks and balled-up tissues, and I thrived on finding remotely déclassé or embarrassing items in the background of Maggie's shots. I pored over the visual crumbs to fit together the interior of her flat like a crazed fan.

Sitting in the dark, wearing a milk-stained pair of Nick's pyjamas because my own no longer closed over the empty spare tire of flesh around my middle, I wondered just how much mystique I had left. My hair was lank, my pedicure chipped. My skin had a looseness it hadn't before pregnancy and my clothes a tightness.

It wasn't only the number of likes Maggie's pictures had, it was the comments underneath them from the girls in the office, from designers and PRs I knew, from readers – comments that made it perfectly clear, to my sleep-deprived, restlessly suspicious mind, that the sort of social life I had never had was developing between them and their new fashion editor. Once again, I felt the pinch of playground whispers, of not being invited, of being stared at rather than spoken to.

The feeling receded during the day, when my attention was absorbed with Lila, her mews and snuffles, waving fingers and catlike mouth; when I strolled through the park with the pram, bathing her in the low-shining late-summer sun; when I met up with Sofia, Adele, and Gemma from our parenting class, with whom I exchanged not so much conversation as a series of lists: wake-up times, feeding intervals, number of nappies.

Around the kitchen table in one of their houses, all filled with exactly the same bouncers, breast pumps, and sheepskins on which some of our babies now lay, we talked about the women who were not in the room but were always with us – the ones doing the jobs we had left behind at the doors to the maternity ward.

'They gave mine to my assistant, who was my intern before that,' said Gemma, blowing her fringe off her face as her baby fed. 'She's eight years younger than me. On my last day, she asked me to hand over my set of keys to the stock cupboard and told me she didn't want things going missing – as if I'd be nicking stuff while I was off!'

We others tutted and rolled our eyes, the biscuit plate was handed round again, and Adele chimed in.

'They kept my colleague's maternity cover on, so she's doing mine too. Massive suck-up, the boss's pet, completely insufferable. She made a complaint about me on my last day, said I groaned every time I sat down and it was distracting her.'

Laughter and grimaces: the memories of heavy pregnant bodies were not yet distant enough to have become fond ones.

'Mine's the boss's girlfriend!' sighed Sofia. 'He couldn't wait for me to leave. So I think we know how *that's* going to turn out when I go back.'

'What about yours, Margot?' Gemma asked. 'Fashion must be so bitchy, did they find some size-zero total cow?'

They turned to look at me, interested and expectant, and my criticisms of Maggie evaporated on my tongue. Now that I had an opportunity to air them, they seemed so petty.

'Mine is . . . I chose mine myself,' I stuttered, and they aahed at the enlightenment of it. 'She's kind of a friend. So that's good.'

I could sense their disappointment but felt glad to have remained above the fray. I needed to be less sensitive to Maggie – she was just getting on with the job.

The women started talking about a recent TV drama in which a maternity cover had tried to kill the mother she was temping for. I had stopped watching after the first episode, because it had made me feel such a profound sense of unease.

'Tell me you're giving up on that because it's crap, rather than because it's too close to the bone,' Nick had said when I changed the channel.

I had told him what his rational mind wanted to hear.

It took me by surprise when, a week later, almost everybody on my Instagram feed decamped to New York. I had come to know the biannual rhythm of the shows as well as I once had the school year: instead of a new pencil case every September, I bought a pair of shoes; instead of going skiing every February, I now packed for a month on the road. This season had kicked off without me, and I was still wearing the same leggings and denim shirt I had for the past twelve weeks.

I followed Maggie's progress ever more closely during the shows. Though I had no wish to leave Lila's side and take up my place on the front row – the thought of facing my peers as

I was now, moonfaced and bloated! – I nevertheless craved the excitement of fashion week. The buzz of filing into a venue, be it a gilded ballroom in the centre of town or a dusty, edgy warehouse in the next yet-to-be-gentrified district, of trying to guess what the designer had in store for the audience. The thump of the music, the adolescent thrill of recognising the track, the first glimpse of the heels, the lines, the silhouette, the hair, and the makeup. The first look at the next big thing.

I had always been amazed by fashion shows. Their big budgets and production costs rivalled those of West End shows, but these were costume dramas played out in miniature: they lasted no longer than fifteen minutes. Quarter of an hour in which to evoke a mood, a context, an emotion. I had been to shows that sent shivers down the spine and had editors in tears.

My nervousness had made me tough and gruff when I first arrived at *Haute:* you'd never catch me crying at clothes. Since then I had welled up countless times at sweetly nostalgic visions of girlhood, at the quiet power of femininity, at knowing references that raised the humdrum to an art form. I cried hardest at a coat that reminded me of one my mother used to have, long and black with double buttons, its elegance undercut by the maternal grin that was her constant accessory.

Maggie just wouldn't get it. She'll think it's all glitz and celebs and star-fucking, she won't see the beauty – only the narcissism. And there was a lot of that. Self-regard by the bucketload; the shallow, the pompous, the cringe-inducingly vacuous. Fashion week brought on plenty of the wrong types of shivers, too.

By the time Maggie reached Paris, her Instagram, Twitter, and Facebook profiles were my most visited. My phone had archived my growing neuroses and helpfully presented them to me as quick links every time I went online, that they might sink their claws in further. I was like a dieter with a dessert menu, unable to push it away unread.

One click and I was absorbed into the show schedule I knew as well as Lila's routine, able to visualise exactly Maggie's whereabouts, the canapés she'd be nibbling, the seat she'd be in (mine). Through Maggie, I sat front row from my chair in the nursery – short, slo-mo videos of the ripple of gown as a model passed by; lingering shots of a name card that should have displayed mine rather than Maggie's; the must-have and must-share £200 baked potato topped with glittering beluga for dinner at Caviar Kaspia. I ate a bowl of cereal standing up today.

I checked in as I fed Lila, as the baby slept, as Nick slept, when I was supposed to be asleep myself. I would blink my gaze from the brightness of the screen to see Lila's navy blue eyes, more iris than white, staring murkily up at me – trying to fathom me – and clouded with the sort of devotion that only comes of utter reliance.

Maggie looked so well, giddy with her own success, exhilarated – surprisingly well dressed – wearing a crop top in one selfie that made me want to curl up and die. I felt like Dorian Gray's portrait by comparison. I was tired, clumsy, and ravaged: struggling not only under the weight of the new emotions Lila had seeded within me when she arrived, but also with the relentless ache of old wounds – both physical and mental – that the end of my oldest friendship had reopened.

For as surely as I kept tabs on Maggie's movements, I refreshed Winnie's feed every bit as often. Between the two women who I felt held the two strands of my identity in their hands, I lost myself for afternoons at a time, waking to my own existence only when fresh squawks rose from Lila's basket.

I had developed a habit of flicking through old photos of me and Winnie on Facebook, taken in the days when four a.m. was going-home time and babies were unthought of. My new habit didn't alleviate my grief and sense of loss, but it stopped my brain from spinning over Maggie, stopped the increasing sense that I had somehow invented all those years of closeness and memories of shared happiness.

I wasn't surprised when, just before sunrise one morning, I saw Winnie had unfriended me on Facebook. Wasn't surprised, though it came as yet another jolt to a body that was still raw with new motherhood.

Our history just wasn't there anymore, and the search for Winnie Clough yielded only a thumbnail image next to the name, with an option to add her as a friend. The message was clear enough. Sorrow welled and with it, irritation. She's treating me like I wronged her. All I did was have a baby.

But I knew that was not exactly true.

It was a Tuesday when I first saw Winnie in my neighbourhood.

I had taken Lila in the buggy to the slightly desultory row of shops near our house, partly because the sun was out and partly because I didn't know how else to pass the time that morning.

Maggie was at the Marc Moreau show, I had seen earlier, wearing what appeared to be a £2,000 suit by the designer himself. That's the suit Penny promised me before I was pregnant. Even worse, scrolling through umpteen versions of the same image posted by all the fashion people I followed, I saw that Marc had placed one of his famous cashmere cardigans on each gilded chair, its label personalised with the attendee's name and seat number, their presence at the show woven into history. An heirloom! I've only missed out on a fucking heirloom!

This was my inner monologue as I walked along the pavement, and I was glad nobody else could hear it. I'm a terrible person. There were limits to how much of it I could complain to Nick about; even he had begun to looked pained when I brought up the subject of Maggie. I could tell he'd be glad when the shows were over and Maggie was stuck behind a computer again. Well, so would I. I was thoroughly sick of myself.

My route, carefully calibrated to last as long as it took for Lila to fall asleep and then complete a nap, took me past the shops, past several primary schools I was already anxious wouldn't be good enough – if . . . – and up to the hill towards the old Victorian cemetery.

It was impressively gothic in its overgrown state of disrepair. Cracked slabs lay at angles on the graves they had once covered, as if the occupants had just popped out. Broken urns sat where they had fallen between resting places. Hooded figures, their hands the victims of acidic rainwater, raised pitted wrists to the sky. They went to all that trouble, and you can't even read their names.

There was a modern area, a greener, jollier spot where the headstones read more like lonely hearts than Tennyson's 'In Memoriam.' 'Darling Steve,' 'always a joker,' 'gone to the great am dram soc in the sky.' This contemporary version of death was warm and affectionate, with none of the nineteenth century's arcane pomp. And there she was.

Winnie knelt in front of one of the stones, her ginger hair, the same colour as the turning leaves along the path, clearly visible above it. I didn't need to see my friend's face to know it was her. I felt her proximity like an electric current. Without thinking, I quickened my pace until I reached the next copse of misshapen tombs, took the nearest exit, and went straight home. I held Lila so tightly for the rest of the day, the baby was relieved to go to her father when he arrived.

I felt watched whenever I left the house after that. I spent my days walking as if with blinkers on, refusing to look anywhere but forward. I saw Winnie's ginger curls whenever I turned my head, so I trained myself not to. Whether my friend was there or not – whether she had ever been there – became irrelevant.

She knows what I am doing. She knows when I do it wrong. She knows when Lila is crying, and she knows that it is my fault.

'Why don't we have a Christmas party?' suggested Nick, clearly worried about my reduced social life.

Christmas was six weeks away and I hadn't made any plans to celebrate it, beyond buying Lila a little corduroy pinafore covered in holly sprigs. Usually Winnie and I met up during the break – always in London, never the city we grew up in. Even though our parents still lived within walking distance, there were too many memories up there to ignore.

We would be in London for it this year, just me, Nick, and Lila. A newborn had proved the perfect excuse to stay away from the streets of my adolescence – where Winnie might also be. This would be her first Christmas as a mother, too; my heart ached for her at the thought of how our days would differ, of how much of the celebrations were focused around children.

'Let's get everyone together,' my husband was saying. 'I tell you what, why don't you invite Maggie? You know you like her really.'

An invited Maggie would be easier to deal with than an unexpected Winnie, I decided.

10

Maggie

She really knew what it meant, that expression about your feet not touching the ground, after a month of fashion week. Maggie was fashion *weak*. She might have clipped across Milanese marble and clopped over Parisian parquet, but she had been spirited along by a mixture of adrenaline and alcohol, fuelled by her own enthusiasm.

The day after she arrived home, Maggie came down with the worst cold she'd ever had. All she wanted to do was lie on the sofa and watch TV.

Cath laughed at the turnaround in her fabulousness. 'From two-hundred-pound baked potato to the home-cooked version. What's on that one then, more caviar?'

'Beans and cheese,' Maggie jeered back. 'And fuck off.'

She spent the next month or so keeping a low profile, refusing dinner invitations from PRs she'd been raucously drunk with during the shows, turning down drinks with the girls from the office who wanted to hear all about it. She needed to conserve her energy if she was going to continue to impress Emily Moffatt.

On her first day back at work, Maggie arrived at her desk to find the girls had decorated her computer screen with yellow Post-its cut out to look like bunting and bought her a net bag of oranges so she could work on her fatigue and booze-related vitamin C deficit. Holly had written 'Welcome home, Number 1!' across the little paper tags, which made Maggie laugh. A famously terse editor at the American edition of *Haute,* whom she'd seen across the catwalk but not spoken to, insisted on being referred to as 'Number 1' at all times by her staffers. They'd jokingly decided after a few drinks that this was what the fashion team should christen Maggie. Technically, she was their boss. But in reality she'd become a friend.

It gave her a little glow that they'd gone to the trouble, so she took a picture of the scene and posted it on Instagram. When she saw on her phone a few minutes later that Margot had liked it, Maggie wondered what that little pink heart had cost her. Would Margot be jealous of their camaraderie? Irritated or unsettled that her replacement was making friends in the office? Or was she genuinely pleased that Maggie was getting on so well with her – Margot's – team?

If Maggie was being honest, she was aware that what she was doing was a sort of power play even before she pressed 'share' on that post. Putting up an image of Margot's desk – even though Maggie hadn't thought of it as such for some time now – wreathed in something *her* colleagues had done for *Maggie* was an incursion onto Margot's territory, a minor act of aggression perhaps. On some level – one she wasn't particularly proud of – Maggie wanted her predecessor to know she was doing well, that she was fitting in. Did Maggie want her to worry? Maybe.

She still felt grateful to Margot, she really did. But as the halfway point of Maggie's year in her shoes approached, the new girl was beginning to feel a tide of resentment, too. The burning feeling in her chest from the secret that she had whispered across the Paris rooftops hadn't abated; the prospect of Margot strolling back in and taking all this from her made Maggie feel sick and angry.

It made her hate Margot sometimes.

She knew full well that this was exactly what she had signed up for, that it was in her contract to bow out gracefully when

Margot was ready to return, but emotions don't tend to read the small print, she reminded herself.

That was why Maggie uploaded the picture of Holly's 'Number 1': she wanted to hurt Margot for hanging over her head like the sword of Damocles, for being a blot on the horizon – and for making her feel inadequate along the way. Every day that Maggie worried about whether or not she was living up to the woman whose place she had taken was a day less in the job she was coming to love more and more. Maggie wanted Margot out of the picture, but she still wanted to impress her. And still wanted to be her friend. It was . . . complicated.

There was something umbilical about the whole situation, this bond between Margot and her. Maggie's doing this job relied on Margot's staying away; Margot's returning to it relied on Maggie's leaving again. They were tethered by this dysfunctional debt of gratitude, bound by necessity but also mistrust. To top it all off, they were similar people. Given their senses of humour and worldview, they should have been friends; under any other circumstances, they would have been. But they couldn't be because of this unspoken awkwardness, like ex-girlfriends to the same guy tussling for superiority. They were like friends who had gone beyond familiarity and into contempt but refused to admit it to each other.

In those quiet weeks after the shows, there was only one invitation that had piqued Maggie's interest, and that was Margot's Christmas party. Could she make it? She'd be there with bells on. Maggie might have come to an unfortunate conclusion about her and Margot's interests being best described as incompatible when it came to the job they were sharing (although she was the only one actually doing it right now), but she wasn't about to let that get in the way of a good old snoop at her rival's house and husband.

Maggie didn't mean to sound ungrateful. She was only too aware of the favour Margot had done her in putting her up for the job – and it'd be really nice to see her and the baby – but since Maggie had been wearing Margot's shoes and walking her walk, she found herself even more intrigued by the other fashion editor. She had thought that by putting on Margot's skin, she'd find out that she was made of the same corruptible flesh as the rest of them – thought that sitting at Margot's desk might be a bit like moving in with her, that inevitable shift in a relationship from making an effort to no longer policing your real self. From pre-fart to post-fart, if you will, although she was sure Margot had never done anything so uncouth.

But Margot remained an enigma. The girls in the office barely knew Margot beyond her coffee order – decaf tea, what even was that? – and all the fashion types Maggie had been out with described the other woman as 'cool' or 'nice,' which even Maggie could tell was damning by faint praise. In fashion, people were either amazing or vile – anything in between and you were a nonentity.

Which Margot Jones clearly wasn't – she was a terrific writer, gorgeous, funny, but it was as though something was missing. Friends, maybe, or a social life. A backstory.

Hence Maggie's excitement about Margot's party. The invitation had come via email to Maggie's phone rather than hand-embossed and through her letterbox – a few brief but jokey lines long and signed off from 'Nick and Margot'. Interesting that his name had come first, she thought, when Margot had clearly been the one to write it. Maggie could tell from the self-deprecating comment about their being 'fuddy-duddy parents' these days.

What do you wear to a fashion editor's house? Maggie thought she might have got better at this, several months and several armfuls of new clothes down the line, but Margot brought out in her the same old insecurities: trussed up, galumphing, too much makeup, Not Cool.

Whatever outfit Maggie chose, Margot would appraise it, drinking it in with her eyes the way a professional wine taster swills for quality and provenance. Her replacement wanted something that would linger on the palate in the right way, something Margot could neither pity nor patronise her for.

Maggie wondered about wearing her Moreau suit (her *le smoking*, to give it what she now knew was its proper name) one more time. She had pretty much lived in it since it arrived in its logoed hanging bag (which she zipped it back into lovingly after every wear), but it felt a bit try-hard for a drinks party. Civilians didn't understand the concept of a fashionable trouser suit; they'd just think she worked in a bank. Or that Margot had hired her as a project manager for the afternoon.

There was no dress code on the invite; Margot wasn't one of those Chelsea types. In fact, she was in the hipster mortgage-and-child belt somewhere southeast. Definitely taxi territory. Maggie assumed the vibe for the party would be that all-too-intangible point between dressy and scruffy. In short, impossible if you don't know how and invisible if you don't really care. The men would wear jeans or chinos; the women would agonise – and then wear jeans.

Maggie settled on a red silk wrap dress over a pale blue pair: dressy *and* scruffy, and a look she'd admired on several other street-stylers over various fashion weeks. It was funny how she had got used to seeing a trend or a certain styling quirk that recurred so often in those rarefied front-row circles that she'd almost stopped noticing it, but when she took it out into real life she was stared at as though she'd just landed from another planet. She'd almost forgotten that, given so many people wore a suit to work all week and then the same sweater and jeans all weekend, a slinky dress over a pair of jeans was a bit of a leap, the sort of thing one's father might be baffled by.

As she climbed out of her Uber – a black cabbie had refused to take her to the south-of-the-river postcode – Maggie looked up at the redbrick Victorian terrace in front of her with a tingling curiosity. Glowing lights through shuttered windows; a small and tidy front garden. It seemed so ordinary, although noticeably immaculate – with its grey door, matching window frames, and squared-off box hedge – for a house on the sort of London road where the pavements were still littered with burger boxes as well as winter leaves.

Who were Margot's neighbours, Maggie wondered. Did they know they lived next door to a fashion editor? She some-times felt that way on the bus: what would the people next to her say if they realised she had one of those fairy-tale jobs that others only dreamed of?

Maggie tucked her hair behind one ear and smoothed her dress. She walked through a wooden slatted gate in the low redbrick wall, along the black-and-white tiled path to the door, and pressed the brass button for the bell. She heard it peal out a *drrrrring* inside above the hubbub of voices and felt her stomach contract with nerves.

A beat. Two – then the ratchet noise of the catch and the door swung open, invitingly inwards.

'You must be Maggie!' A male voice, and a smile within it: Nick.

He was tall, Maggie noticed instantly, much taller than her and very slim. Having failed to find Margot's husband in any of her social feeds (she had taxed herself with the coin jar for looking), Maggie had half thought Nick would be of the rugby player variety, one of those meaty, dimple-chinned boys who had resolutely ignored her at university in search of longer legs and more symmetrical faces.

In fact, Nick was edgier than she had expected, dressed in dark jeans and a T-shirt decorated with an abstract insignia. A record label, she presumed, or an artisanal brewery. Something deliberately obscure and cliquey – she could tell by the dark-rimmed designer glasses and expensive sneakers he was wearing with it. She knew men like him – they pushed buggies in the park near her own flat while listening to podcasts, sported sleeping babies in papooses at the pub.

That said, Nick looked less like the fatherly provider she had pictured, all shoulders and shirtsleeves, and more like an overgrown student. But perhaps that was just the can of beer he was holding.

He was handsome, too: somewhere between chiselled and boyish, but without the haughtiness that comes of growing up good-looking. She found herself imagining what it would be like to climb into bed with him every night – nothing more. His grin was lopsided, his eyes crinkled authentically with the force of it. Maggie couldn't help but smile back warmly.

'I certainly am.' She stepped across the threshold. 'Pleased to meet you, Nick. I like your Christmas decorations.'

The hallway twinkled with the dim light of candles of various sizes in jars and sconces, warming up the darkening afternoon outside. A row of small apothecary vases filled with sprigs of holly, mistletoe, and eucalyptus lined a shelf along one side of the hallway. On a marble console table stood a deep golden bowl filled with clove-pricked orange pomanders. The rich and oaky sweet scent they gave off was so evocative of perfect Christmases – so unlike the TV-centric, argumentative ones she tended to share with her own family – that Maggie was nearly knocked sideways by a wave of yearning. Of envy.

Of course Margot Jones didn't do tinsel and glitter like everybody else at this time of year.

The place looked like a hotel. A warm, welcoming, wonderfully luxurious hotel. One that Maggie would find it hard to check out of.

'Thank you,' said Nick, holding up his hands. 'Obviously I had nothing to do with making the place look this nice.'

'I guessed as much,' she laughed. 'Margot has such amazing taste, doesn't she?'

She meant what she said, even as it pinched her heart to say it aloud. The scene was transcendentally perfect, like one of Moff's heavily art-directed shoots, from the tiny children running here and there between the bustling eat-in kitchen at one end of the hall (herringbone parquet; bare plaster walls left a naturally modish shade of calamine) and the sitting room to Maggie's right (oak floorboards, wood-burning stove, thick wool rug), where people were milling and chatting.

Nick and Maggie shared another smile, amateur aesthetes in the presence of a master tastemaker. From the bare brass pendant light in the hallway hung a solitary sprig of mistletoe.

'Right,' Nick said, turning away from it to lead the way. 'Come through and meet people.'

Maggie suddenly felt overdressed in her silk and heels. Margot's clique were obviously sophisticated and urbane enough not to goggle as though they'd just arrived from the provinces – they were no doubt used to seeing their host dressed in a similarly eye-catching way – but Maggie noticed the odd look flicked towards her from the corners of eyes and lingering, if not out of judgment then definitely out of curiosity.

They weren't a fashion-y bunch: this much she'd expected from the fact that she was the only one invited from the office. Margot's friends – and Nick's friends, Maggie supposed – were a selection of the sort of creative-looking, tortoiseshell-spectacled crowd who worked in design, publishing, architecture. Tidy, neat people in expensive utilitarian clothes that were once designed for toil but had been co-opted as a leisure uniform for the intelligentsia and given matching price tags: paper-bag-waist chinos and twill dungarees for the women, French worker jackets and chambray shirts for the men.

They stood chatting around a teak dining table laden with cheese and cold meats, some leaning down to hear what the inevitably high proportion of heavily pregnant women seated on the matching Quaker dining chairs were saying.

'Maggie, hi!' Margot appeared from behind a check-shirted shoulder and squeezed through to kiss her replacement's cheek as Nick began speaking to another man on his left. She was wearing black cropped flares and a shimmering blue sweater that Maggie recognised instantly as being by a much-hyped new Belgian designer. She must have preordered it, surely – was Margot really going to designer boutiques with a buggy in tow? Maggie felt a lurch of insecurity.

'Something a bit Christmassy!' Margot explained with a jokey shrug of the shoulders designed to hide what Maggie decided was nervousness. 'Although every fashion editor knows that sparkle isn't just for evening!' She rolled her eyes at the cliché. Quite a good idea though, really. 'How are you, Maggie? Let's get you a drink, and then tell me all about everything!'

As Margot guided her towards the kitchen and ladled mulled wine into a gold-rimmed mug, Maggie noted gleefully that she hadn't lost much of the baby weight, and then instantly hated herself.

'How's Moff? And Holly? You survived the shows, did you have fun?' Margot's patter was as fluent as her hostessing, but her eyes slid around the light and airy open-plan room (they had a skylighted extension, Maggie mentally jotted down enviously, and knowingly retro cork tiles on the floor) until they found what they were looking for: the baby. Margot visibly relaxed to see the child being capably jiggled by a tall man in a striped T-shirt.

'Things are good!' Maggie gushed. 'Everybody in the office is great, everyone sends their love. The shows, wow, I mean – intense, sure, but what fun. So amazing to see it all. And Moff . . . Moff is Moff.'

She searched Margot's face for anxiety, for that brief bitchy look she'd glimpsed on it all those months ago, when the fashion editor had seemed annoyed her cover hadn't been taken down a peg or two, but Margot kept on smiling beatifically, as though things as ephemeral as office politics merely washed over her now that she was a Mother. Perhaps they did – the suspicion had crossed Maggie's mind before as she put up her Instagram posts and sent her tweets, trying to provoke jealousy like a scorned lover baits their ex, that Margot probably didn't even notice these small acts of spite because she was operating on a higher level these days. The realisation had not made Maggie feel good.

'Anyway, pfffft, here I am talking about work when you've done something incredible – where's that gorgeous baby daughter of yours?' Maggie swivelled around as though she hadn't already seen Lila. 'She's even more adorable than in the pictures! Do you think she'll let me have a cuddle?'

She wasn't overreacting – Lila really was a beautiful baby: golden ringlets that fuzzed out from her head in a messy corona, big blue Disney eyes, and fat pink cheeks. Lila didn't exactly set Maggie's ovaries twanging, but there was a little tug in her heart that suggested her body hadn't quite given up on the idea of having one of its own. Although when or how it thought that might happen was anybody's guess.

'She's just been hanging out with her uncle Tim.' Margot patted the stripey man's arm.

'Well, hello there!' Maggie cooed, stretching out her arms to relieve him of the wriggling load. Lila had begun to kick her froggy legs, smiling gummily.

'I haven't managed to get a grin out of her this whole time,' said Uncle Tim, mock crestfallen.

Broad-shouldered and thatchy-haired, with dark eyes, a sharp jaw, and a clipped baritone, he was one of the most handsome men Maggie had ever met. Much more handsome than anybody she'd ever gone out with. Far more so, for instance, than any of the men she'd ever met on a dating app.

'So you're Nick's brother, is that right?' she asked him, reasoning dejectedly that family was probably off-limits to someone currently moonlighting as Margot in her second-most-important job.

'Oh no, just a friend,' he replied, grinning.

'His best friend.' Margot looked up at Tim affectionately, made a top-up gesture towards somebody behind her, and disappeared back into the throng.

That was two weeks ago. Since then, she had seen Tim Pritchard three more times – a great ratio. Maggie might have decided on a dating ban, but what she'd meant was a dating *app* ban. When somebody single and normal turns up in front of you, real flesh and blood with warm skin and an even warmer smile, you'd be a madwoman to turn them away.

The real-life meet-cute, the friend-of-a-friend, the oh-we-got-together-at-a-party: these things are the holy grail of single life. When you've been by yourself for as long as Maggie had, you begin to wonder whether they really exist or if they were invented by the breeders to keep you in a state of false consciousness so you don't realise the only option to procreate is with men who list pizza on their profile as one of their interests.

Tim did like pizza – they went for sourdough ones on their first date – but there was more to him than that. He was kind, funny, a real grown-up. He liked cycling and he did his own laundry, which was always a good sign. Maggie had seen the evidence on a clotheshorse when she first stayed over, which made her wonder whether he had a secret girlfriend or a female flatmate, but he assured her: neither.

Annoyingly he lived in the same bit of southeast London as Margot and Nick – just round the corner from them, in fact. Annoying not because they were so nearby, but because it was a hassle to reach from her place in Camden, and because people who lived in North London automatically looked down on people who lived in South London. It was a positive, really: Tim already lived in the land of pregnancy yoga and primary schools, so he must have been looking for all that too. But Maggie was getting ahead of herself.

It was unfortunate timing. Just last week, she had pitched a piece to Moff about how great it was to be single, an uplifting, happy-alone sort of thing, and the editor really went for it. Maggie didn't know whether to tell Tim about that up front – although that seemed sort of presumptuous, given it had only been two weeks – or to let him see the article when the magazine came out and risk his being offended that she still considered herself unattached. She was definitely getting ahead of herself: the mag wouldn't be out for another month.

Maggie had let Margot know after the party that Tim had asked for her number, and the other woman had seemed enthusiastic. But Maggie couldn't help wondering whether her face as she typed her reply had worn that same slightly annoyed look. If Maggie was with Tim, wouldn't it be much harder for Margot to disappear her replacement when she returned to work?

That wasn't the main reason Maggie was so into Tim, of course, but it definitely helped.

11

Margot

It took me a couple of days to get round to opening the cellophane envelope that contained the new issue of *Haute*. Since
it had thumped onto the doormat after Christmas, I had been
in a spin of sleeplessness and worry that was almost welcome,
hingeing as it did on the next stage of Lila's development
rather than anything my own imagination could conjure.

My daughter had forgotten how to go back to sleep by
herself in the middle of the night. After a few weeks of Lila's
only needing one feed in the small hours, sitting up rocking
her to sleep three times before dawn felt like several steps
backwards. All very natural, the websites I checked assured
me, not to mention temporary, but brain-addling while it
lasted. On top of all that, it was time to persuade Lila to try
food other than the milk I produced for her, which gave rise
to endless questions of safety, hygiene, and whether I was
doing it right or failing completely.

Winnie would know. I stamped on the inner voice as soon as
it bubbled up; I tried to limit my time spent thinking this way
to the afternoon walk I always took with the pram. That way,
I had fresh air and distractions, rather than the deadening
reverb of my own spiralling thoughts for company. *She would,
though, and she'd be able to tell me what to do.*

I missed my friend. Even though it had been nine months
– a gestation – since I had heard her voice, since we'd laughed
together or spent time together, I felt Winnie's absence daily.
Not only during the moments when I craved reassurance that

I was looking after Lila correctly, but when I caught my daughter's comic expressions, like those of a little troll-faced old man, or the squawky dinosaur noises she now made, and just wanted to share them with somebody else I knew would appreciate the minutiae of this life I had created.

I missed Winnie in the moments I forgot how to be myself, the self I had been before Lila, and needed reminding of what I had once been like. *Would the old me have laughed at that? Been annoyed by that? Or is this something that the new me does?*

On quiet days – of which I had many – I ached for company while at the same time rejecting it. I didn't want to go out and make an effort with women I barely knew; I craved that easy bond, a link that went way back, forged in years of experiencing each other, in years of being each other's confidantes to the exclusion of everybody else. I wanted Winnie, but Winnie didn't want me. I'd forgotten that feeling. Now I remembered it too well.

I hadn't seen her again, had begun to wonder whether, in fact, I had ever had that glimpse of her at the cemetery. I remembered years ago regularly catching sight of my ex-boyfriend in the weeks after the relationship had ended, following the back of his head through crowds only to find it was a man who bore only a slight resemblance to him, an astral projection of the humming and insistent one-note melody bouncing around the inside of my own head. Had I imagined Winnie into existence because, thanks to my interior monologue, she felt as constant a companion as Lila, even though her profile on Facebook remained blank and inaccessible, like that of a stranger's?

So I assumed the brisk knock at the front door a few weeks into January would be yet another courier delivering more baby stuff. There was so much that seemed urgent as I ordered in the middle of the night but that almost always turned out to be just another waste of money – rendered obsolete by Lila's constantly changing needs – as soon as it arrived. I always cursed myself the day after I'd bought anything, because I hated answering the door to deliverymen when I was home alone – a fact I tended to forget when Nick was asleep next to me.

Charles jumped slightly when I opened the door, as if he were as startled as I was at the fact of his being there on our front step. My first thought: I wondered if Winnie knew her husband had come here, whether she had sent him. Or had he come without telling her?

'I owe you an apology,' he said as he took a seat at the kitchen table and looked around quizzically for any sign of Lila among the empty bouncy chair and toys scattered on the cork tiles.

'She's asleep upstairs,' I explained, and he nodded, looked at the time on the microwave clock: one p.m.

'Of course she is,' he replied tightly. 'Lunch nap.'

His brown hair was longer, floppier, than I had seen before, his face more gaunt than it used to be, but he was tidy. The pale blue Oxford shirt and navy chinos he wore under his smart black coat were spotlessly clean and pressed. I inwardly tsked myself for being so patronising: Charles had lost a baby, not his marbles.

'I'll make it quick then,' he continued with a smile. 'I know downtime must be precious at the moment.'

He played with a spoon that was lying on the table. It was dirty, but I hadn't had a chance to clear it away.

'I wanted to ask you to be patient,' he said after a pause. His eyes didn't meet mine and I realised how hard this must be for him. Jack had been dead nearly ten months. 'With Winnie. I know how she's been with you since . . . recently. It must have been hurtful. I know how close you two have always been over the years.'

I tried hard not to let my expression change, yet my insides turned very cold at the mention of the past. *Does Charles know? Did she tell him?*

'But she's just going through so much at the moment,' he continued, looking up. 'It's been so hard for us both, of course, but Winnie's . . . Winnie's a mother with no child, and she'll just need some time to figure things out. So I wanted to tell you that I was sorry about how she'd been with you, and to say just hang in there for her. I know this must have been upsetting for you as well.'

I wanted to thank him for noticing, even in the depths of grief and mourning for his son, that their terrible loss might have had an effect on me, too. I had told myself so often that my feelings didn't matter in the face of what Winnie and Charles were going through that the acknowledgment of that felt like a balm.

'And also to say congratulations!' he added, and gave a crooked smile. 'Any chance of a peek at her?'

I spoke before I had really considered his question: 'I'm sorry, but she's such a light sleeper, she wakes at the slightest noise so I'd rather not disturb her.'

I didn't know where that had come from – Lila could sleep through police sirens screeching down our road, through the washing machine in turbo mode, through a plane taking off from next door. *That was selfish of you.* Nevertheless, I was glad of my quick reaction. I was happy to see Charles, grateful for the empathy he had offered. But I didn't want him near Lila. I still felt too sick about Winnie.

He left after that, promising to keep in touch, and when Lila woke up, I held her and held her.

I noticed that the moments I spent feeling grateful for my daughter – feeling arbitrarily blessed where Winnie and Charles had not been, wondering for how much longer my beloved baby and I might cheat tragedy – helped to take away some of the bitterness I felt about my replacement.

Seeing her at our party reminded me that Maggie was just Maggie, gawky and kindly, done up in an outfit clearly inspired by the bloggers she'd seen at the shows. I had to admit she'd looked good – just the right blend of cool and pretty. No wonder Tim had been interested – to my amusement, he'd checked as he helped Nick and me clear up afterwards whether dresses over jeans were 'a Thing.'

'Don't ask me!' I'd laughed. 'The only fashion I know about right now is of the leggings-and-cardigan variety.'

My pre-pregnancy wardrobe still felt as remote as my old life, not just because of the risk of covering designer silks in pureed sweet potato but because I suspected (I didn't dare check) that most of it would no longer fasten over my still-domed stomach, my newly rounded hips, and a bottom that I could now feel jiggling behind me as I walked.

Pick your battles, Margot. You can torture yourself either over Winnie or over being fat, but you don't have the energy for both.

Since I appeared to be powerless to stop my former friend's name from beating in my brain like the chorus of a catchy song, I had decided to put dieting on hold. My weight always crept up when I was worried, as though the metaphorical burden on my shoulders somehow registered on the bath-room scales. It had been the same at school, thanks to Helen, and now my breastfeeding body seemed to hoard whatever I nourished it with as if expecting famine or drought.

I couldn't help but notice at our Christmas party how slim Maggie looked. I recognised it as the slenderness that comes from living off coffee, adrenaline, and not quite enough sleep. I was hardly banking eight hours a night myself, but the effect insomnia had had on *my* looks was rather different.

I had tried my best to compartmentalise my angst over the inevitable comparisons made between us both at work, but my replacement began crowding into my home life as well.

'Maggie's so much fun!' Nick had declared one night a few weeks ago as he sat at the bottom of the stairs and unlaced his sneakers. He had left me with Lila and gone for a drink with his friend, only to find Maggie sharing a wooden bench with him in our local, too.

'What was she doing there?' I asked my husband sharply, and he looked up with a mischievous grin.

'What do you think?' He winked.

Of course I'm the last to know.

'She's witty, she's got great stories. Real life and soul, isn't she? I can see how you had such a great time in Iceland together.' He smiled, the delight for his best friend writ large on his clean-cut features.

No doubt Maggie's new slimline figure would now be topped up with the jittery first flush of whatever was going on between her and Tim.

Was I annoyed at the relationship? Absolutely. Tim was Nick's best friend. Did Maggie's sudden ubiquity, present if not in person then in almost every conversation Nick and I had that wasn't about Lila, prickle my spine with irritation? Plans for the weekend, brunching as a foursome, asking them over for dinner. Of course. I acknowledged it as yet another personal failing of mine that I couldn't muster the enthusiasm that Nick had for his closest friend's new relationship.

I, who had never been described as the life and soul of anything, had winced and replied mechanically, 'Yeah. Maggie's great.'

Is it not enough that she's taken my desk? Does she have to take my seat in the pub too?

When Nick and I had first got together, Tim had been a welcome third wheel in our relationship. We'd spent hours in the pub most nights of the week, chatting, playing cards, delighting in our shared sense of humour, the niche references we all got. I hadn't been for a drink with Nick and Tim since Lila was born – it seemed crazy to pay for a babysitter for the sort of evening that felt even less enticing than watching TV on the sofa. Nor would it make sense for me to see Tim without

Nick: an awkwardness that had never afflicted us as a three would have crept in – he was Nick's friend, not mine.

Instead of finding a new way to socialise, they've just found a new me.

I felt forgotten, erased. Replaced. Just as I had when I saw Maggie's picture from work on Instagram, my old desk decorated with a display of jocular friendship that I had never been the recipient of. *Number 1? Where does that put me? Am I even in the top ten?*

The first time Nick invited Tim and Maggie over for dinner, I spent it with what I thought of as a clown grin plastered onto my face: one drawn over the scowl beneath. Sitting up late with them as they drank beers and I lingered over a glass of tap water meant I'd be tired in the morning, when Lila woke as the dawn broke. Nick would offer to help, but he couldn't feed her and there was little point in both of us being awake. *Nature's lie-in.*

But I could no more go to bed and leave the three of them together for another hour or so than I could ignore Lila's cries or stop myself from scrolling through Maggie's Instagram feed. I couldn't quite articulate the sense – *jealousy? danger? what did we say before FOMO?* – but I knew that to give my replacement at work a run at the space I occupied at home as well was a bad idea. I had left Winnie once, all those years ago with Helen, and look what had happened.

Maggie sat in the chair I usually occupied when we had guests, regaling my husband and Tim with funny anecdotes from cool and smart places where I would no longer have fitted in, about people to whom I'd have had nothing to say. She talked and laughed about the news, about current affairs that I no longer knew enough about to share my own opinions alongside theirs.

They discussed countries far away where terrible things were happening and I, no time for the headlines anymore, could only nod along in theatrical outrage. They were people of the world, these three dynamic occupants of my newly upholstered vintage dining chairs; the farthest I had gone that day was to a café two streets away. Remaining and not contributing made me feel pathetic, but leaving them – pleading nursery rhyme fatigue and tomorrow's childcare – would have felt worse. Maggie seemed only too ready to pick up the slack in my home as well as behind my desk.

Suddenly I hated Maggie with an intensity that filled me with sadness. My replacement's easy charm and ability to make friends, and Winnie's accusation, her implied judgment and disapproval, fused in my brain into comprehensive proof of my own selfishness and flawed character. Pride, narcissism, thoughtlessness piled into a constant feeling of guilt I pushed around with me just as I did Lila's buggy. A reminder of the reasons I was never chosen, never number one, always on the outside. The reasons that had led to what happened at school.

I continued to scrutinise Maggie's digital life: more breakfasts, more selfies, more shoes. I watched and rewatched a video loop of Maggie dancing in front of a wall of blue disco balls with Holly and Amma, at the sort of industry party I had given up attending soon after I met Nick because they were full of office juniors and thrusting types who were dissatisfied with their jobs. I was running *Haute*'s fashion desk by then, and all I wanted to do was cosy up on the sofa with my new boyfriend.

Winnie had come to a couple of fashion parties with me at the very beginning. We'd cobbled together outfits between us that we were convinced looked impressive: cheap vintage, faded hand-me-downs, ancient T-shirts that we slashed and customised. We went on other people's invitations, senior members of the team at *Haute* who I knew would never use them because they were old and lazy and had kids or other unfathomable reasons for passing up the multitude of invitations to eye-widening events that were couriered to their desks.

They were just like I am now – of course they didn't bloody want to go.

But Winnie was right, I never fitted in at those things anyway.

Back on Maggie's feed, I baulked at a picture of her wearing the pink version of the blue sparkly sweater I had ordered in Paris while pregnant and then worn for our party. I was irritated but felt smugly superior, too: Maggie was following my lead even now. I fumed after recognising a stylised shot of a flat white in an earthenware cup beside a milk-bottle vase of wild-flowers as having been taken in the new coffee shop down the road, and then reading the caption: 'they do good coffee in suburbia!' *Sneering at my life, even as you try to make it your own?*

One night, my phone glowing on my knee as I fed Lila back into a deep sleep, I noticed the pink sweater in a piece on the *Haute* website, with the headline 'Sparkle isn't just for evening!', and gave a short, hot gasp of indignation. *I can't decide whether I'm more annoyed that she ripped off my idea or that she ripped off an idea that I said as a joke.*

Beneath it, a lone comment – nobody ever commented on the website – under the username HelenKnows: 'long live Maggie Beecher! Let's hope that boring Margot never comes back.'

I tried not to think about it.

At the end of January, I would be halfway through my maternity leave and I was heartbroken at the prospect of leaving Lila. For me, time was slipping through my fingers, but Maggie was using it to shore up her position.

I texted Moff the next day, just a one-line 'How's things?', the equivalent of clearing one's throat in a meeting to remind people of one's existence. And I was crushed when, three days later, I got the reply: 'all great, don't worry about us. Maggie such fun!'

I flung my phone down onto the sitting room carpet next to where Lila lay and wept so loudly and for so long that my daughter stopped batting at the dangling toys above her and flicked wide, worried eyes towards her mother.

'Oh, my precious, I'm okay,' I sobbed, scooping Lila into a hold and snuggling into the folds of her soft baby-skin neck. I noticed the new issue of the magazine on the sideboard as I did so, still in the cellophane wrap it had arrived in. *I used to know what was going on every page of it.*

This month, I didn't even know who was on the cover.

It was rare for Moff to find somebody among the horde she thought of as 'civilians' that she deemed attractive enough to put on the cover of the magazine. My boss was an exacting body fascist, unashamed of the high aesthetic standards that made her title one of the most prestigious on the newsstands.

After the first shoot in which I had had my picture taken for the magazine, Moff explained reassuringly, out of nowhere, that she'd arrange for my cheeks to be slimmed in Photoshop afterwards. When I saw the final images, the small but insistent fat pad under my chin and the tops of my thighs had also vanished, and my eyelids had been lifted. Evidence enough that Moff didn't consider me cover material, had I ever expected the chance.

The face that shone out from the glossy front page of this month's issue wasn't the usual bronzed Hollywood actress or youthful neon pop star. In fact, it took several moments for me to recognise it, to transliterate it from the woman who had sat at my dining table only last weekend, offering toast crusts to Lila, to the woman in the photograph, hip cocked and eyebrow raised, cleavage displayed in skintight gold chain mail, the epitome of glitz, glamour, sophistication, and worldly success. *Cover stars are the people everybody else wants to be.*

SINGLES ON TOP, ran the cover line. WHY I DON'T NEED A BABY TO HAVE IT ALL.

I had the sudden sensation of falling down a deep hole that had opened up within me. My heart beat in my temples, my vision throbbed. My eyes stung with tears of jealous anger. If this wasn't a direct assault, what else could it be? This was Maggie saying in no uncertain terms that she'd won: beautiful, confident, thin, young looking, and, most important, childless, the way fashion editors are supposed to be. The way Moff wanted them to be. These were the qualities she looked for in her staffers, not saggy tummies and laughter lines; Moff was Maggie's champion now, not mine.

Maggie was living her dream job on the most coveted spot in the magazine. I might have been the most in love I had ever been in my life – in many ways, the happiest and most contented during my hours with Lila – but I couldn't quite remember anymore who I was. Most days, I felt as though I and the baby were the same person: freshly hatched and intensely vulnerable to every new shock.

I remembered when I used to press onto the train alongside the rest of the rush-hour crowd, used to elbow my way through the mob to my front-row seats at fashion week as a matter of course, and couldn't believe these two versions of me were related, let alone sharing the same body. Then again, that body looked so very different now anyway: heavy and mottled around the thighs and stomach, with pendulous, veined breasts that hung to my rib cage rather than sitting pert on my sternum. *Hardly a cover girl, barely even a young woman anymore.*

I studied my face at length in the bathroom mirror. A purple bag under each eye, broken thread veins along the swoop of my nose, high red patches on the apples of both cheeks. I was tired and unhealthy, the unrest in my head manifest in the way the world saw me. I looked dreadful: I looked like a loser. No wonder Maggie had won.

'Won what?' Nick said later, after I had shown him the magazine. 'She's scored a cover, sure, and that'll be great for her career once you go back and she no longer has a full-time job.'

'But it's a dig!' I wailed. 'A dig against me, because I had a baby and I'm not fabulous or single anymore.'

'I for one am very glad you're not single anymore,' he said, pulling me close, and gave me the sort of lingering kiss that would have thrilled me once but now just made me impatient. 'Have you actually read the piece? It really doesn't seem like a dig to me. She hardly mentions babies, really. It's more about how being single doesn't have to mean feeling sad. That's what Tim said, anyway.'

'You knew about this?' I couldn't believe Nick hadn't said anything. I remembered Winnie's text: *you could have warned me.* Was this how she had felt? As though someone else's happiness had excavated her insides?

'Look, 'Go, she told him about it a while back because she wrote it before they met and obviously now she isn't really single anymore. I didn't know about the cover. Doesn't it make you feel better that she's all single and fabulous here, but in reality she's bonking a man who thinks cycling shorts are the last word in cool?'

I gave a wobbly smile: Nick was right – another overreaction. Just as my nightmares about Winnie and her poor dead baby loomed large in the dark but receded during daylight so as to seem almost hyperbolically ridiculous, so the panic and anxieties about Maggie that I worked up during the long hours spent alone with Lila could be defused merely by voicing them. They crumbled to nothing when Nick was around, even though they had seemed so incontrovertible, so terminal and dreadful, when I was by myself.

'I appreciate you feel weird about Maggie,' Nick continued, stroking my hair, 'but why don't you just try taking her at face value for a while and try to like her as a person rather than hating the idea of her? She's even offered to look after Lila for a few hours so you can have some time to yourself – why don't you let her? She adores Lila, and Lila's pretty into her as well.'

I had to admit this was true. Over brunch the other week-end, Lila had gurgled merrily on Maggie's lap, as I clenched my fists under the table at the woman with my haircut, who was wearing my sparkly sweater, sitting on my chair, using my cutlery, my crockery, and now, entertaining my baby.

But the baby's contented happiness whenever she was in Maggie's arms was the only thing I couldn't hold against the woman I felt was assimilating my life. It brought out far less of the territorial streak that Maggie usually pricked, because Lila always looked so genuinely delighted in her company, pure joy unadulterated by the suspicion and stupid, selfish para-noia that had come to characterise her mother's moods. *Perhaps babies see the real person, not the layers they've wrapped themselves in.*

Nick was right; he was always right. My demons were reaching out from my dreams – the memories of that sicken-ing plunge and my grief over Winnie's anger had fused into terrors almost every night now. I was so worn down by them that I had failed to recognise Maggie wasn't one of them, merely a symptom of my own anxiety. The cure was to be happy for Maggie; to be positive and embrace her and purge the bad feeling. That much was within my control.

I practiced swallowing my reactions to the profusion of fans who sprang up online as the magazine and its cover star swept through my circle of colleagues and industry acquaintances. They gushed in comments under the image on Maggie's Facebook page, exclaiming over how wonderful she looked, over how interesting the piece was. Almost everybody from the office reposted the picture captioned with kapows, love hearts, and red-hot flames.

When the cover went viral – *Moff will be over the moon* – Maggie was invited onto women's radio shows and TV segments to discuss her thesis on a way of life that I knew, because of her connection to Tim, she wasn't really living anymore. *I could really mess this up for her if I tweeted that.* But I'd learned long ago it wasn't worth it to use people's deeds against them. Talking others down only left you in the dirt, not them. The injustice of it, and the irritation, remained, and I struggled not to dwell on it.

Some days were harder than others.

Helen Knows @HelenKnows: Looking great on the cover @itsmaggiebetches. I wonder how @ hautemargot feels in her maternity jeans?

It aimed to wound. And it hit home perfectly.

'Hang on,' protested Nick when I thrust my phone into his face the moment he was through the door that evening. 'You don't know it's her. It's a pretty weird thing to do, in the depths of grief, to start trolling your best friend online.' He unbuttoned his coat and put his arms around me.

'It's exactly what you do in the depths of grief, isn't it? When you're tormented by the fact your friend has had a baby so soon after yours d—' I couldn't bring myself to say the word *died*.

'Besides, you don't know anyone called Helen,' he murmured into my hair.

Not anymore.

Again I told myself that Nick was right. My absence from the magazine and the fact of Lila's birth were both in the public realm, on social media. The situation I and Maggie found ourselves in, as though at either end of a seesaw, one able to rise only with the other's fall, was surely commonplace when women left their jobs to have children. Whoever was behind this Twitter troll was perceptive and spiteful, but they didn't have access to my inner world, nor to my darkest fears.

Why haven't I blocked you yet?

I clicked the option on the drop-down menu that would hide any more bile from HelenKnows from me, then texted Maggie. I congratulated my rival and cheers-ed her with a glass of red (water for me) the next time she and Tim came over for supper – almost a twice-a-month occurrence these days.

I told myself it was nice to have the company, and sometimes it was. But I would find myself drifting in and out of conversation. Maggie seemed so comfortable in our home now – she moved around my kitchen with the familiarity of a roommate or lodger, retrieving items from various drawers in order to set the table as I watched from the doorway.

She's just trying to help. So why do I want to smash all those wine glasses she's so thoughtfully set out for everybody but me?

One evening I found Maggie writing her and Tim's names onto the calendar that hung in our kitchen for Sunday lunch the following month. 'A rematch,' she told me, and smiled at my slightly stunned expression.

Nevertheless, I took Maggie up on the offer of looking after Lila, so that I might have a head-clearing afternoon off. I booked my place in one of the faddish but effective, expensive spin classes I used to go to and dug out some gym clothes that would provide enough coverage for the extra flesh I now carried. And surprisingly, I began to feel positively light at the prospect, eager for my first taste of time alone since Lila's arrival – since before my pregnancy, technically. Any residual guilt about not appreciating my daughter ebbed away as I realised having the class on the horizon was making me happier, less tense, and more engaged with Lila. Humming, I took a picture of the baby playing on her patterned quilt in a beam of sunlight, gums bared in a smile that split her round face open like a Halloween pumpkin and wispy hair sprouting wild in golden tendrils, before posting it on Instagram with a slew of pink hearts beneath.

I was pottering in the kitchen during Lila's nap when I heard the double *ping* of a comment being posted alongside it. I tapped in my phone's security code in an unconscious motion before I saw who it was from. When I did, my stomach caved in on itself and I crouched against the cupboards, eyes frozen on the screen.

@HelenKnows: Just another self-indulgent new mum? You're not fit to bring up a child.

I shuddered as though electrified as the phone buzzed again in my hand and another note appeared underneath it.

@HelenKnows: I know what happened, Margot. I know what you did.

12

Maggie

Maggie got a shock when she next saw Margot. When she opened her front door and ushered Maggie inside, her face seemed different. Despite the insistent purple bags that had become a feature beneath the new mother's eyes, there was an energy there hadn't been to her prior state of permanent-seeming glumness. Maggie couldn't quite put her finger on it, and then it clicked: Margot seemed weirdly excited.

Margot's eyes were bright and her steps brisk as she gestured left and right to various bits Maggie might need while looking after Lila; she'd left a note of the various times that the baby needed to eat and to sleep, she said. And oddly, Margot seemed more herself than she had in the past months, more like the woman Maggie had made friends with in Iceland, less sad-eyed and withdrawn. It was a strange thing to think, given everything Margot was talking about was inherently domestic – how to boil Lila's formula, which little crackers the baby preferred – but, to Maggie, Margot seemed professional again. She half expected Margot to finish up with a PowerPoint presentation.

When she asked if there were any questions, Maggie had a sudden revelation. This was just like the few days they'd shared in the office before the handover. Margot had been in a position of not exactly power over her replacement, but of advanced expertise. And now – like then – she positively glowed with it.

Maggie felt herself bristle and then remembered she was there to do Margot a favour.

She'd have been lying if she said she hadn't felt a little guilty about the last time they'd met. She and Tim had gone round for dinner just after the magazine had come out. She'd meant to tell Margot about it in advance, but she had honestly just sort of forgot. Perhaps it was a convenient amnesia, because she'd known it'd be awkward, however she raised it:

'By the way, Margot, next month I'm on the cover of the magazine you used to work at.'

Or:

'Margot, have you ever been on the cover? No? Well, I'm going to be.'

Maggie felt a small thrill at having managed something her predecessor hadn't. Yet whichever way she tried to phrase it in a message felt like either a rebuke or a boast. So she'd put her phone away, decided to try again later, and then just never got round to it. As soon as Maggie saw Margot that night, she realised how hurtful the omission must have been; *I should have warned her,* she thought.

'Maggie, hi!' Margot had said as she came into the dining room after putting Lila to bed upstairs. Tim was having a drink with Nick, and Maggie was setting the table. Margot pulled at the slightly splodged grey T-shirt she was wearing and smoothed it over the spot where her pregnant belly had once been. It was much smaller now, but not quite gone: what a poet would call liminal space and something, Maggie imagined, new – and not so new – mothers thought about both subconsciously and self-consciously all the time.

'You look so amazing on the cover of the mag this month!' Margot's smile didn't even reach the edges of her lips, let alone her cheeks or eyes. In fact, her eyes watered slightly, perhaps from tiredness. 'Congratulations, you're *Haute*'s new star!'

She leaned over the table, picked up the glass of water Maggie had poured, and held it out for her to clink. When the two connected and the women made eye contact, Maggie saw there, in their depths, how much of an effort it had been for the former fashion editor to be pleased for the new girl.

'Thanks, Margot, I—' She fought the urge to apologise with every fibre of her being. She wasn't even sure why she felt the need to, or what it was she'd be saying sorry for, but Margot's very presence was like that of a sainted martyr: enough to make you feel bad for feeling good, Maggie thought resentfully.

Maggie had an impulse to tell her then about the day she'd found out she was going to be on the magazine's cover. In her head, she now thought of it as 'my magazine': *I might have to give this job back, but that issue is something that will always be mine.*

She had scarcely believed it when Moff had told her. Maggie was walking past the editor's door to the printer when she was beckoned into the corner office with a fingernail manicured in glossy dark brown. Always the same shade from the same brand – Holly had said it was called Chocolate Lab.

'About your single piece,' Moff said, her eyes back on the computer screen, where she was replying to an email. She rarely sent messages longer than a few sentences, mainly staccato opinions or commands.

'I've been let down by Sarah Mara's agent,' she continued. Sarah Mara was the film star slated for the cover of the issue Maggie's article would be in, a svelte sort of blond amazon who specialised in making comic book movies more palatable to women, while catering amply to their male audience too. 'They can't do the shoot date now, and we don't have time to find anyone else. So. You'll be on there instead.'

At first Maggie thought this was some kind of ludicrous test. She hadn't forgotten how delighted Moff had looked when she had made that slip-up in the interview about Margot's name: this woman revelled in egos being punctured, and here was a prime opportunity to string her new fashion editor along in an elaborate practical joke. But the tall, thin woman on the other side of the desk seemed totally serious.

'Of course, we'll need to amp up what you're saying. It's all very nice that you're single and happy blah blah blah, but we need you to sound happier than anyone else. A manifesto. Or a battle cry.'

It wasn't until Maggie saw the cover copy that she really understood what Moff had meant. She'd made it tribal: Maggie against the breeders. She felt a little sick at that, especially now that she was gunning to be on the other team, having met Tim. Yes, okay, she'd already thought about having kids with him; she admitted it.

It would have taken superhuman strength not to: meet someone in your early thirties and doesn't every sentence you utter have the unspoken phrase 'and do you think you might want children?' hanging off the end of it? Really, once you're over the age of twenty-seven, there should be a rule that you both drink truth serum on a first date instead of sauvignon blanc just to make sure you're on the same page.

Maggie had never been in denial about wanting that stuff – the big white dress (but actually maybe a silver one), the house, the babies. It had just been so long since she had believed it might actually be coming her way, she'd persuaded herself to forget it all. Now it seemed constantly at the forefront of her mind, especially given how much time they were spending with Margot and Nick, whose every conversational opener was to do with Lila or some piece of equipment the baby seemed to need.

It hadn't made Maggie any less interested at work, though; if anything, it galvanised her to try even harder. How, after all, would she afford a baby if she were forced back into freelance penury after Margot swooped back in and sat down at the desk she was currently occupying?

Maggie had to make sure that didn't happen.

It had been difficult to consider her future when she'd been counting the pennies day to day. Being Margot's replacement had finally given Maggie the unexpected luxury of a long-term plan. And this cover story was just the latest step in proving to Moff that Maggie would still need her around after Margot returned.

Was it possible their editor had Margot in mind when she added that bit about not *needing* a baby? Probably not: Moff rarely thought beyond magazine circulation numbers to the impact stories might have when they hit too close to home.

Maggie wanted to explain to Margot that she had never meant it to be like that, hadn't pitched the article with the two of them in mind, but to voice it would be to acknowledge all the weirdness there was already writhing just below the surface in their relationship. So she didn't.

If Maggie was being honest, she barely recognised the woman staring out from the front of that month's *Haute*. In fact, she barely recognised quite a lot about herself these days. The blond hair, the sharp jawline, the overflowing closet, the boyfriend, the weekends spent in South London wondering how long it'd take Tim to suggest she move down this way. Too long if she didn't make sure she spent a few more nights in the Camden flat, she told herself.

She had stayed at his that Friday so she could get to Margot's easily the next morning, once he and Nick headed off to the football match. Maggie had been offering to take Lila for an afternoon for ages and Margot had seemed reluctant to take her up on it.

At first, Margot had smiled and thanked her when Maggie suggested she could have some time by herself, but she didn't raise it again. Maggie appreciated it must be weird, leaving your child with someone else – a bit like leaving your job with someone else – but Lila and she had struck up such a bond, surely Margot could see there was no reason to worry about her looking after the baby.

So Maggie kept suggesting it, but Margot kept putting her off; the more she did, the more determined Maggie became to give the tired new mum a bit of time off. She was covering one job for Margot, she might as well have a go at the other, right?

This was the line she had laughingly used when she finally mentioned it to Nick. Maggie knew instinctively that she needed to endear herself not to Margot but to her husband, so he would champion her both with his best friend and when the time came for Margot to return to work. Nick, she realised, was key to both of the projects most dear to her heart.

So she suggested it to him in the pub one night: wouldn't it be great if she, Maggie, could give Margot a bit of time – an afternoon, say – to herself? She could tell immediately that Nick was grateful to her. He would never say his wife had been difficult company – he was far too loyal – but all the words he didn't say implied that Margot was more immersed in the baby at the moment than she was in their relationship.

Without the need for much digging, he told her that Margot had been a little anxious and Maggie pushed down the suspicion that some of that might have been her fault. She had just been getting on with her own life, she told herself: *Margot's mental health isn't my job – my job is to do her job. For now, at least.*

'How are things in the office?' Margot asked as she pulled a tailored camel coat on over her sweater and jeans, then gave the baby one last hug.

'Same old rush to find ideas, same deadlines that come round too quickly.' Maggie shrugged and laughed, dangling a toy in front of Lila on the cushion where her mother had placed her. 'The girls can't wait to see pictures from my afternoon with this one, though.'

Margot gave a tight smile at that and reached for her keys from the hall stand.

Maggie was still playing with Lila on the carpet in the front room when Margot left. She didn't want to make a fuss about it, in case the baby started crying, just picked up her gym bag and closed the door behind her.

'Well, Lila, what shall we do together?' Maggie said. The baby gurgled and pushed a blue wooden block into her mouth, her rosebud lips forming a wet smile around it and melting her babysitter's heart utterly.

Maggie had never really done childcare before, not one-to-one of an age where she couldn't just resort to the telly. She was exhausted after half an hour. No, not exhausted, that's not quite right. Bored. She was bored stiff after half an hour. How on earth did Margot cope all day?

It wasn't Lila's fault – she was a peach. That fluffy blond hair sticking out at comical angles as if she'd put her finger in a socket; her flawless blue eyes; the crinkle at the top of her nose when she laughed, which was often. No, Lila was a lovely baby – it was just the monotony of sitting on the floor, with Maggie moving her toys around and keeping up a monologue in her best sunbeams-and-strawberries voice, that got tiresome.

After an hour or so, Maggie decided to strap the baby into her pushchair and take her to the café down the road. It'd be busy on a Saturday, but it was a baby-friendly sort of place. Where wasn't, round there?

They took the long way, past the old Victorian cemetery that Tim had told her about. Now, in an early February thaw, there were snowdrops at the foot of the gravestones Maggie could see from the road, and the beginnings of crocuses on the grassy lawns.

Lila chatted in a tongue known only to herself from the buggy and Maggie tried to imagine what Margot's days must be like, steering this thing around with its precious cargo, attention always on it, but the mind with freedom to wander. What did Margot think about Nick? Or Maggie? She knew Margot was viewing the pictures she had put on Instagram.

The fact of them was a small prick on Maggie's conscience every day, but that didn't stop her from posting. When the moment came to click 'share,' Maggie found she always had a solid reason beyond baiting Margot to share whatever it was – a shoe, a piece she'd written, a bouquet of peonies she'd been sent. These were tokens of Maggie's life, she reasoned, not a comment on Margot's – everybody was on social media, there was no reason for one woman to take it personally, right?

As she strolled, Maggie thought of her predecessor wandering, free, in the fresh air as she, Maggie, sat at the desk she hadn't thought of as Margot's for some time now from dawn until dusk, toiling for Moff. Maternity leave had its upsides.

She wasn't tiring of the job, but she was tired from it, especially now that she was spending so much time with Tim. Not getting those early nights she'd forced herself to have at the beginning, not sleeping in her own flat, not quite staying on top of things.

Maggie suddenly envied Margot her settled existence, her comforts, the stable knowledge of who she was and where she belonged every night. Life, Maggie decided, must be less existentially exhausting once you're married. After all, so many things have fallen into place by then. You aren't expected to juggle them all constantly like you were before you settled down.

The spare pair of knickers, shoes, and washbag full of travel-sized toiletries she now always carried with her in various designer logoed canvas totes cadged from the fashion cupboard seemed emblematic of her disarrayed mental state. By contrast, the carefully compartmentalised bag that hung from Lila's pram and contained the baby's nappies and wipes, milk, a change of clothes, a sun hat, and a bottle of Tylenol spoke of a serene and settled mind. Or of a psychopath, Maggie supposed, repressing a smile.

By the time they reached the café, the afternoon sun had dropped and, with it, the temperature. The lights shone through its fogged windows the way those of inns did to high-waymen traveling along misty moors. Lila and Maggie weren't quite saddle sore, but the baby was impatient to be out and her babysitter was ready for a sit.

Maggie found a small, round table in one corner not far from the counter and parked Lila's buggy there, giving her one of the rice cakes Margot had packed to appease her until she'd ordered. As she stood in line, Maggie gurned at the little pink face and bounced up and down, bending her knees and waggling her fingers to make the baby laugh. Lila seemed more interested in the snack.

Maggie ordered from the girl at the counter, then went back to the table. As she unfastened Lila from the straps of the pram and lifted her into a wooden high chair, a woman at the next table watched intently, ignoring the book open before her.

'What a beautiful child,' she said.

The stranger's face was youthful, but there was age in it; her curly auburn hair was pulled back in an untidy bun. She wasn't wearing much makeup, but the little she did have on made her look even younger. It sat on top of her clear skin, not quite blended, as though it had been inexpertly but enthusias-tically patted on. As though she hadn't quite committed to being around people that day.

Children were the sole talking point among strangers in this city now that fewer and fewer of its inhabitants had the need to ask one another for matches or a lighter. Maggie was usually the one giving the compliment – now, on the receiving end, she found herself responding unthinkingly with a warm grin and a scrunching of her nose: the universal signal that translates as both 'thanks for noticing' and 'of course she is'. Lila *was* a beautiful baby.

The woman smiled back.

Maggie's order was called and she went to retrieve it from the counter, ending the brief interaction. *How many of these do you have,* she wondered, *when you have a baby?* It was a window into the spontaneous community of motherhood, one of the few real-life tribes that still existed in the digital age. Then again, what use was a smile in a café when you were on your own with a screaming child in the dead of the night? Maybe social media wasn't all bad.

The server dithered, having confused her herbal tea with another customer's. It took only a minute or so, but suddenly she felt nervous. She shouldn't have turned her back on Lila for more than a few seconds.

But she needn't have worried: when Maggie spun round, heart hammering, cup and plate in hand, she saw the woman had been making faces at Lila, disappearing and reemerging from behind a paper menu. Maggie gave her another smile as she slid back into the seat next to Lila, and the woman returned it, before resuming her book.

Lila chewed her rice snacks, burbled and fiddled with a napkin while Maggie drank her tea and ate her carrot cake. Was this what parental competency looked like? After ten minutes or so, as Maggie gathered up the last few crumbs from her plate with a fingertip, Lila began to fidget. When she checked her phone, Maggie had a message. Margot had texted a few moments earlier to say she was home.

Baby and sitter clattered through the grey front door ten minutes later, stepping from the blue evening into yellow house light, the shadows retreating from their faces at the same rate the smile dawned on the mother's as she swept up her daughter in her arms. Lila bleated joyously to be reunited.

Maggie felt a prickling behind her eyes: how strong the bond was between them, how much they revelled in the sight of each other. Would anyone ever feel that way about her?

She left Margot throwing Lila up in the air and catching her in a hail of giggles and nipped upstairs to use the bathroom. As she washed her hands, Maggie looked at herself in the mirror. She'd stopped wearing her red lipstick – not entirely, but mostly not on weekends – and she looked less fierce without it. She'd toned down the cleavage a bit, too.

Maggie took the opportunity to put a bit more makeup on. She was about to go back to meet Tim, and although he really wasn't the sort to mind or even to notice if she wasn't freshly scrubbed up, it was still early enough days that she felt a little self-conscious when she wasn't. As she lined and plumped, blended and patted, Maggie looked along the wooden shelves over the bath, where lurid bath toys mingled with expensive potions in flat, round jars and fashionably anonymous brown chemist's bottles. She recognised them as the fruit of the beauty desk's treats table, where they laid out the products they'd tested and discarded or had no more use for.

Of course, Margot didn't have to scavenge from the table the way the others did: she had a hotline to the beauty editor because of her rank, and it meant she got first dibs on what was up for grabs. It was a relationship Maggie had tried to strike up too, but she had received a distinctly chilly reception from Trina.

To women with children, the maternity cover was just another 'other woman', and Trina treated this one accordingly. Her assistant, however, had slid Maggie a few bits on the QT, and she had them displayed every bit as proudly in her own bathroom, albeit alongside Cath's Clearasil. Did Margot neglect to use any of these fabulously expensive unguents because her old garden-variety moisturiser actually worked better on her skin? Probably not: Margot's skin looked like it had expensive taste – at least, it had used to.

Maggie packed up her makeup, stepped onto the landing, and walked past the open door to Margot and Nick's bedroom, dark and cosy looking. From the top of the steep stairs, she could see Margot standing at the bottom, Lila balanced on one hip.

Maggie saw immediately from her posture that something had happened – Margot's shoulders were hunched and her back doubled over like an old woman's, her right arm across her body as though she'd been punched, and Lila folded into her side.

But it was the other woman's face, as it turned to look up at her on the stairs, that sent a chill through Maggie. Margot's mouth was slack and black inside, open in a silent scream. Her eyes were sharp and wary, the blue in them darkened to deep, empty pools, the brows above slanted at such an angle as to drag her features down towards a terrible gape of pain.

A quiet but high-pitched rasping sound was coming from the other woman's throat.

Margot looked a hundred years old. She looked haunted. No, not that – she looked *hunted*.

13

Margot

'Met the new girl today.'

There was a time when the message would have been completely normal. When I would have been smug at the little villagelike community in which my young family and I lived, in my friendships overlapping like juggling balls in midarc. Now though, those arcs felt like concentric circles squeezing the air out of me as I drowned.

I know what you did.

That my oldest friend could terrify me like this felt ludicrous, surreal, but then the hollow sensation in my stomach curdled into an anxiety that bordered on nausea. I remembered it too well. *It's been a long time since I felt scared of you, Winnie.*

Before I could process quite the order of things that must have happened to lead to Winnie – silent, bitter, grieving Winnie, whom I hadn't spoken to since before Jack had died and who hadn't been in touch since that final reproachful text – sending me a picture of herself with Lila gurgling next to her, Maggie had reappeared at the top of the flight of stairs, her legs and torso refracted by the angle, so that it was mainly my cover's shocked and worried face I could see.

Maggie. What did she have to do with all this?

I had been reluctant to hand my baby over to a woman I already resented so much. Maggie had by degrees so inveigled herself into the entirety of my life, both professional and domestic, that I sometimes found it difficult to breathe around her. But I had told myself I was being overly sensitive. To refuse would hurt Maggie's feelings.

Nick had taken pains to point out to me, at great length, the many flaws in my theory that Maggie was determined to usurp me in my own life, and I had relented: he would go to a football match with Tim and I would leave Lila with Maggie. I wondered now that I could ever have entrusted Lila to a woman I half liked, half feared for the sake of appearing polite and felt it as a judgment on my care of Lila. I wondered that Nick could have put Maggie's feelings ahead of my instincts as a mother, ahead of the safety of our child.

Now this. Not for the first time, I felt the bleaching, corrosive sensation of being intently scrutinised. I gasped as I realised I had been crouching as though somebody had struck me in the stomach. I had been physically winded by the photo's arrival.

'Where did you go?' I spat out. 'Where did you take her? Who have you been with?'

My voice was a violent rasp that made me think of cartoon villains. I forced an airy laugh. I didn't want Maggie to know how unhinged I felt. *Bit late for that.*

'Margot, are you okay?' Maggie started down the stairs, her concerned eyes sliding between my pale face and Lila's rosy one. My daughter's gummy smile was clouded over with that veil of the doubtful anxiety children seem to absorb when those around them are suffering. 'Has something happened? Margot? Was it your phone? Is it that creepy troll again?'

So she knows about HelenKnows. Is it her?

I could feel Maggie's dark pupils sweeping over my face, searching for something, waiting for me to speak.

The eyes. The stares. The open mouths.

This was the moment to tell Maggie, to explain who Winnie was and what she had done. What *we* had done. That we had been friends – the very best of friends – for years until Jack's death and Lila's birth, until that silly, thoughtless photo that had so wounded Winnie. Except that wasn't quite it, was it?

There was so much more to it than that, so much that couldn't be condensed into the sort of empty, neutral chitchat that I felt comfortable with around Maggie. And if I told Maggie – Maggie who also exerted this bizarre hold over me, a gentle but insistent pressure on the very foundations of my identity ... Well, then Maggie would know my weakness. Maggie would know something that I hadn't even told Nick. Something that was too terrible to tell anyone.

My replacement had burrowed so far in already; I couldn't let her get to the core of me.

'No, look, it's nothing,' I managed to say, my voice more steady and back at its usual pitch. 'Just a stupid thing from my mum that I wasn't expecting. Where did you two go? Did Lila enjoy it? Did you stop for a drink somewhere? Did you meet anybody?'

I knew I was asking more questions than was logical or sounded casual. I knew I was leading the witness, but I had to know what had gone on in the last few hours that had once more made my future happiness prey to Winnie's vindictive streak.

I jiggled the baby with forced jollity and carried her through to the sitting room, where I set her upon the carpet surrounded by toys. Lila peered up between the faces of the women standing over her, her expression as grave as one and as bewildered as the other.

'We just went to that café along the road,' Maggie answered eventually, her eyes searching my face as though it were a map to a destination she had never heard of. 'We took the long way round, had a walk, then a quick cuppa. Everyone was cooing over gorgeous Lila, as usual.'

I turned away. Winnie must have taken the picture without Maggie's seeing. Had she left Lila and gone to the loo? How long had Lila been alone for? I felt a wave of nausea at what could have happened to the most precious part of my very being, followed immediately by a hot anger with myself for having let my child out of my sight.

'Then I saw your message and we came straight back,' Maggie finished, and dug her hands into the back pockets of her jeans. *High waisted and fashionably cropped, not the skinnies she used to wear.* 'But look, are you sure you're okay? Did something just happen?'

Here it was again, the chance to unburden, but I still didn't take it.

That's exactly what she wants – something to hold over me.

I didn't even know whether I was thinking of Maggie or Winnie anymore, but my lips stayed closed, my breathing shallow. I shook my head.

'I'm fine, Maggie, thank you,' I lied, affecting bashfulness. 'I guess I just haven't left Lila for that long before and I got a bit anxious, that's all. Quite highly strung at the best of times.'

It was only an extended version of the truth, but I played up to the stereotype. The new-mum demographic is so expected to career around fuelled by angst and unreasonable panic that had I revealed what I really felt – an increasingly cool, detached sense of fear and an increasingly logical urge to protect myself – Maggie probably would have been even more concerned. Women with babies are not supposed to be capable of detachment or logic, only berserk, reactive mood swings and tears. I hadn't cried for weeks; the salt water inside seemed to have evaporated under the heat of my constant anxiety.

When Maggie had slipped her leopard-print coat back on and the door had swung shut behind her, I reached immediately for my phone. I placed Lila among her toys once more, then opened my messages. Winnie's face, gaunt, but recognisably the girl I had known since the age of twelve, looked out at me. Directly above it was the grovelling apology I had sent to

Winnie's last text; above that were the months' worth of unanswered upbeat banalities I had sent in an effort to prolong our
relationship.

Winnie's face was level with my daughter's as she leaned in
towards the café's wooden high chair until their temples were
touching. One arm outstretched with the phone and the other
around my baby's chubby bulk, my friend looked directly into
the camera, while Lila's eyes were fixed on the image of herself
on the screen. One guileless pudgy fist reached towards it to
try to touch it. Winnie's lips were set in a smile; Lila's rosebud
lips formed an appreciative 'ooh' and the permanent patch of
dribble on her chin glistened in the light.

Her expression seemed genuine enough: Winnie looked
delighted to be with Lila, to have encountered her unexpect-
edly while out and about. The little globe-round face smiled
back at me too, the flaxen curls blending into Winnie's own
coppery halo where their heads were bent together to fit the
frame. My insides felt cold.

What would Nick say if I showed him this?

He'd be delighted, I was certain of it. He'd see it as the
beginning of a reconciliation, the renewal of a friendship that
had lasted so long and been through so much. *So much he
doesn't know about.*

What would Nick say if I told him how frightened I am?

He'd cajole me into feeling less troubled. As much as I
longed for the special sort of absolution my calm and rational
husband could always provide, it was the opposite of what I
needed, to relax into complacency just at the point when
Winnie had me – and Lila – in her sights. I had to stay sharp
for this, which meant Nick couldn't know. For now.

*Clever Winnie to make it all look so ordinary. You'd have to
know everything to understand the threat she was sending.*

I checked my watch: six-thirty, and time to give Lila her
bath. I had become adept at blocking things out while I cared

for my daughter – just as I had with Nick in years before – and I let my nerves unwind into the familiar routine now.

The kettle on, the formula mixed, and the bottle placed in cold water to cool. The bath running, the thundering of the tap's plume into the tub a version of white noise that both Lila and I had come to love. The baby kicked on her back, her changing mat brought through to the bathroom floor, while the water came up to temperature.

There is no perspective to raising a child. Everything is immediate. A child's needs are absolute – whatever else the world asks must wait. The sense that my rib cage might burst with joy had never left me even as I felt the sky could fall in on me. I had heard of the women who couldn't connect with their babies, who cared for them as automata until the love kicked in. I wasn't one of them – there was nothing mechanical about my reactions to Lila. To me, they were the most perfect expression of being human, a pendulum between ecstasy and worry.

What I resented was the rest of the world creeping in, seeping through the cracks, like ecto-slime from a horror film, to fill up a mould around me and my baby. I couldn't bear this, the most expansive range of emotions I had ever felt, to be sculpted by the life I had had before them. By work and Maggie; by friends and Winnie; by Nick? No, Nick was different. I knew that he had, as I had, recognised another dimension to himself from the moment of Lila's arrival.

He doesn't have to fit her in the way I do. It's enough for him to have his life and her as well. I have to change my outline to let her in.

Gazing down at Lila, freshly towel-dried and popped into a fuzzy sleepsuit that rendered her even more like a little teddy, I felt the usual blissful drag on my heart. I savoured the moment of gently depositing Lila into her cot as the final few seconds before I had to deal with real life again.

The nursery door closed, the monitor on and a small, breathy, supine figure flickering on its screen, I found my phone again and sat on the sofa downstairs with it, and a glass of wine that, tonight, I didn't feel guilty about. There was no one around to judge. It'd be out of my system long before Lila's next feed anyway.

Just as there was no punctuation in Winnie's message, so there was no overt animosity. Her first move was a blank, an empty version of how we both felt, a step taken in the dark without knowing whether there was firm ground to land on.

And yet everything about it made me feel uncomfortable. There was nothing warm about it. It had been intended to catch me off guard and to leave a chill. *To remind.*

The new girl in question was Lila, but we had used that term years ago, to refer to somebody else. *Helen.*

The hairs on my arms and the back of my neck had stood on end when I received it.

I drafted and redrafted my response – not in the message screen, in case it sent before I was ready or notified Winnie that I was *typing* ... a detail I had always found ominous – until I had done more rewrites for this than I ever had done for Moff.

I would send my reply in the morning. I knew well enough from my own dating career, Triassic period though it felt by comparison to the many complex apps and arrangements Maggie talked of, that it was never a good idea to send a weighted text ahead of a night one hoped to spend sleeping. Not that I did much of that anymore anyway.

I poured some sweet Gavi into a wine glass from a set Nick and I had been given as a wedding present, and flicked from the Notes app on my phone to Instagram. Maggie was on there again, a picture of two gin and tonics on a wooden table I recognised as one in our local pub, the Abbess.

When will she come clean about Tim?

I wondered whether there was a way – subtly, of course, and swiftly followed up with a 'silly me' apology – of outing my replacement's relationship, so that all the hundreds of followers Maggie had gained in the wake of her 'singles on top' piece could finally see her for the fraud she was. A comment beneath the picture perhaps? @-ing Tim and telling the lovebirds to have a fun evening together?

Too obvious.

Such were the mechanics of the seesaw I found myself on opposite Maggie. Whatever either of us did rebounded on the other, even if it was unintentional. An act of deliberate sabotage would be seen instantly for what it was: jealousy, envy, pathetic spite.

I flicked past pictures of toothless baby grins posted by the women from my parenting classes and arty shots of cocktails from PRs I had known in a former life, past country-house vistas from some of my colleagues, and carefully curated modern and minimalist interiors from the others, those who projected status with their London pads rather than their ancestral piles.

Idly, I opened Facebook, less full of my London life and more full of the people Winnie and I had shared classrooms with – plus Maggie. On here, her gin-and-tonic post was subtly different, a shot that featured Tim's hand on hers in the foreground, subtitled with the word *happy*. I felt a whoosh of disappointment that Maggie had got there before me and gone public, that whatever tiny hold I had had over my replacement was gone.

I had known Tim for the best part of a decade, could see he was happier now than at any point during those years. I had sometimes felt him looking at the relationship I had with his best friend, my husband, with a yearning – nothing remotely sexual, more a desire to have what we had. Now that he'd found it, I felt myself depleted in his eyes. Maggie had taken that from me, too.

Running a hand self-consciously through my unwashed hair, I recognised within myself a simultaneous swooping sense of excitement for Maggie, a woman on the brink of what might be the most important relationship of her life, and a bitter scorn that she felt the need to share it with the reassuring clamor of a remote audience.

What you do every day with pictures of Lila, you mean? Maggie's voice taunted me.

This was life now: the only other way was to turn off the lights and pretend you'd gone out, as Winnie had done. Was I more disturbed by Maggie's needy availability or Winnie's sudden disappearance? Impossible to say.

An icon flared red in the corner of the screen, of my eye, and I clicked it without thinking: a friend request.

There was the idiotic picture again, those stupid joke sunglasses.

'HelenKnows wants to be your friend,' the request read.

Setting my wine glass down so abruptly it spilled onto the rug, I mused in silent horror. What exactly was it that this person might want from me? Several things, I noted, she had taken already: my peace of mind, my self-esteem, my attention from my infant daughter, the supposedly impenetrable bubble of love in which Lila and I had once existed. Precisely the things that Maggie and Winnie were steadily dismantling, too.

Ignoring the spilled wine, I revisited the Twitter profile. The troll continued to bombard female public figures with vitriolic comments about their appearance and their professional standing. She had recently got into an online fight with a popular news anchorwoman about the colour of a suit she had worn to read the headlines. With every malicious post I read, many of them sent in great clusters during the small hours – *You're awake then too, are you?* – I felt my own sense of

dread subside. HelenKnows was a troubled individual, spit-
ting bile at any target she could find. The communications
with me, though seemingly personal, were part of a wider
crusade rather than a witch hunt.

With this latest though, she felt closer to home; I couldn't
shake the feeling, a small current humming along my skin,
that she was watching me even though the shutters were
closed. Although I seldom used Facebook, it was a personal
account, not a public profile like the others. On there, this
friend request felt like a sudden knock at my door.

A click on HelenKnows's page revealed nothing – no other
friends, no messages, no posts. I hesitated before choosing to
report her, with the sense all the while that she would know
the moment I did so. I worried I would be goading her with it,
how she might react to the perceived slight. Then I remembered my tormentor had been the one to get in touch with me,
that it was *her* aggression; she had elbowed her way into my
memories, shattered my solace.

*Whatever she thinks she knows can only have come from one
person: Winnie.*

I hadn't thought about Helen since school, not in an active
way. It was all in there under the surface, but I had learned not
to pay attention to it directly. Whenever I fizzed with anxiety
and worry – which was often – I attributed it to whatever was
in front of me, not the insistent drone that was always within.

*The eyes. The stares. The open mouths. The scream as she fell.
And the noise she made as she landed.*

I shook my head forcefully. Too much Helen had got in.

I clicked 'delete' to her request and refreshed my Facebook
feed once again. At the top, Maggie's latest picture had several
likes and a ladder of comments underneath it.

'Awwhhh cheers hun!'

'You deserve it!'

'Bon weekend, Mags!'

What must it have been like to live a life that brimmed over with good feeling, where people spouted positivity for positivity's sake? The scorn I felt for Maggie's online existence wobbled. For so long now, mine had been defined by loss and death and fear.

You could have warned me.

The phrase floated into my head and I remembered my reply to Winnie, waiting to be sent in the morning. It niggled at me, a blade in the flesh that I needed to remove before the wound could heal. Opening my messages, I paged to beneath the photo Winnie had sent a few hours ago – *Was that all?* – and typed my response:

'You always were better at making friends than me.'

I clicked 'send' and closed my phone down entirely, draining the glass I held in my other hand. For the first time in months, I felt the illusion of being in control. I knew nothing had changed, but I had stopped wondering how I had angered my old friend, was no longer waiting to hear from her, no longer scraping before Winnie even at a distance, apologetic for circumstances over which I had no say – the death of one child and the burgeoning life of another. And something that had happened years ago.

After months of feeling remorseful and ashamed, I now felt angry.

Winnie specialised in making others feel guilty; that was how she had dealt with what she had done. Winnie had a talent for doling out shame, always calm, always serene, always ever so slightly disappointed and resigned. After it was all over with Helen, Winnie had made it clear that no one else could ever come close, that I would always be the second choice she hadn't intended to make.

Well, now I've made mine: no more of this.

Filled with purpose and suddenly upright with an energy I had forgotten had ever existed within me after months of nightmares and the minimal sleep Lila allowed me, I set my empty glass down and stood.

It had grown dark, the evening gloaming replaced with blacker night, and the shadows in the hallway stretched along the walls. The top of the stairs was an acute angle in the darkness. What I needed was up there.

I decided to delete myself. I would take myself off all the online outlets that I felt had made the leap from my screen into my soul and, in doing so, had lowered my defenses to Maggie, to Winnie, to this Twitter troll, whoever she was. I would do it on Nick's computer, the giant inch-thick screen that occupied most of the spare room, where he had often worked in the evenings before Lila was born, creating glyphs and logos for his clients.

I'd been horrified when he bought it and I found out its price tag – an echo from my thrifty youth – but I'd also been secretly pleased. Nick's acquisition was the stuff of Manhattan lofts, that screen, the hip designer dream, something my teenage self would have longed for, had she had a clue that brushed steel could look so good.

I could just have removed the app from my phone, but I wanted it to be final, wanted to make sure I had done it properly. Slightly drunk, I reasoned that killing myself online should be done with a certain amount of ceremony. My sober self also knew that, for the same reason I sometimes saw the interns at work stifle a giggle at my out-of-touch tech questions, I still saw desktops like Nick's as the only means of doing what I thought of as 'business'.

First time I've sat at a desk since Lila was born; I'm almost excited.

I flicked the light at the bottom of the stairs and climbed them decisively. From the sitting room at my back, I could hear the low hum of the baby monitor as it relayed the image from the camera trained on Lila in the nursery – *Yes, 'the nursery.*' From behind her door at the top of the stairs, there came every so often – much less often than I was strictly happy with, I had realised after her birth – a small, irregular gust of an out-breath and the rustle of a tiny body shifting in its sleeping bag.

In the spare room, Nick's screen winked, always on, always ready. It reminded me of myself during the night, motionless, with all the appearance of sleep but ready at a moment's notice to perform whatever task Lila required of me. I clicked the light on at the wall, picked my way through the boxes we still hadn't quite got round to unpacking – *two years on* – and the bags of baby clothes that Lila had already grown out of, waiting to be passed on.

'Mummy's bags of heartbreak,' Nick called them, teaching me about my sentimental attachment to the tiny things Lila had first worn. He always seemed excited about whatever the next phase of Lila's development was, I noticed, whereas I marked every new learning, every rite, as a little death: a step further away from the time when Lila and I had been the same person. I hadn't much enjoyed being pregnant, but I couldn't bear the idea of it becoming part of our distant past.

Lowering myself into the chair in front of the desk – a chair that had cost almost as much as the screen but that we both had fallen in love with for its retro appeal as much as we had delighted in the space-age look of what sat on the desk above it – I waved the mouse to wake the computer. The black expanse, wider than my head by several feet each side, sprang into luminous pixels.

I found I was looking at a pinkness that stunned me. The shadow of a fold here, the tail end of a smear there. A fingernail, an eyelash came into focus. Then a hat – and a bunny. The picture of Jack taken soon after his birth, and his death – the picture that Nick had deleted from my phone – took up the huge screen.

I often giggled at Lila's ability to be shocked long after whatever it was that had caused it had passed. Her startled jump coming several seconds after a loud noise or someone entering the room had made me laugh. But now I felt a similar delay as my mind struggled to process the image before me.

And when it did, I leaped from the chair as if it were hot on the back of my legs and let out a cry that was somewhere between a gasp of disbelief and a wail of horror.

This was gone, this picture; Nick had deleted it.

I grasped, still reeling, for all the reasonable explanations for why it was on his screen, but there weren't any. Nick was the only person who used this computer, was the only other person who'd been up here in weeks.

Except for Maggie.

Maggie had been in our house alone all afternoon but had come upstairs specifically after dropping Lila off in the evening. Just after I'd had the message from Winnie.

Now I thought about the moments immediately before I received Winnie's picture. Maggie had spent far longer up here than she needed to. And I had hardly been in a state to notice which rooms she'd been into. The door to the spare room was right next to the bathroom, after all.

Maggie had done this. Maggie, who was taking my job, my friends, my life – and now, it seemed, my sanity.

Maggie had put this picture here for me to find. But why?

Winnie. Who had been in the café, who had posed for a picture with my daughter – my lovely, rosy-cheeked, healthy baby. Winnie had asked Maggie to do it.

PART TWO

Winnie Clough

I

A world without children is a world with no future.

And given how hard I have worked to forget the past, where does that leave me?

These are the thoughts on repeat in my brain, in time with my steps as I pace the streets trying to forget. No, not forget – I won't allow the image of my son to fade, yet I can already feel the details of him escaping me.

The scent of him, rust and caramel, is evaporating as if on a breeze. The noises he made, the soft rasping snuffles before the harsher noises began, are fading as the days whizz by without him in them. The humbling sense of completeness that Charles and I felt as we held him – that won't go. But I worry that the profound emptiness that hangs like a weight in my arms never will, either.

I walk the streets trying to numb myself, not to forget. To take the remorseless edge off what has happened to me. As if by putting one foot in front of the other over and over I can somehow wear down the razor's edge of my feelings.

During the week, I get up at dawn to catch the train with the city crowd. Chancery Lane, St Paul's, Aldgate, Bank, Canary Wharf. Grey streets lined with grey buildings where grey people walk to work. I go there just to exist. In the office districts, you aren't assaulted by prams and the women who wheel them around every corner. A pedestrian in London's pinstripe postcodes is just that – not a man or a woman or a wife. Not a mother.

In these childless streets, I seek to remember myself. The feeling never goes, even if I can banish the visuals for a short time. There's no room for anything else, for everything else. For things I used to think I needed. For people I used to think I cared about. For the mistakes I've made and the secrets I've kept.

Maybe that's why I feel them bubbling towards the surface again after all this time.

On the weekend, I can't escape as easily. I risk bumping into people – families, fortunate and whole – heading for the shops, the museums, the theatres. Places you go when life is something to be enjoyed rather than endured.

Sometimes I walk near our house, but that's difficult when you live, deliberately, in a part of town that people move to, deliberately, when they want to start a family. I never for an instant thought that we'd be any different from the rest of them, the ones who come home with a car seat full of bundle topped off with a little white hat. We brought ours back with us too, only Charles had stuffed his bloodstained shirt into it. That was what we carried over our threshold.

I can't say it is getting easier. I can't even say it is getting less hard. The physical signs have gone now. My breasts were taut with milk that went undrunk for nearly two weeks; the pain of it, like somebody kneeling on my chest, came as a relief, something to focus on other than the constant nebulous ache. The skin of my stomach sagged for months even though all I could face filling it with was the protein shakes Charles wordlessly passed me. I forced them down like fuel because I wanted my body to be ready again.

Little by little, it is healing. After I put on the weight I had lost, my periods came back as the frost melted, with the first crocus buds that grow in a ring around the base of the tree outside our house. My lustrous pregnancy hair fell out and regrew in short tufts above my ears – these velvet antlers that curl out when I pull my hair back are the only thing I have in common with other mothers. I see them, patting theirs back down, tutting and fussing, but I twist mine around my fingers endlessly: they started growing with his first breath, they are proof he existed, their length is the span of mine and Charles's new lives without him.

I tried to be happy for Margot when her baby came, but when she didn't tell me – warn me – before posting it online, I realised I couldn't. I couldn't stand her complacency. She had no idea how lucky she was, how close she'd stepped to disaster. No woman in childbirth does, because they're all assured beforehand that it's as simple as having a tooth out. They have to believe it, I suppose, because you'd go mad with the thought that carrying life inside you came with the very real possibility of its death or yours. But you don't hear people sobbing in a dental clinic.

In the very darkest days, I thought a lot about my and Margot's past. The days when all I could do was endlessly look at the few photos I had of him on my phone until either its battery ran out or mine did.

This wasn't the first time someone had been taken away from me as I stood on the brink of sharing a new life with them. And it wasn't the first time that Margot had moved on as though nothing had happened.

Helen arrived when we were sixteen. She was in our year at school but a few months older and easily the most sophisticated person Margot and I had ever come across in what was, admittedly, a rather slight social circle. She had a frizz of dark hair that she kept closely cropped to her head, and her school tie was permanently and boldly askew. Within a few weeks, I had started wearing mine that way, too.

Margot and I weren't used to having to share each other. Nobody else at St Dominic's held any interest for us. They were too quick to laugh at our jokes, too slow to follow our wit, too much a part of the surroundings we both had plans to leave behind as soon as we possibly could.

Margot was tall and skinny, something her fashion colleagues later lapped up but at school our peers ridiculed her for: being a young woman with no breasts in the north of England is a tough gig. I had ginger corkscrew curls – that's a cross to bear the world over. I clamped them down every morning under a hair slide that tended to work its way loose throughout the day.

But what we lacked in the looks department, we made up for with senses of humour so perfectly matched to each other's, so nuanced, that the bond between us sometimes felt like telepathy.

No one has ever made me laugh the way Margot did – not even Charles. I left that gasping, gulping, helpless-with-tears schoolgirl humour behind with my textbooks and pencil case when I finished at St Dominic's, but back then Margot could bring it on with as little as a look, an eyebrow raise, or this weird trick she had of hitching her upper lip over her teeth and blinking rapidly. I'd be a puddle on the floor within seconds; one term, our teachers had to separate us in every subject, for every lesson.

I remember with a fondness tinged with anxiety the aching cheeks after we'd spent a break time together conjugating some ridiculous involved joke or inventing a new character for our repertoire. Those giggling fits always had an edge to them, a breathlessness, a lack of control that brought with it a certain sense of rising panic.

Once I set Margot off during a choir concert, with such force that the notes she was singing came out as a deep, tuneless bellow that echoed round the hall in stark contrast to the reedy sopranos we were surrounded by. After that, all either of us needed to do was hum the opening bars of the song to crack us both up into convulsions.

Every break time, we escaped our peers up a decrepit spiral staircase to the dusty music practice rooms housed within the roof space of the brutalist main building. There were no prodigies among the few students who dutifully croaked along in the school clarinet band to challenge us there, so we sprawled on the dilapidated sofa, scrawled our idiolect on the chalkboards, and picked at the flaking paint and patches of dry rot that held together our special sanctuary.

We discovered an opening at one end of a room with a wheezing old piano in it: a small, not-quite-person-height door that lay behind a sheaf of two-dimensional thatched cottages left over from the set of some drama production in years long forgotten.

The prac rooms were dingy, but this door opened into glorious sunshine. The panes of the refectory's giant skylights were only a few meters above our heads, the scrape of chairs and clink of local Sheffield-forged cutlery on plates rising from below. It wasn't a room but a balcony – a minstrels' gallery above the dining hall that had fallen into sad disuse through St Dominic's total lack of anything even approaching a musician, let alone an event with enough pomp to require accompaniment.

For two girls longing for the chance to escape, gazing down on the rest of the student body as it stuffed itself on bland meals was both invigorating and depressing. We lay on our stomachs so we wouldn't be seen above the railings, the wooden spindles of which were so rotten many had broken or crumbled clean away, and gossiped callously about the cliques spread beneath us.

Margot and I learned to hide ourselves by raising only the tops of our heads above the lower skirt of the railings, where the wooden struts were attached to the floor. We came to know by heart where the slats were gap-toothed and how to avoid being seen through them. We'd learned not to brace ourselves against any of them – they splintered easily and bowed at the slightest touch.

From above, we watched bonds form, friendships dissolve, and kept an eye out for the more outrageous table manners. Margot and I took it in turns to narrate, as though we were watching a BBC nature documentary, and found ourselves so amusing that we had to stop regularly to catch our breath and wipe the tears from our eyes.

We made ourselves a nest up there in the eaves, wove it from schoolgirl giggles and small-town daydreams. Margot and I barely ever spoke to the other pupils; we were an exclusive club of two. By the time Helen arrived, it had been years since anybody else had bothered trying to join.

Helen hadn't tried – perhaps that was what made her intriguing. She'd just shown up one day – it was a Wednesday, I remember; Helen was so exotic she didn't even start on a Monday – and sat, aloof, in the form room while the teacher introduced her. She was freckled and substantial – not big or plump, but womanly in a way Margot and I wouldn't become for several years. Helen wasn't as tall as either of us, but she drew glances because she held herself straight-backed and with her chin high. She made eye contact like a painting does, with everybody and at all angles. Hazel searchlights winkling out secrets and a thin-lipped smile as though she found herself funny.

Helen spent her first day not with her dark, curly head down trying to fit in, but competently answering questions in biology, French, and geography as though she didn't care what the rest of us thought of her.

It wasn't until I went to university and met other students from private schools that I realised what had shaped Helen into the sort of mature and confident young individual rarely seen among the breeze blocks, prefabs, and chips on the shoulder at St Dominic's. She had never mentioned it, and we had never thought to ask.

Nobody else in our class had the social skills, so Margot and I introduced ourselves to her on her second morning. I say 'Margot and I': I was always the more self-assured of the two of us. I gave Helen our names with all the anticipation of handing a child a much-longed-for Christmas present. She received them with a steady expression, but gratitude – and curiosity – twinkled behind her eyes.

'How are you finding it then?' I asked as nonchalantly as a sixteen-year-old can manage.

I leaned on the desk at which Helen was sitting alone, the book she was voluntarily reading marking her outsider status, while she waited for the bell to ring for registration. Margot loitered to one side, unsure how to stand in order to look at once approachable but also occupied, not too available. (This was the reason why, in years to come, she would smoke until she was thirty.)

'Not bad, thanks. Having some mates might improve things a bit though. Do you guys fancy going to the Peppercorn at lunchtime?'

And like that, Helen established a new ritual. I could see that Margot ached at how easily and how fluently the new girl had turned her own weakness, her own indebtedness, into a position of strength with that invitation, handed out with all the grace of a socialite, even if it was just to the tatty café along the road from the school.

I never forgot how casually Helen had done it, either. That deftness was one of the first things that drew me to her. I've often wondered whether the new girl even realised she was manipulating the pair of us, or whether it just came naturally to her.

It wasn't long afterwards that Helen followed us up to the prac rooms.

I had just dropped my rucksack onto the floor and pitched myself down on that sagging sofa. Margot was sitting at the ancient piano, repeatedly pressing the very highest key, trying to discern the sound of the note from the noise of the hammer.

'Why do they even have this one?' she grumbled as a crashing noise came from beyond the door to the staircase.

We jumped in unison: nobody had ever disturbed us here. We weren't convinced that many of the staff even knew about these rooms, either.

Helen careened through the door, dust powdering her hair and a spiderweb streaking along the sleeves of her green school blazer. When she tumbled into the room that day, it was the first time I'd seen anything other than studied boredom cross her features.

'This place is amazing!' She brushed her fingers along a blurb of our bubble writing on one of the chalkboards.

'Did you follow us up here?' Margot asked, uselessly, from the end of the room. Of course she had.

'Yeah, sorry for being creepy.' Helen shrugged mischievously. 'I wanted to know why I could never find you two at lunch. Where you were hiding.' She gazed around the drab room with its bits of scenery dotted here and there and haywire old music stands with their broken antennae as though it were filled with glistering treasure. 'Does anybody else ever come up here? They don't know what they're missing.'

Margot spoke next, and I was glad. I didn't yet know how to deal with the situation; Margot and I had constructed so much of our personalities up in the prac rooms that Helen's unexpected arrival in there somehow felt like far more of an intrusion than the way she had crash-landed into our friendship.

'Actually, there's more,' Margot said, standing up from the piano stool and shifting aside the backdrops propped at one end of the instrument.

She pushed open the half-height hatch onto the gallery and gestured through it. 'Stay down though. Don't let anybody see you.'

Margot and I followed Helen through at a crouch and our eyes met over her back. I had the sense we had opened the door to more than just the balcony.

I watched Helen take in the scene: the vast windows onto the sky and the view into the busy cafeteria below. I couldn't help but feel a burst of pride – or smugness, perhaps – that we had been the ones to introduce her to it.

'This. Is. Soooo. Cool,' Helen breathed. 'Oh my God, we're going to have so much fun up here.'

Behind her, I saw Margot's face go slack.

So why were we surprised when we found Helen waiting for us the next time we made our way up the decaying steps?

'I thought we could rearrange some of the furniture.' Helen had already dragged a chair in from the anteroom, placed the piano stool between it and the sofa like a coffee table. 'Give it a new look.'

'You've cleaned all our stuff off the boards.' Margot spoke through what sounded like a mouthful of sawdust as she took in the walls, denuded of our chalky jargon. 'You had no right to do that.'

Helen looked surprised at her tone and, with it, a little impressed. 'Oh, sorry! I thought it was just old doodles. Are we cool?'

I had never seen Margot look less enthusiastic when she nodded in reply, but it seemed enough to satisfy Helen, a cuckoo in the nest Margot and I had fashioned for ourselves.

We started going to the café every lunchtime instead. The practice rooms now looked scruffy and sad by comparison: a childhood den versus what we thought of then as a sophisticated refuge.

Margot and I drank milkshakes and Helen had peppermint tea, something I could tell Margot regarded as an affectation. I tried it but had to swallow my first mouthful with a badly stifled gag.

'It's good for your skin,' Helen said, laughing.

Helen wasn't funny the way Margot was. She was too self-possessed to ever give herself over to the gales of giggles the two of us used to share. When she did laugh – one sharp and sceptical outbreath through both nostrils – I felt delighted to have wrung it from her, and such was my preoccupation with repeating the triumph, I began to find Margot less amusing.

After school, we three would decamp to someone's house, ostensibly to do our homework, but more often to watch MTV and read magazines. Helen had a stack of well-thumbed glossies that nestled in a nook in the corner of her bedroom that had once been a fireplace. Her house was an old barn that had been converted; neither of the postwar semis that Margot and I had grown up in had anything that resembled the crannies that Helen's home did.

Margot's own slightly tattered collection – inherited from the waiting room at her father's dental practice – rivalled Helen's, though, and we flipped through them as we lay on the floral bedspread, the fluffy blue carpet, the burger-shaped beanbag, feigning knowledge. Helen wanted to be a barrister; I had it in my head to be a gallerist, simply because I thought the word sounded sophisticated. Margot said she just wanted to write about people who were more interesting than anyone she had ever met – even Helen, she didn't quite say.

Margot used to unleash my hair from the clip that held it on those afternoons and try to twist it into new styles while Helen gave instructions. One day I started to paint Margot's nails while she did mine, our hands spread out in a yin-yang of us both as we always had. Helen was content to watch for a time but then insisted we try it as a trio, and it descended into Rouge Noir smudges across all of our knuckles. The difference between Margot and me was that I found it funny.

The seasons changed as the dynamic did. We found one day that it was spring and the three of us had become inseparable. We marauded as a threesome, swapped clothes, and made tapes for one another, carefully copying an extra each time, so we could all listen to the same compilation at once.

Mine were gutsy and guitarish, Margot's full of pop tunes we could make up dances to. Helen, whose elder sister was on her year abroad in Marseille, peppered hers with French songs that we sang along to phonetically. I didn't much like the tunes, but I knew that wasn't where their value lay. Years later, when Charles mentioned him casually on one of our early dates, I'd be grateful for that basic grounding in MC Solaar. It wasn't until then that I realised the accretion of culture could be accidental, and cynical.

I forgot that Helen was the new girl, had ever been a stranger, until one day when I was off school sick and the two of them, Margot and Helen, went to the café together without me. I knew Margot well enough to know she'd feel uncomfortable without me there as a backstop, and it made me feel protective and contemptuous of her in equal amounts.

What Margot has never understood about herself is that three is an ideal number for her: enough to deflect some of her intensity, enough to take off the self-imposed pressure to carry a conversation, enough for her even to seem garrulous. She could have thrived in a three, but I knew how desperately she wanted us to be a two again – just as I recognised that I was enjoying the way Helen had opened up the rather airless friendship that Margot and I had shared before.

In Helen, I saw a recklessness I'd always strived for but had been too scared to embrace alone. Margot liked to be safe and quiet, warm and cosy, but I wanted to feel the chill of high-altitude decisions, to stand in the blowing gale of a life lived on the edge. Helen never even seemed worried about the drop.

The day I was ill, conversation between the two of them would take more effort than usual; I knew that. I imagined it as I lay on the sofa at home, covered with a knitted blanket my grandmother had made, the TV droning in the background. Margot would be tongue-tied and self-conscious without me, at a loss for what to say next. The harder she had to search for sentences, the less likely she'd be to find any that intrigued Helen. Our three-way friendship was based on my translating Helen into something Margot could understand and respond to. For Helen, it was that she liked me, and Margot came as an inseparable part of the package.

When the doorbell rang an hour after the end of the school day, I knew it would be Helen on our front step even before my mum showed her into the sitting room. She let her ruck-sack fall to the floor, shrugged her blazer off and dropped into the armchair opposite me.

'I told Margot I had to help my mum with something at home,' Helen said, looking at me levelly, as though trying to watch my thoughts as my brain projected them on the inside of my head. 'We didn't have much to say to each other, really.'

She stared at the frayed cuff of her school sweater, and I shifted on my pillows. I was acutely aware of how childish I must have looked to her in my tartan pyjamas: hair unwashed, pale faced, and sniffly.

It struck me that Helen had done a very mature thing in coming to see me when I was ill. It was the sort of thing I supposed grown women did to look out for each other, the sort that live by themselves in flats made of glass and steel with balconies and potted plants. They'd pop round with shopping for each other, offer to put a wash on: the careful and considerate overlap of independent adult existence. Margot and I were still at the stage when our mothers called up the school to explain an absence and we'd be content to see each other the next day. Helen seemed to have so much more autonomy than us, and I was all the more impressed with her for it.

'Margot's a funny one, isn't she?' Though Helen's attention was seemingly on the invisible loose threads on her sweater, her voice was suggestive, her body tensed for my reply. I understood she was trying to prod me into saying something disloyal.

I knew, too, how Margot must have felt relieved to have had their afternoon together cut short – and that she'd be devastated to learn it had ended with Helen's coming to see me.

'She gets very nervous.' I tried to defend my best friend, without feeling much enthusiasm for the task. I thought of Helen, lying so easily, then slipping off to get the bus to my house. It never would have occurred to Margot to do anything other than go straight home. In that moment, Helen seemed to care for me in a way that was immediate and genuine, sincere rather than giggly, serious instead of a catchphrase and a silly voice.

I gave a nonchalant shrug that I hoped would belie my pyjamas and pigtails, the empty soup bowl on the tray my mum had brought through at lunchtime, the kids' programmes flickering on the TV with the sound turned down. I said what I thought I'd say if we were having the conversation at a polished chrome bar, legs crossed in sheer tights beneath it after a long day at work, fingers picking olives off toothpicks from tall vaselike glasses. 'She's just a bit young, I suppose,' I said.

Helen looked delighted with me, and the warmth that rose in my torso melted the heavy, nagging suspicion that I had let Margot down, had told the new girl a secret that wasn't mine to give away.

When Margot phoned later to see how I was, I didn't mention my visitor.

3

All it took was that one holiday. A week off school at the end of term because her parents could get the cottage cheaper that way. I stood and waved Margot off from Helen's front door, the pair of us silhouetted against the light from the hallway as she trudged down the drive, diligently turning back every few paces to check we were still watching. She had to head home early that Friday evening to pack her suitcase, as they were leaving before the sun came up the next day.

She looked uneasy as she left, her eyes flitting anxiously between our two faces as she made us promise to text her while she was away. Margot's complex blend of insecurities, combined with her shyness and an almost pathological curiosity for anything that happened in her absence, had made for a heady draught of desperation in those last few weeks with Helen, but this was the first time I noticed how it hung about her, heavy and cloying.

As she rounded the corner out of sight at the end of the drive, Helen turned to me with a slow-spreading smile.

'Right then,' she said. 'Shall we have some real fun? Call your mum and tell her you're staying here tonight.'

I'd never been drunk before – and I probably wasn't very that night, not by grown-up standards – but I felt as though my every sense was intoxicated with what Helen had to offer. We swiped our pudgy girlish faces into mature contours with her big sister's cast-off cosmetics; she drew silver eyeliner onto my lids that forked into lightning bolts on each side and outlined my lips in matte maroon. She fished a silky scarlet camisole out of a drawer and showed me how to stuff my bra with wads of toilet paper until two perfect half-moons of flesh appeared over the top of it.

Helen took the schoolmarmish barrette out of my hair – 'I'm confiscating this!' – and curled my hair in front of the mirror she kept propped against the wall in her bedroom, and I watched both of us in it as she did so. I didn't recognise the me inside the reflection – it would have taken even Margot a few moments to twig whose that pout was – but I felt more myself than I ever had before. Why hadn't I met this girl yet? Helen had found her for me.

We had a shot of everything in her parents' bar, a large oak bookcase with a fold-down cabinet at its centre where the bottles sat. We played the mixtapes we had made for each other and danced on the sofas. Then we got on the bus at the end of her road and went to a club that I didn't know existed but that Helen said would let us in.

There we danced more, sharing sugary bottles with alcoholic lemon bubbles and the tang of additives inside them. When the lights came on, we went outside and Helen found us a taxi while I breathed out fog into the starry sky and contemplated this, the beginning of my new life.

Did I think of Margot? Not until the next morning, when my mind kicked in again and, dry-mouthed, I peeled my head from one of the pillows on Helen's double bed. Margot and I only had singles, so we'd had to top-and-tail whenever we stayed over with each other. That morning, I'd woken up beside Helen, as though I were her wife.

I had woken up a grown-up, and I couldn't wait to do it all again.

Margot never stood a chance.

* * *

It had rained in Normandy, she said when she got back to school, and they'd been stuck indoors. Margot had quickly finished the books she had brought to read and zipped through the money she'd put on her chunky old mobile phone, texting me mostly but Helen too. I've lost count of the number of times since then that I've wondered whether things would have been different if group chats, or social media, had been invented then.

She messaged out of a compulsion to keep herself in our minds, asking questions to which she knew the answers, sending meandering thoughts on meaningless things. She even made up anecdotes about her family that she thought might amuse the two of us, but when her credit ran out, so did our replies.

By the time Margot returned home, Helen and I had changed, infinitesimally perhaps, and invisibly to anyone else, but irretrievably. Remarks Margot made that would usually have earned her a giggle sank into the silent air between us. Questions she asked were met with a sigh before they were answered. When she spoke, a flicker would pass between her oldest friend and her newest; the more she tried to ingratiate herself, the less interested and more irritated we became.

I told her all about our night out when she got back from holiday – a rare moment when it was just the two of us. Down the road, Helen was lying, mouth open, in the chair at Margot's father's dental practice. His daughter lay with her head in my lap as I tweezed her already perfect eyebrows into a pair of modish tadpoles – the perfect angle from which to see her icy blue eyes darken with worry.

'How could you afford it? What did you tell your mum? What if somebody had spiked your drink?'

I watched as her cautious mind built every obstacle to fun it could think of, the very same obstacles I had so enjoyed scaling with Helen by my side. I knew then that I had outgrown what there had been between Margot and me.

It wasn't like anything had even happened between us – until it did.

Margot noticed one break time that I was listening to a hand-labelled mix cassette that Helen hadn't made a copy of for her: of songs we had danced to on our night out together. At the school gates that lunchtime neither of us waited for her, and when she arrived alone at the Peppercorn, I was sipping a peppermint tea.

I know now, as the mother of a dead child, that cruelty is at its worst when it is arbitrary. When it can't be reasoned into part of a logical equation of cause and effect. I wondered, when Jack died, whether it had happened because of the things I had done wrong over the course of my life, but Charles, rightly, told me to stop being superstitious.

I remember Margot asking me one day how she'd offended me, why Helen and I didn't want her around anymore, why we were shutting her out – and I remember shrugging. There wasn't a reason, we just could; that's how cruel we were, that's how teenage girls work.

The day after we'd left her behind, Margot approached me and Helen at the top gate at the end of classes and I made a sort of half apology.

'We got paired in French while you were away, and Helen's going to help me practice for the oral test,' I mumbled, my eyes on the ground. 'You know how good she is.'

Margot's smile wobbled. 'Oh yes! Of course. Well, I could wait while you do that, I've got some stuff I need to do, too. Just get on with it, while you're . . .'

But she could see from our expressions that we were waiting for her to finish speaking rather than listening to what she was saying. I felt her watching our backs all the way up the hill, before she turned to catch the bus, her cheeks burning with the humiliation of it, throat lacerated with acidic tears she managed to stopper until she got home.

When we got to Helen's half-timbered house on a leafy avenue lined with driveways much longer than the ones on my road, she showed me a letter she'd typed up on the computer that sat in a nook in the landing. It was for Margot: a brief but businesslike character assassination, an agenda of flaws, intended, Helen told me, to help her grow up a bit so she could hang out with us again.

' ... *too worried what people think,*' I read, scrolling as sickness broke inside me like waves, my hands cold and slippery on the mouse. '*Being shy isn't an excuse ... could do with being more spontaneous ... juvenile ... spineless ... embarrassing ... Does everything have to be a joke?*'

It didn't exactly feel right, but Helen's observations spoke to my own. I wouldn't have said any of it to Margot's face, but I had been exasperated by many of the same complaints behind her back – especially recently. I saw it as yet more evidence of Helen's maturity, of her wanting to solve a problem rather than let it bed in. She seemed genuinely upset at the prospect that Margot could lose touch with us.

'What do you think?' she asked me, running one hand through her short hair and chewing on a fingernail. 'I just want to make sure she understands that she has the chance to save our friendship if she wants to. Don't you?'

She printed it off, put it in an envelope with a clear plastic window that she found in the top drawer of the desk and held it out to me.

'You should give it to her in maths tomorrow, Win,' Helen said reluctantly. 'She'll take it better from you.'

Then we went downstairs to watch Australian soaps, a couple of cheerful little psychopaths able to switch without pause from breaking our friend's heart to discussing which actress's hair we preferred.

*   *   *

I gave Margot the letter in the next lesson we had together. I slipped it to her as I sat down and she looked at me quizzically: an 'et tu Brute' across the desk. I could feel her reading it next to me, her shoulders hunching her smaller with every paragraph, the page trembling in her grasp. My insides roiled as she scanned it, and I realised with a jolt that it was less with empathy than exhilaration.

When the bell rang, Margot scooped up her belongings silently and left the room ahead of me. By the time I reached the corridor, she was lost in the swarm of heads and Helen was waiting for me.

She shrugged and gestured down the hallway, pursed her lips: 'She didn't take it very well, did she?'

4

It couldn't have come at a worse time, really. I've often wondered, in the decades since then, whether if Helen had shown up a year or two earlier, things would have gone differently. It wouldn't have been too late – in a school where most students didn't stay on for sixth form – for Margot to meld herself into one of the other cliques. She could have carried on as normal, bruised from the experience but not forever scarred by it.

As it was, our year group was counting the months until our exams finished at the end of the term and we were free to go our own way beyond the gates. Nobody was interested in making new friends at that point. Margot could hardly blame the rest of our cohort; she wasn't particularly interested in them, either.

I barely even saw her during the weeks after the letter and before what happened next. When I called her at home the night after she'd read it, her mother told me – a new crispness to her local burr – that Margot was busy and couldn't come to the phone.

One day, Margot met me as I came out of a lesson she knew I was in without Helen, had come to ask me what was going on. It was maybe a month after she'd come back from holiday, after my and Helen's night out and the letter, and we'd been avoiding her, cutting her out of our plans, stonewalling her attempts to start up a conversation with the two of us.

At first I had felt guilty about it, but her desperation to win us back became intoxicating, and I began to enjoy the power that being unavailable to her gave me.

She'd made me a mixtape, a gesture so tragic that it made me want to laugh in her face the moment she handed it over. As she held it out to me, Helen came out of a classroom upstairs and down the upper flight to find us talking.

'What are you doing, Margot? You know she doesn't want to speak to you. Neither of us do.' Helen's voice was cold but it had that calm, reasonable edge that teenagers think lends credibility to terrible behaviour. As if she were simply stating facts.

'I haven't come to talk to you,' Margot mumbled, looking at the floor. In that instant, I willed her to make eye contact at least, to show a bit of backbone, to deny Helen a reason to despise her any more.

I was embarrassed for her, this nervous girl whose friends had deserted her, for her being sad that they'd gone even though they'd been so unkind, for her missing them although they continued to wound her. It was an embarrassment that bordered on pity but that contained no compassion, only contempt.

'Well, I don't have anything to say to you, Margot,' I replied. 'And you certainly don't seem to have very much to say for yourself – as ever.' I did a theatrical eye-roll at Helen, who sniggered appreciatively.

'She's not worth it, Win,' Helen would say, always by my side during our estrangement, the few times Margot tried to greet me and start a conversation. 'Leave it. Don't bother.' Or, 'It's sad, really, isn't it?'

We didn't pick on Margot, taunt her, call her names, or even try to intimidate her – and that was perhaps the worst thing about it. We were just . . . *indifferent*. I remember sort of shrugging my shoulders apologetically, as if to say, 'It is sad, Helen, yes. It's sad that someone could be such a dreadful loser and have to sit by themselves all the time because nobody else wants to be their friend.'

After that, Margot became silent. She was hardly in a mood to make small talk. I knew the only thought that pulsed around her head was that life had been better once, that she had been happy at one time, that things had been easier – before Helen.

I knew without checking there that Margot had gone back up to the practice rooms. She spent morning breaks listening to her Walkman and waited out her lunch breaks reading on the sofa we used to share, rather than sitting under the beady eye of the poisonous librarian. She brought books in from home, chosen specifically from the shelves of her mother's study for their tortured-sounding titles. *Samson Agonistes. Les Misérables. De Profundis.* She told me years later that the latter had actually gone some way to making her feel better, while it was in front of her, at least.

When the bell rang, she had to force herself up and back down and onto the landings, crisscrossed with stairways that were crammed with bodies between lessons like an Escher-Lowry megamix.

It didn't strike me until several years afterwards that perhaps Helen felt guilty about the letter as well. Teenage girls don't do culpability. We didn't want to think about how Margot felt, so we froze her out. Looking after her wasn't my job, I told myself, even though I had a dragging feeling that I had failed my old friend.

I resented her for it: I just wanted to be able to enjoy the future that was opening up ahead of me with Helen. Why did Margot insist on being a constant reminder of the childhood I was leaving behind – and of a lapse in judgment that would haunt us both for years?

The letter. There was an unspoken agreement that it would never be mentioned again. Even then, thinking about it made me squirm; I knew how unkind we had been. Helen seemed supremely bored by Margot anyway. I got the impression Margot was relieved by our indifference: that we weren't

about to bring up her failings for everyone around us at school
to hear.

And ears were pricked, eyes peeled. Though the rest of St
Dominic's had written the pair of us – and Helen once she'd
arrived – off as snooty, clever posh girls, with our weird private
jokes and our funny made-up language, they were only too
eager to congregate and watch as the ties that had bound us
so closely began to unravel. It became a live soap opera, a
tragedy with the student body as chorus. Areas of the hallways
and grounds fell to a hush whenever the three of us were in
proximity, in case any words passed between us were missed.

The new girl, meanwhile, acted like she had been there for
years. She walked through the halls and classrooms as though
she owned the place, a confidence I was constantly reminded
of when I came up against Helen's kind at Cambridge and
then from behind my desk in the gallery. Rich, self-assured
people who had been educated to believe they counted, rather
than schooled to take up as little space as possible.

What someone like Helen was doing at St Dominic's was a
mystery, I realised much later. I've spent years projecting
imagined scandal onto her solicitor father – bankruptcy, fraud,
witness protection. But at the time, the new girl was far more
at ease in a school she had attended for three months than
Margot ever had been, even though she'd started there alongside me wearing a blazer that was far too large and a rucksack
almost as big as she was. She had never quite grown into either
of them.

Margot had always looked up to me, but who did I ever
have to look up to? In Helen, I found someone more worldly
than me, whose opinion really counted for something. Who
would help me find the woman I wanted so desperately to
become.

5

A couple of weeks later, Helen and I went out again. When I left my house to stay at hers, a rucksack full of outfits and makeup on one shoulder, I told my mum that we'd put on a film and eat pizza, play Ping-Pong in Helen's games room. We were only just on the cusp of that not being believable anymore: half children, half women. Femmes fatales who still watched cartoons.

I was excited to meet that new girl again – not Helen, but the one within me who had stared out from the mirror at me, burnished with silver at her temples, kissed with cherry on her lips. The girl who had danced on a stage, who had climbed the security barrier at its edge and hung from it over the crowd as the notes swelled around her.

It was as exhilarating as it had been the first time round, everything from the rituals of getting ready – Helen pilfered a bottle of cheap and fizzy sugary wine from a cupboard downstairs – to shivering in the queue outside the club as we each muttered the fake birth dates we'd need to recite if the bouncer asked us for them.

Where I had sometimes felt self-conscious in front of Margot – as though we were children trying out adulthood – I never did with Helen, because her maturity wasn't an act. It lent my own shaky version a feeling of authenticity. Back then I didn't realise that she was every bit as uncertain of the steps as I was. All I wanted was for life to open my eyes as wide as they had been the last time, when Helen and I had claimed our first night as almost-women.

There was a noisy cluster of other teenagers a few groups behind us in the queue, and, peering around, I recognised some of them from school. Initially irritated that our haunt had been discovered by others – specifically, others I had built my entire personality in antithesis to – I reasoned it wouldn't do my reputation any harm if I was seen by them to be already au fait with the nighttime economy.

At first, I barely noticed her, but as my eyes travelled over the heads of the girls behind us, the ash blonde on their periphery caught my attention. Margot was in my direct eyeline and stared back through the queue at me expressionlessly. My body remembered enough of our friendship to be delighted to see her on a reflexive, muscular level; a smile rose on my lips and my throat almost called out a greeting.

'What. Is *she*. Doing. Here.' Helen's voice was scathing.

'Looks like she's got some new mates.' I shrugged and turned back to face the front, but that magical feeling of liberation, of newness, of being on the cusp of . . . something, had fizzled and was no longer there.

It didn't take me long to realise that was because *she* was. Margot knew me inside out and I hated her for looking at me as though she didn't recognise me. How could I be that new girl with my old life looking on?

It was no surprise, really, that she didn't get in: Margot was practically faint with terror at the prospect of lying to the doorman, her face as transparently readable as a toddler's. We gleefully saw her being turned away as we waited in line for the cloakroom, and as the cordon came down in front of her, Margot caught my eye. I felt like I was closing a door on a crying child.

The old Winnie would have dropped back from the cashier's till and gone home with her, seething but honourable. The new Winnie hesitated for just a moment longer than was necessary, and then—

'She can make her own way, Win!' Helen shouted in my ear over the music. 'Come on!'

I don't know how long we had been in there when I saw her again. Time went out of the window in that place, because there weren't any – nor was there a sense of the minutes passing while the music blared. We'd danced to maybe ten or eleven songs when I noticed Margot standing on the other side of the bar as I went to get another drink.

She had gone to a shop, bought a bottle of vodka, and drunk it as she queued again. She'd rolled her T-shirt up and tucked it under her bra to change her outfit. Her stomach was the pale board I remembered unsuccessfully trying to rub a crappy tattoo transfer of a rose onto a couple of years before, before we'd given up and thrown a tennis ball back and forth for a couple of hours.

She had borrowed somebody's lipstick so she would look different to the doorman. I doubt he would have noticed either way: another girl, another face, another body. We're all the same in the dark.

I found that I was impressed. Shocked, but impressed. I'd even say relieved. I thought, for a moment, that we'd have fun together that night, that she'd come round to Helen, that maybe everything would work out among the three of us.

How stupid I was.

Margot swayed slightly on her feet, and I realised she was drunk.

'You left me,' she slurred, and hiccuped a bit of vomit.

I was mortified at the prospect of her puking there and then, of the acidic puddle and accompanying waft that would mark us out as the young amateurs we were, so I hustled her over to a banquette along the edge of the dark dance floor and pushed her down onto it. Her eyes were closing even as she hit the pleather with a soft bounce.

'She okay?' came a male voice through the dingy haze.

'Just needs a disco break,' I said, and went back to Helen, who was gyrating to a familiar guitar riff a few meters away.

I meant to keep an eye on her. Not in a clucking mother-hen sort of way, but just to flick a glance every now and then to check she hadn't tipped over into a pool of vomit. But the next time I looked over, Margot was gone. My groan of frustration was so loud it must have sounded as though I was singing along to the blaring music. How had she become my responsibility yet again?

I gestured to Helen that I was going to the loo, and she waved me off confidently, deep in a jocular back-and-forth that she was shouting directly into the ear of a man with long hair and no shirt on.

The nightclub was dank and steamy, the air so thick with dry ice and cigarette smoke that I felt I was combing it for Margot not only with my eyes but with my hands too. Fuming at having had to leave the dance floor, where Helen and I had been having fun, I could feel righteous anger building up – it wasn't my problem Margot had got so drunk she could barely stand up, but here I was doing the right thing. In my head, I composed what I'd say when I found her, my silly, callow friend – a sharp reproof for wasting my time. But then I realised she'd probably be in no fit state to hear it.

Pushing through throngs of people clustered around bottles and badly hidden baggies of powders that I didn't yet quite recognise, I felt like the prince hacking back briars to reach the princess at the heart of the forest.

The deeper I went, the more coldhearted I began to feel. Margot never had been any good at looking after herself; it had always fallen to me. No wonder I was out of patience with her.

I tried the toilets, recalling from our last visit a closed cubicle door with one comatose foot sticking out from underneath it, and hoped, more for my sake than for hers, that Margot had

made it there before the inevitable torrent had shot forth.
There was no response to my calls. And no sign of that blond
head among the gaggle of women, all older than me, who were
doing their makeup and narrating their domestic situations to
whoever might listen.

Next, the bar, by this hour ringed with the desperate who
needed no more but were intent on buying it, and the chem-
ically enhanced – astonishingly active dancers who were
drinking water as though they'd been deprived of it for weeks.

I checked under a pile of coats wadded up against a wall
and, to my surprise and disgust, found another woman asleep,
her eyes half closed and her mouth open, a string of drool
attached to her glittery top. I wondered what the Middle Ages
had looked like, substituting sequins for sackcloth in my head,
and came up with a scene not dissimilar. I was relieved to see
it wasn't my friend under there but noted with annoyance that
the time was ticking down until the night – my night – would
be over.

Eventually I came to a standstill near the corridor that led
back out onto the street and stood, chewing my lip. Had
Margot gone home? That was the most sensible option, but
she hadn't seemed in a state to decide when I'd last seen her.
As I pondered, I became aware of laughter coming from
behind me, seeping through the door to the club's office: the
hearty but heartless humour of men confronted with vulner-
ability. My stomach turned over at it.

I opened the door, just a crack at first, and put my eye to the
gap, through which the brightness of strip lights made dusty
shapes in the filthy dark air. Through the slit, I saw two broad,
dark backs standing on sturdy feet encased in Doc Martens.
Ducking for a better view, and peering between their legs, I
saw another set of heavy-duty boots, tangled between a pair
of white Converse, now streaked black with beer mud. Margot
had bought them only a few weeks ago.

'Proper jailbait, that,' I heard one of the two backs growl, and rasp a husky laugh that they all three joined in with.

Had I stopped to think about the safest way to proceed, I doubt I would have done what was absolutely necessary in that instant, which was to remove Margot from the situation. Instead, I barged through the door, blinking in the bright light and shouting: 'Margot, time to go now, your dad's outside!'

'What the f—' The backs leaped aside as I barrelled in, and I saw for the first time the sport they had been spectating on.

Slumped on a chair, Margot's head hung heavy on her chest, her face in as deep a shadow as the rest of her was almost unbearably well lit. Her T-shirt had been ripped from neckline to navel, her small, girlish breasts tipped out of the soft cotton bra she was wearing underneath. Her denim skirt was shoved up to her waist, her pale pink knickers accusingly childish for both the context and those men's intentions.

The very grounds on which Helen and I had frozen her out had come to this room to thaw: here, under fluorescent lights that mercilessly highlighted the greasy pores and ingrown hairs on the doughy faces leering down at her, Margot looked every inch the bewildered little girl she had every right to be at the age of sixteen.

The third man had been in the act of leaning over her and unzipping his fly but had stopped where he was, bending over Margot, with one hand rummaging inside his trousers.

'What the fuck do you think you're doing?' a voice behind me said, low and snarling. 'You're not supposed to be in here.'

The sweat I had worked up dancing suddenly seemed very cold on my skin. Margot raised her head at the sound, and for the first time, I saw a trickle of blood running from one nostril, as shiny and as vital as the terror in her eyes when they met mine.

Shame and regret rushed at me for having despised Margot for being naïve, for being nervous, and for not trying to hide it under the blanket of worldly-wise cynicism that Helen and I had endeavoured to cultivate. For playing the tiresome ingénue to our jaded alter egos.

'Your dad's here, Margot,' I insisted, not wanting to interact with anyone in the room but her. What do you say to the men you've been warned about your entire life? How do you reason them out of doing everything you're most afraid of?

'It's time to leave,' I added.

'Go on then.' The man leaning over had moved back, and jerked his head and a hand at me, at the exit. A gesture that usually accompanies someone holding a door for you, this time waving through a lucky, bloodied girl who had only been half molested.

Margot moved quickly then. She grabbed her bag from the desk behind him as she passed and bundled straight into me at the precise moment a gob of spit landed in the back of her hair.

'Fuck off, you little slag,' called one of the men as we stumbled out of the room.

Outside in the corridor, the night was over. The lights were coming up over the steamy dance floor and the party rubble strewn across it. Under the strip lights, the club that had been so full of wondrous possibilities was revealed as a windowless room filled with tired people and the rubbish they'd generated.

Margot sank to the ground, sobbing. Her T-shirt flapped baggily open to reveal the immature underwear underneath. Her coat was gone, and so was her trust, I realised – in me, in herself, in the people who milled nearby as they left the venue, their shoes making patterns around us as they wondered whether to pause and help this crying girl.

'Drunk,' one of them said.

'Jailbait,' another laughed in return, and I whirled around, certain that those broad backs had followed us, but it was someone else. I had never heard the term before that night but I was beginning to recognise the type of man who used it as currency.

Margot came with me to Helen's house. She had to, because the girls she'd come with had left without her. They were bound by curfews set earlier than Helen's mother's – I wasn't sure Helen even had one at all. Back in that fashionably rustic kitchen, at the wide wooden table with mugs of tea, disconcerted by her tears, I asked: 'Do you want to talk about it?'

Margot shook her head. 'Not while she's here,' she said quietly, and Helen rolled her eyes.

6

The next morning, Margot washed the blood from her face and shampooed the cigarette smoke out of her hair three times before she went home, scarcely speaking to me and Helen as she collected up her belongings and pushed the ripped T-shirt deep into the bottom of her bag. When the door banged shut behind her, Helen and I exchanged a look and breathed out a breath we hadn't even realised we'd been holding in.

I didn't hear from Margot all weekend, although I called and texted again and again. I couldn't stop thinking about her head nodding in the chair. I kept seeing the largest of the men leaning over. But what haunted me the most was the sense of her acceptance of what had been about to happen. I was horrified by it – not because I thought she should have fought harder, but because her acceptance struck me as the brutal reality between men and women beneath the veneer of civilisation we rely on.

One summer a few years later, when I was working in a supermarket between university terms, an older colleague shut the doors to the stockroom while I was in there and showed me his dick as though it were part of the fresh produce I was supposed to be checking over. It wasn't the fact of seeing it that pulled me sharply awake in the middle of the night for months afterwards – or that made me blink and shudder with hot shame when I recalled it – it was my terror: that split-second moment when I didn't know whether I would leave that back room a whole person again. Whether what happened in there would travel with me, uninvited, for the rest of my life.

We carry these men with us, although we might not realise it. The stray hands and too-close lips, the eyes that look too long and the steps that sound too close. They're the reason we walk the long way round, why we can't use our parks after dark, why we clutch our keys like a weapon. Most of them we slough off like winter skin eventually, even though they take us off with their jackets that night. I'm sure that grocery dick guy doesn't even remember me. He probably has a baby of his own now, but imagining somebody else's babies into being is even harder than willing your own back to life.

I was five years older than Margot had been when that happened. I knew how men were supposed to treat you, to talk to you, to touch you, and how nice it could feel. At sixteen, she had no such comparison to make, didn't know how to process it. The way the casual violence done to her – brutality dressed up as a bro – found its outlet would echo through the rest of her life and mine.

On the Sunday night, ahead of school the next day, Margot finally texted me back: 'meet me in the prac rooms at lunch.'

I fobbed Helen off, as she once had Margot, with a line about having a detention and rushed up the staircase to our old haunt. We greeted each other like a brittle Victorian couple, in love but constrained by politesse: her characteristic awkwardness was galvanised with anger and sorrow; my guilt at how I had treated her stayed my tongue. After a few brief moments just staring at each other, I hurled myself into Margot's arms and was so relieved to feel them tighten around me that I started crying.

'I'm so sorry, 'Go,' I sobbed into her hair. 'I'm so, so sorry. I was such a stupid cow, and you – you—'

She held me and said she had missed me. She thanked me for getting her out of that room. Then, on the sponge-spewing sofa that we'd loafed on and laughed on countless times, Margot told me what had happened.

She'd woken up in a corridor with a man on top of her, she said, more worried by the heaviness of him than by what was happening to her. Worried that his weight would push all the air out of her and no more would ever get back in again.

In the end, his friend had dragged him away: he'd found two girls willing to go home with them instead. Smiling, drink-blurred faces with responsive bodies. Luckily for Margot, they were a more exciting offer than an unconscious sixteen-year-old lying on a filthy floor with her top torn and her skirt hiked up.

One of the doormen had helped her to her feet and into the office, saying he'd fetch her some water, but returned with two other men she'd never seen before. One had punched her as she'd tried to get away. After that, she'd sagged back into the chair and tried to pretend she was somewhere else.

We became friends again that lunchtime, in the attic space that had witnessed so many years of us already.

'But,' Margot said, softly yet sternly, as I agreed to tell Helen the fact of our reconciliation but not the rest of the story. 'But. I don't want her around.'

The terms were hardly difficult to agree to. Everything that had drawn me to Helen – the glamour, the rebellion, the sophisticated subversion – was now tainted with my and Margot's experience of what cost they came with. The seediness, the fear, the ugliness. Helen was no more an adult than we were. And I was more than ready to once again inhabit a world where schoolgirls were a protected species, rather than prey.

'I promise,' I told Margot. 'I'll explain that she was out of order. We go way back, you and me, Helen's got to understand that.'

★   ★   ★

We found her sitting in the doorway of one of the maths blocks, headphones in and chewing gum. I was barely a handful of words into my declaration before she cut me off, eyeing Margot by my side with an expression that morphed from distaste into empty-eyed boredom as she spoke.

'Don't tell me – she's back, your little shadow. She gets herself roughed up because she doesn't know any better, and suddenly she's interesting? Pathetic.'

'Come on, Helen,' I tried. 'Me and Margot are—'

'*You're* not much better, you know!' she blazed. 'With that librarian hairdo and your constant fussing. "Ooh, Helen, you're so grown-up", "Ooh, I can't stay out late, me mam would kill me",'

Her mockery of my hated curls and local accent made her accusations sting all the more. I knew how she felt about the people who lived round here, and now I was mortified to learn what she really thought of me. Beside me Margot was cringing too; Helen hadn't even needed to stand up in order to face us down.

'Christ, you're such a pair of little losers!' she spat. 'Is there anyone at this school who is actually cool?'

She gestured for us to leave her in a way that reminded me of something. It was the same arm the doorman had extended over Margot as he 'let' her get up from that chair. Helen plugged the buds back into her ears and looked away with set jaw. She was done with us.

I had assumed the new girl would at least try to slot back into a threesome with Margot and me. I'd foreseen afternoons of awkwardly trying to chaperone a game of conversational tennis between two people determined to hit aces at each other every time. Instead, I was profoundly relieved Helen had ditched us, even though I was still reeling from how poisonous her real assessment of us had been.

I squirmed to think that Helen had inwardly despised me as some yokel even as I had been revelling in her company. What a delightfully useful idiot I had been for the new girl, selling my oldest friend down the river on her suggestion and – I now realised – for her own entertainment.

I had far less reason to dislike her than Margot did, but my feelings towards Helen burned with a fierce intensity that was stoked by my embarrassment at having been duped. I would never forgive her, I knew, for looking down on me, for withering my fledgling self-confidence. I was a zealous convert to hating her.

Later, Helen told whoever she could that she wanted nothing more to do with us. We were weirdos. We were a pair of sappy kids who didn't know how to have real fun, how to be cool, how to drink – who were bankrupt of street cred. Reputations being what they were at that school, our classmates were delighted to believe her.

The stories she told that stung the most weren't the snide lesbian fibs designed to embarrass, they were the truths we had bared to her about our ambitions, our dreams beyond the perimeter fence – bubbles of hope for our futures that were all too easily pricked by the cheery scorn of those who had no such aspirations. Margot and I had laughed off their bafflement before, but we had always had the upper hand; now we were openly mocked.

We spent more and more time in the practice rooms. The low-ceilinged spaces felt increasingly like bunkers in which to dodge the artillery of our peers; we peered over the edge of the balcony at them as if from the trenches. We could relax there without feeling the weight of Helen's contemptuous stare. We'd lie on the floorboards of the musicians' gallery and watch the rest of the school at its business below.

Bobby Davis rubbing mushy peas into his mate's hair. Mandy Elton giving the finger behind a teacher's back. And Helen, of course, whose presence we felt like a chill in the air whenever we had to share a space with her, but who from this angle looked sad and lonely, a little girl quickly eating her sandwich with a book covering her face and her headphones permanently jammed on.

'I feel a bit sorry for her,' I said, a month or so after Margot and I had made up, as we watched Helen watching the rest of the room from behind *The Catcher in the Rye*. 'She's so messed up, she wanted to mess us up, too.'

'I don't,' said Margot coolly. Sometimes, after the incident in the club, her face and voice were so cold and blank that I'd feel a pinch of fear. 'She deserves everything she gets.'

7

Once you've seen someone in their most fundamental state of grief, it's like you've seen them naked. No, more than that – like you've seen them without their skin, all their blood vessels and organs exposed. There's a power imbalance afterwards. It takes time to come back from that, to be able to talk about what's for tea or what the weather is doing, or to ask if they think their heart will ever mend.

In the moments before Jack's little chest stopped moving – I had never seen a baby's tiny rib cage fluttering close up before and it seemed every breath would exhaust him it was so hard fought for – Charles and I wrung out all our human longing, all our desperation, let all our despair loose in that hospital room.

It was there in our sobs, the relentless shaking of our heads as if we could command the inevitable not to happen. I kept saying it, no no no, but Charles was silent until the end. When he shouted as Jack left us – Jack, the little boy he'd hoped and planned for, a name he'd chosen years ago for the son we surely would eventually have – the one word he cried out was 'Don't!' A bark of a command, an order any father might give to his child if it strayed too close to danger, but in this case forever destined to go unobeyed.

There is something about sharing a moment with some-one when the veil of civility that we drape over our lives is tugged loose to reveal everything visceral and base lurking underneath. The smell of mortality, Shakespeare called it. It makes ordinary interaction difficult to resume. For a while, at least.

That's how it was after Helen.

I saw her immediately – that frizz of dark curls looking down on the midday morass below, scanning and rescanning for the two heads that weren't up there alongside her. Helen hadn't really hidden herself, just sat down behind the wooden hand-rail. It meant I witnessed the precise half second she saw me and Margot as we entered the hall together before veering to the right to climb the stairs ourselves.

That day, Margot had suggested the two of us walk up the hill to the Peppercorn and order our sandwiches in paper bags to take back and eat in the dusty rooms at the top of the spiral staircase.

Helen was too far away for me to tell whether there was a wounded note in her expression, but no distance could dilute the look of undisguised rage she wore at the fact that Margot and I hadn't been where she had expected to find us, that she wasn't privy to our plans anymore and no longer knew the rhythm of our lives.

Standing, Helen glowered down at us. That was the moment when Margot slipped her arm through mine and waved up at Helen, a thin smirk across her features.

I turned to my friend, puzzled.

When I realised, I felt cold all over.

Those stages clicked past quickly, like a camera shutter flicking through shots; the next sequence seemed to drag on forever, even though there was no time to undo it.

Then, even as my heart screamed in protest, Helen leaned against the handrail in front of her.

A noise, then, like the first bowing of a cello during tuning: wooden and scratchy.

There was a pause, a beat. The instant before the drop on a record, after the cymbals in 'Blue Monday,' which Margot had put on a tape for both of us only a few months earlier. It can't even have been a second, but it felt like much longer.

Helen pitched forward as the rail gave way beneath her hands, the sourness wiped from her face by a terrible surprise, not at all like the insouciance we'd found so irresistible.

If the groan of rotten timber hadn't alerted the audience below to the tragedy that was happening above their heads, the shriek that rang out soon focused their minds. The sound hung over us all as jarringly as the broken balcony. The racket hushed in an instant, just in time for a noise like a bunch of thick celery stalks snapping as Helen hit the floor, twenty feet below where she had been only moments before, inches from where Margot and I stood.

And then the screams began.

Students and teachers rushed to encircle Helen, to see what they could do for her.

'It wasn't my fault,' Margot whispered, motionless with fear.

Watching the blood trickle towards the tip of her shoe, I said: 'I know what you did.'

The police wanted to speak to us even before we had been delivered into the arms of our parents that afternoon. After the initial hush and the horror came the inexorable, grinding process of rooting out the truth.

'What happened, girls? Tell me what happened.' Ashen-faced, Mrs Wilson yanked us up the couple of steps onto the dais in front of the headmaster and deputy's offices.

What had happened? One minute Margot and I had been talking, the next a misstep, a tremble, a note of panic, and air where there had been a girl. Black blood on the green lino floor.

There was only one option. To say anything else would only lead to more questions. Questions about why and how, about where we had been and who knew what.

'We never even knew she was up there,' I told our teacher, clear and dead eyed. 'We'd only just walked in with our sandwiches.'

It was easy, really.

All I knew, I told the sergeant who questioned me on the chintz sofa in my parents' sitting room, was not only did we not know Helen was in the prac rooms at the time, we hadn't even been aware of the minstrels' gallery.

Had we ever been up the spiral staircase? Of course, everybody had. Had we lingered? No thanks, too spooky. What secret door?

And that was what Margot said, too – that old telepathy again, only this time neither of us was laughing.

The police officer made notes and asked more questions. He doubled back to certain moments and tested from other angles. He never seemed to doubt my words; his rigour was simply part of a professional habit that had been honed on detainees far more likely to deceive him than the stunned, shocked schoolgirl who faced him on the settee.

By the time my interview was over, I was shaking so violently my teeth chattered and I couldn't keep my knees still, whether under the intensity of the scrutiny or with the effort of uphold-ing something I knew to be untrue, it was hard to tell. All I wanted was for the policeman to leave. Once he was gone, I told myself, I would be able to relax and catch my breath, to stay my shaking limbs and wait for the adrenaline to leave my body.

They wrapped everything up so quickly it was unseemly, my mother said, but the school wanted it all sorted before that balcony – and the rest of that rickety old shithole – became a health and safety target for the local press. So our version of events stood, and life went back to normal. Almost.

As soon as Helen's body struck the floor, Margot and I were a two once more, every bit as intensely bound as we had been before, only this time by what we had done – what we had let happen, what we hadn't said. Before we had only needed each other – now, each of us had only one need from the other: silence.

I let Margot understand that if she ever left me, I could ruin her life at a stroke. All I needed to do was change my statement with the police: '*you were taunting her. I know what you did.*' I'd always been the one in charge of our friendship, the one who decided where we went on a Saturday and what we bought, what music we liked, how we cut our hair, or what colour we painted our nails. Now I was in charge of her future, too.

I realise now – as Charles has told me so regularly over the years – that I made a rod for my own back. That threat, the lingering chance that I might change my story, made Margot even more anxious, even more needy, so that I ended up devoting much of my adult life to clearing up her messes and soothing her fears. The number of times Charles and I have sat down to dinner, only for the phone to ring or the doorbell to go and for it to be Margot, white faced with that cowlike expression, saying, 'Sorry, I just need some help', 'Sorry, but can you listen', 'Sorry, I don't seem to be able to function by myself'.

I never liked to think about why she was always so jumpy, about what might have happened to make her doubt her own judgment even as a successful, grown woman. I certainly didn't like to think about what my part in that might have been.

I never did find out where Helen went, only that the rehab facility most suited to her injuries was near London, where her family had come from in the first place. My parents and the few teachers who ever spoke about the incident to me mentioned words such as *traction* and *bed rest*. One told me Helen would live in a hospital for the best part of a year. The bones in her legs had shattered and there were fractures in her spine that would mean she needed to lie still for at least three months.

They said she needed a halo vest, which I thought was darkly comic given how she'd treated Margot, until I looked it up and found out they screw those into your head. There was nothing funny about that.

It would take months before she could sit up again, I was told, then years possibly before she'd walk – but she would one day, and in all likelihood without lasting damage eventually. Anyone who knew her as an adult would probably never even realise what she'd been through, Mrs Wilson told me on my first day back at school after it all happened.

'Can I write to her?' I asked then.

I already knew what I would send: mixtapes and coded notes, whispers by post, sniggers in envelopes that would suffice until we could see each other again.

'I'm afraid her parents have asked us not to pass on their new address, sweetheart,' she replied. 'Helen wants to start afresh where she is now.'

And that was that.

Afterwards, it was like being friends with a war vet, someone haunted by what they have done and had done in return. The camaraderie was gone, the joy too. The innocence. There was no more laughter. Margot and I didn't go out again, we simply clung to each other like ballast for the final two years of school, before we could go to university.

Cambridge was a relief for me. New friends, uncomplicated friends – at least, uncomplicated by monstrous reality: the usual wealth, beauty, and status niggles were all there. Simple anxieties for adult-sized children as yet untouched by the world. Fun with them didn't feel like a millstone around my neck. I revelled in being young with them, because what had happened with Margot and Helen felt like it had aged me by several decades even before my seventeenth birthday.

We were the only people who knew the truth about why Helen had fallen, and we shared the heft between us like pallbearers. Although we never spoke of it directly, there was a comfort to be had in our guilt, mutual if unequal, as I'd come to think of it. In the carefully balanced scales in which our friendship sat, loaded and lethal, safe only if we both kept to the bargain we had made.

That's why we stayed in touch all those years. We had shared interests and similar personalities – and we did care for each other – but it was the fault line at the heart of us both that glued the pair of us together. I tried to distance myself from

Margot as much as I could, but the pattern was set: I could never turn her away when she needed me.

When she told me she was pregnant a few months after I had dropped her a line saying the same, it felt like a wholesome new beginning. Flowers growing on a rubbish heap. As we compared notes and shopped and planned, closeness sprang up again. We were as thick as thieves; the old telepathy returned. She called me once straight after I'd felt a Braxton Hicks.

But when Jack died, all that disappeared overnight. I didn't want her anywhere near me. I hated Margot. I loathed her for her unknowing smugness, for her life's carrying on the way mine was supposed to, her abundant body ripening while mine was a sterile husk incubating only this terrible sense of loss.

Jack's death fretted at something distant in me, the way raindrops on the surface of a pond eventually stir up the silt below. The feelings I'd pushed deep down within since school came rushing back up to the surface, familiar resentment and remembered wrongs, like Greek Furies at the window.

I told myself, when I saw the picture of Lila that she posted on Instagram, that I'd just been hurt by Margot's thoughtlessness, by her inconsiderate flaunting of her own healthy, happy baby. But I was lying to myself. I wasn't wounded by it, I was incensed.

The tufting hair a crown of hay-bale yellow beneath a little woollen hood. Nick's face, but Margot's eyes. I had spent a lifetime looking into those eyes and they had always wanted something back from me. Now they demanded devotion. I knew the baby in the café was theirs at the precise moment I knew she had my heart forever, this fluffy chick in expensive miniature knitwear that I could tell, just from looking at it, her mother had been delighted to buy for her. My gorge rose at so simple a pleasure, denied to me but given to Margot. Even after what she did.

With other types of bereavement, they tell you time is a great healer, that distance from the event can give you perspective on it. Not when you lose a child. The death of a child is so unfathomable that time and distance simply give you more opportunity to rage against the injustice of it, to contemplate how unnecessary it is, to muse on who they might have been and what they might have achieved. There are people at some of the support groups I tried going to at the beginning who have been attending those sessions for over thirty years.

No, the only thing that can help you get over losing a child is having another one.

PART THREE

I

Maggie

When Maggie left Margot's house and walked back to the main road, she heard a female voice calling to her, a regional accent with throaty depth carried on the cold night air.

'Excuse me! Hallo!'

Maggie turned to face the direction the call came from. She saw the woman from the café striding towards her, pulling her green parka tighter across her middle and bending into the slight breeze.

'I hoped I'd find you,' the woman said. 'You left this on the table, and I hoped I might be able to catch you up.'

The woman held out Lila's iridescent purple sippy cup. Maggie assumed she'd left it in the bottom of the buggy but she must have forgotten to scoop it up along with the baby and all her many other accoutrements. She hoped Margot wouldn't be too annoyed at its disappearance; she would take it round to her when they went for dinner next week. Give her a bit of space for now after whatever it was that had just happened back there.

'Oh, thank you! How kind,' she replied. 'Not used to carting all this baby kit around – I was just looking after her for a friend. Handed her back now.'

Maggie shrugged in a way that she hoped conveyed equal parts affection and relief.

'I did wonder.' The woman shuffled her feet from side to side on the pavement. 'Because – and sorry if this is either really lame or really creepy – aren't you the woman on the front of *Haute* this month?' She gave an apologetic grimace, smiled, and tightened her crossed-arm grip on the opposite elbows of her faded army surplus coat.

Well! Maggie couldn't pretend she wasn't intensely pleased at having been recognised. Her first time in the wild. If she'd had feathers, she would have preened and fluffed them in delight.

'I am, yes!' she said back warmly, and presented her right hand. 'Maggie Beecher. I hope you enjoyed the piece?'

The woman gave a short huff of laughter as the tension, and the embarrassment of the question, left her body. She matched Maggie's hand and shook it firmly.

'Winnie Clough. I really did, actually. I mean, I'm married myself, but there was so much in there that I recognised from before. And that you don't need—'

An ambulance screeched past, and Winnie broke off the sentence, glanced at her watch. 'Well, I'll let you get going now . . .'

'Lovely to meet you, and thanks so much for this,' said Maggie, holding aloft the plastic beaker, and they turned in opposite directions.

Honestly, Maggie didn't want to spend her night in the pub with Tim talking about Margot. She was as sick of the woman she seemed to share her life with as Margot must have been of her replacement: the other half of the balancing act at work and now at home.

Sometimes she felt not a minute went by without her thinking about the woman whose maternity leave she was covering, wondering what Margot thought of her, whether she'd ever be free of her shadow at work, whether she'd be spending another evening with her, or a morning; a coffee, a lunch, a babysitting gig.

The thing was, Maggie had been sort of shaken by Margot today, by the way Margot had acted, how glitchy she'd been,

by how little connection there seemed to be between the petrified expression on the woman's face and the platitudes she
was speaking in, by how she didn't seem to sense what a bad
job she was doing of hiding the fact there was so obviously
something wrong.

Maggie had thought, by the time Margot had hustled her
out of the door, the other woman had convinced herself that
she'd pulled it off, that she'd persuaded her visitor that she
was fine and that was the end of it. It wasn't for Maggie to pry,
but given the way their lives had grown around each other
these days, like ivy through an iron fence, she felt a duty to
look out for this stricken woman.

So no, she didn't want to spend her night talking about
Margot, but it ended up happening anyway.

'I'm a bit worried about her, actually,' she confessed to Tim
after they'd kissed hello and found themselves a table. He'd
asked about how she'd got on with Lila. On that front Maggie
had no worries; they'd had such a lovely afternoon together.

She told him about their carpet time and a joke they'd
shared knocking down the wooden baby blocks, carefully
omitting quite how quickly she'd tired of stacking and restack-
ing them; about their walk and Lila's happy gurgling as Maggie
pushed; and about their trip to the café. She started to tell him
about meeting Winnie, but his eyes had glazed over a bit by
that point, so Maggie just said she'd had her first approach
from a reader. He was so good at being pleased for her, Tim.

She chose her next words carefully to describe Margot. She
had read about the women who sat on the other side of the
room and watched their babies cry for hours without inter-
vening, who held them under the water at bath time, smoth-
ered them just for a moment's peace. Maggie didn't want to
barge straight in and accuse her friend of having postnatal
depression, but she needed to convey how jumpy and
disturbed Margot's behaviour had been.

She wanted Tim to be worried enough to speak to Nick about it, but not to convince him Margot needed to be put on medication or to do anything too severe. People tend to leap to conclusions about new mums. It wouldn't be a good look for Margot's replacement to be the one heading up the intervention. She needed someone else to do it for her.

She also needed not to look too keen on the idea herself; she needed Tim to deliver her message as though he'd come up with it himself, and to persuade him to do that, he had to believe Maggie found it a real wrench to go behind Margot's back.

She demurred a little before launching in, making enough noises about 'betrayal of trust' and 'just between us' to invite Tim to demand Maggie open up to him. Precious Tim, he couldn't figure out whether to be more concerned about Margot or his girlfriend.

'Something's clearly bothering her – maybe someone,' Maggie said, deliberately hesitantly, as if she hadn't run through everything she wanted to say to him in her head already and was just working it out on the spot. 'She's got this horrible woman tweeting at her every so often – I see it because she often puts me on the tweets, too.'

The stuff that the Twitter troll kept putting up was yet another source of awkwardness between her and Margot. They'd never spoken about it – it would have been too mortifying to acknowledge in person because her digs at Margot were always so close to the bone. Maggie replied when she could, to set this woman straight or to stick up for Margot, out of the same sense of duty – and awareness of how things would look – that had her unburdening herself to Tim.

Maggie had been a bit flattered by her, the troll, at the beginning. But as the taunting and the jibes became crueller and more hurtful – about Margot's writing, her career being over, her figure, her looks, even her mothering – the satisfaction that anyone had even noticed Maggie's stepping into the fashion editor's shoes dissipated into pity for the woman they were directed at. Who the hell did she think she was, this Helen or whatever she called herself?

'But, look, I don't really know if that's it or not,' she continued hastily, because Margot's off behaviour couldn't be explained by just one anonymous tweeter. 'She's so nervous all the time, as though she's expecting something bad to happen. And she's secretive, cold – as though I'm prying when I ask if she's okay.'

Tim nodded and sipped his gin and tonic, his eyelashes long over the rim of his glass.

'She's always been a bit private,' he remarked. 'I'm not sure I've ever really found out much about her beyond her life with Nick, and a bit about her job. She doesn't have many friends. There was one, but I don't think they're in touch anymore. She never mentions her family, but they're around. Nick had a Christmas up there with them one year, and he said it was pretty stressful. Don't think they get on.'

'Who does?' Maggie murmured, although the news that perfect Margot didn't come from a perfect family was interesting. She felt, once again, a treacherous thrill of schadenfreude that sprang from all the many resentments she'd pushed deep down inside.

She tried again, careful to introduce a bit of empathy alongside the amateur psychology, so she sounded caring rather than griping. 'I'm not trying to unearth her secrets or get to the bottom of some family feud – I'm just a bit worried that she might be having a tough time. It's hard being with a baby all day. Margot's a go-getter, it's a big change of pace. Maybe she's just got a bit of cabin fever.'

'Yeah,' agreed Tim mildly. 'I'm sure she'll snap out of it soon.'

Jesus Christ, Maggie thought, *am I going to have to spell it out for him?*

She had always assumed the reason men were so crap at feelings was because it suited them and their happy-go-lucky, where's-the-next-beer-and-football-game existence not to acknowledge the big stuff in case it spoiled the banter. But knowing Tim as she did, knowing that he was a sweet, switched-on guy who had the best interests of his friends at heart, and seeing how quickly he tried to gloss over Margot's pain, Maggie wondered whether it just didn't occur to men that the big stuff might actually be changed for the better.

Maybe that was why they didn't talk things over, didn't have it out, why they punched each other when they were sad – so that the lights went out when somebody's cheek hit the pavement and they could go home without having to explore things any further. Perhaps women went too far the other way sometimes – the post-mortem rigour with which they examined the faults of their friends, then the assassin swipe when they decided to act on their conclusions – but at least they noticed when someone had been crying.

'Do you think you could talk to Nick about it?' Maggie pressed. She might as well have just written him a list of stage directions. 'So he knows to look out for her. I mean, I know they're rock solid and everything. But it never hurts to keep an eye on someone, does it?'

Tim's own hazel eyes widened as they registered genuine worry. 'Of course I will,' he said, and his hand came down on top of hers on the wooden table. 'I'll make sure Nick knows we're concerned, and I'll make sure he's checking on Margot.'

Mission accomplished.

She took her phone out and snapped a picture of their hands, together at the base of their glasses. Maggie felt serenity take the place of the harried sensation she'd had since she'd seen Margot's drawn, drained face contorted like a Kabuki tragedy mask.

She just wanted to get rid of the feeling that the strain Margot was under was her fault. Which, of course, it was.

The next morning, on her way to the bakery to buy sourdough for the bacon Tim was cooking at home, Maggie had an unexpected encounter. The loaves there had a certain cachet among the locals, who waited around the block for them, and Maggie had posted a picture of one on Instagram just a couple of weeks ago, tagging the little family business as her location: 'only Earle's will do for Sunday morning sarnies!' The likes had crept up into the thousands, including – of course – one from Margot.

'Hello there,' called Winnie Clough, who joined Maggie once she'd paid for her bundle of fresh bread. 'Do you live round here then?'

In the streets around Maggie's flat in Camden, London was all spilling, shouty pubs; clouds from joints smoked in the corners; flashing neon kebab shop lights at night; and endless, faceless, shouldering bustle. Her neck of the woods was full of renting transients like herself and Cath, no ties to bind. Tim's London – which was Margot's London, too – with its tidy gardens, libraries, and playgrounds, was settled and calm, planned, with a continuity of life that made social investment in the form of well-wishing and small talk among its residents worthwhile.

Still, how small a place was it to see the same person three times over a weekend?

Maggie chuckled to herself. Only a few months ago, she would have scorned all this as so much parochialism – *Cranford* for hipsters – but now she was delighted to be part of it. Delighted and anxiously wistful that it wasn't hers quite yet to officially relax into. Her heart squeezed enviously and her stomach lurched with nervous excitement at the prospect of this everyday, grown-up existence. At knowing where she'd be in five years' time.

'Sort of,' she replied, blushing. 'I'd like to. I'm seeing a guy who's round here, and, well, I suppose we might . . . I hope . . . We haven't really got to that stage.'

'I get it.' Winnie laughed and, hugging the bread to her chest, held up two sets of crossed fingers. 'It's the last taboo, the moving-in chat. You can get yourself a brilliant job, you can travel the world solo, but woe betide any woman who brings up that topic too soon.'

Maggie couldn't have put it better herself. 'It's pathetic, isn't it? We're so conditioned not to scare them off.'

Winnie rolled her eyes. 'The good ones don't scare easily. Look, if you're going to be a neighbour, let's go for a drink sometime.'

'I'd like that,' said Maggie warmly, and took off a glove to tap her number into Winnie's phone.

'Great!' Winnie turned to leave. 'Enjoy your Sunday sarnies.'

She was prompt at getting in touch. Maggie's phone pinged that evening with a message, stacked on the screen between notifications of likes on her latest photo – a pair of eye-water-ingly expensive diamante-encrusted satin heels she had borrowed from the cupboard for a black-tie event at Tim's work that she was attending with him in a few days' time.

'Fancy a bottle of wine at the Abbess one evening this week?' Winnie had posted a row of little clinking champagne-flute emojis alongside her words.

They arranged it for Wednesday, the night before Tim's event. The one before that, Maggie and Tim spent at Nick and Margot's, eating dinner around the teak table again.

Maggie arrived straight from work, a little flustered with rush-ing, having stayed late to receive the delivery she had been wait-ing on tenterhooks all day. Penny had loaned her a dress by Marc Moreau for the reception she was attending with Tim.

The word *dress* didn't really do it justice, truth be told: it was a glittering cocktail gown in icy blue silk, trimmed all over with flashing silver beads. Midi-length hem, long sleeves, high neck: nothing too red carpet, but guaranteed to turn heads as soon as she entered the room. Guaranteed also to be the most expensive piece of clothing at the annual get-together of London's chartered surveyors, Maggie wagered, sending up a private prayer of thanks that it'd be hers gratis, albeit for one night only.

'It's being shipped to a celeb cover shoot in LA the next day,' Penny had warned her, 'so I need it biked back, pristine, the second you wake up.'

Maggie would guard it with her life.

She mock-staggered into the hallway when Nick opened the door to her and made a show of flopping onto one of the dining chairs in exhaustion after a busy day, dropping the tissue-wrapped gown in its starchy designer carrier bag on the floor by her feet. The kitchen was full of a rich coconut aroma, and Margot stood stirring a large casserole dish on the cooker.

'Maggie!' She turned and waved, wooden spoon in hand, and crossed the kitchen to give her guest a hug, eyes alighting on the logoed bag under the table as she did so. 'Lovely to see you. Now, what on earth is in there? A little something from Marc?'

Maggie was watchful for emotion, suppressed or otherwise, in the other woman's face but found none. In fact, she found little there at all. The thought crossed her mind that the blankness of Margot's expression might be the result of a prescription. Tim had told her he'd had a word with Nick about Maggie's fears: on the strength of them, Margot's husband had persuaded her to visit the doctor again.

'Actually yes,' she replied, deliberately shyly, aware that to enthuse might seem boastful, to be crowing about her glamorous social life to a woman tethered to her home by a young baby. 'It's for Tim's big do on Thursday. But shhhh – Moff doesn't know!' Maggie tapped the side of her nose conspiratorially.

Margot cocked her head to one side. 'About the dress or the do?' she asked.

'About either,' Maggie admitted. 'But also about Tim – she still thinks I'm "singles on top." Besides, the dress is due in Hollywood for a shoot on Saturday, so I'm far from the most exciting person it will grace this week.'

'Let me guess,' Margot said, peering into the bag. 'Look twenty-seven?'

Of course she knew the precise dress that Maggie had chosen. Even on maternity leave, Margot knew exactly which of the looks on the catwalk from the main collections were the best, the most photographed, the most influential.

Maggie swallowed a lump of disappointment that had lodged in her throat for reasons she couldn't quite put her finger on. She was still the woman who'd be wearing look 27 to a fancy party that week; Margot would still be at home pureeing vegetables and cooking curry in leggings and a ratty T-shirt. So why did she feel like she'd been upstaged, as though Margot was flaunting her superior knowledge?

'I'd love to have a peek at it after dinner, if you can bear to unwrap it,' Margot said with a wink, and returned to the cooker.

As it was, they finished eating late, after Lila woke up wailing halfway through and refused to go back to sleep.

It wasn't until Maggie got back to Tim's flat that she noticed the radioactive-yellow, turmeric-infused streak that had dripped from Margot's wooden spoon deep down into the bag and stained one side of the dress that she was supposed to be keeping pristine.

2

Margot

When I woke – sweating and gasping for breath, my mouth open in an endless, silent scream – I checked the green numbers on my alarm clock to find out what I already knew: dawn was still some way off, but for me, morning had broken.

The dreams were relentless. I needed something, I was looking for something, there was something I had to hand over – whatever it was was always located at the top of a flight of stairs with no end. Sometimes Lila cried at the bottom while I drove myself upwards to the summit. That variation was particularly hard. Sometimes I was carrying Jack, with his bloody nose and his rabbit, tripping as I climbed and terrified to drop him. That version was even worse.

They had ebbed a little, the dreams, and the intensity had briefly lessened. I had begun to feel a little less glue-eyed in the mornings; my heart shuddered less throughout the day. But they had picked up again since I'd found the photo on the computer, since I'd received the picture from Winnie. There had been no reply to the message I had sent in return.

Four fifty-one a.m.

I had failed to delete my Facebook and Instagram accounts. After the violent shock of little Jack's image on the computer screen, I had reeled back downstairs in search of more wine. My resolve had weakened and I quickly slipped back to checking them frequently. I did so now, with my husband asleep in the dark next to me. I could hear Lila snuffling gently in her room down the corridor.

The two of them, Maggie and Winnie, were so constantly prominent in my mind – as they had been for the best part of a year, unknowingly intertwined with me at the centre of the Venn – that I failed, initially, to understand the top post on my screen even as I read it several times over.

'Maggie Beecher and Winnie Clough are now friends.'

After Helen, I had spoken to a woman called Sheila, who wore a grey linen shirt decorated with a floral brooch, once a week for what felt like long enough to make up a decade.

'And what emotion did that make you feel?' Sheila would ask me, as though feelings could be codified like colours, selected from a pack like felt-tips.

Sadness. Doubt. Isolation. Fear. I intoned them now, although I hadn't seen Sheila for as many years as I had accrued at the time of our regular appointments.

I looked at the words on my phone screen again, as if from a depth below them. I felt a cold, heavy jacket of iron being shrugged around my shoulders by an invisible hand.

'Acknowledge it and move through it,' Sheila recommended, but Sheila didn't really know, hadn't really understood what it was I was dealing with – as a witness, yes, but also the reason why what happened had happened. I was as guilty of causing Helen's fall as if I'd pushed her myself.

I put my phone down again. I knew then that the worry and fatigue I would feel all day was nothing I could blame on Lila, who had begun – after that one disturbed dinner with Maggie and Tim – dozing without a murmur for twelve hours straight each night.

Later that morning, after Lila's clockwork routine of break-fast-nappy-nap-nappy was complete, I strapped her into the buggy with the plan of walking to the park. Fresh, cleansing air for both of us: the bright, cold, sunlit day steamed my breath when I stepped out of the house.

As I wrangled the pushchair over the lip of our front door and then down the step onto the path, I heard something crack and crunch under its rubber tires. Lila was used to being jostled as we made our exit; it was an awkward manoeuvre performed several times a day as we came and went. Today, though, there was something in our way.

Nick and I were no longer surprised by the infinite variety of detritus that was regularly tossed over our garden hedge by passersby – it was part of living in the sort of London neigh-bourhood that was still only halfway to what it eventually might be. Schoolkids ditched their fried chicken bones some-times, unlucky gamblers their betting slips. I once, through our bedroom shutters, watched an after-hours drunk sit on our wall and mix himself a drink at midnight, singing all the while, and came down the next morning to find an empty vodka bottle still sitting there, as if waiting for a bartender to clear it away. Soon after we moved in, someone jettisoned a leather briefcase full of porn mags in our flower bed, and we entertained ourselves with the notion that our front gate had been the setting for a pervert's Damascene moment.

I couldn't see what today's discarded item was from above, but the hard shell of it screeched along the paving stone as I wheeled the buggy round to look underneath. At first I thought it was some giant, wounded insect and recoiled in horror: its shimmering black innards were unspooled on the ground beneath the mesh shopping basket that hung under the baby's seat.

It had been so long since I'd seen one that it took a few moments before I realised what I was looking at. The shiny black intestines were surrounded by crystalline crumbs of plastic: I had crushed and inadvertently disembowelled an old cassette tape. I heard in my mind the click of the deck open-ing, the rattle and slide of the cassette into the chamber, and the clunk of its closing again, and felt nostalgia wash over me.

In my current state, I was sympathetic to an artifact that had been nudged out by something newer and shinier.

As I bent to pick up the pieces, though, the feeling ossified into a cold, beating heaviness. A crescent moon sticker, yellow stars, a red cartoon guitar. A handwritten label now smudged and faded. I stared at the holographic ribbon wrapped around my fingers as though it were blood on my hands.

This was one of our mixtapes. One of the compilations Winnie and Helen and I had made for one another at school. From the indistinct blue ink, it looked like one of the new girl's.

Are you back?

I was in the canteen again, waving up at the girl on the balcony.

I tumbled from my crouch backwards against the front step, and its concrete edge struck me painfully in the lower back. A cool sweat sprang up on my upper lip, my temples, my palms; my eyes strained over the metallic cat's cradle strung out between my hands. I leaned sideways to spit out the bile that had collected behind my teeth.

This wasn't Helen. This was Winnie.

This was a warning.

A plane passed overhead, and Lila mewed at it.

I caught her navy blue eyes over the handrail of her push-chair, smiling but questioning. In an instant, I was back on my feet to reassure her, cooing as I rubbed my wet chin with my sleeve and shook the black lacing from my hands. I dropped the plastic case onto the ground once again and ground it viciously under my heel; I would clear it up later, before Nick got home.

I set off for the park, with the feeling I had been assaulted. The past I had tried so hard to slam the door on had been brought to my front step.

I would tell Nick about Maggie and Winnie when he got home from work. I would tell him all about the selfie, Facebook, the photo on the computer screen. He hadn't mentioned it, but he must have seen it too. The mixtape I would keep to myself; it required more backstory than I was willing to give.

I got as far as telling him that Maggie had met a woman in the café when she was looking after Lila.

'Isn't that great?' my husband said robotically, staring at the television screen as he scooped the vegetables I had roasted into his mouth. 'Maggie's really getting to know the area. Tim's pumped that she's spending so much time here – he thinks she might even want to move down this way.'

'But the woman—' I stuttered. 'Maggie didn't – It wasn't what it sounds like—'

Nick reluctantly turned his head towards my end of the sofa, his expression carefully blank and the warmth in his eyes shut down.

'Please don't,' he said simply. He looked at the fork in his hands and cleared his throat. 'Please, 'Go, not tonight.'

'Why aren't you on my side?' I whined, high-pitched and sad.

'I'm always on your side, Margot. But I don't want you to upset yourself.' He lifted a hand to place it on my arm, but I jerked it away before his fingers landed.

In the old days, if I didn't talk for a while, Nick would always ask me what was wrong. We both knew I used silence as a punishment, an icy reproach. It had been his job after arguments or disagreements to coax me back into speaking again. Now I felt his straining every nerve not to. I could sense his relief when nine-thirty ticked round and he was able to stretch his long arms over his head, announce he couldn't keep his eyes open and was going to bed.

By the time I had finished the washing up and looked in on Lila as she snored softly, Nick was asleep. At least, he was still and his side of the bed was in darkness. I would need to find a different way of getting my message across.

The weekend after Tim's work do, the four of us met in the café by the park to warm our hands on cups of coffee after a stint of pushing Lila on the swings. Nick and Tim had texted the plan into existence by themselves; by the look on Maggie's face, she had been hoping to have her boyfriend to herself for the morning.

'How did the dress go down?' I twinkled at her when we arrived, carefully wiping my features of anything that might be construed as knowing.

'I wore something else in the end,' she said briefly, and I imagined the substantial – and specialist – dry-cleaning bill she must have had to foot.

'We had an amazing time though,' she continued, excited at the memory, and I tried to square the fact that I was pleased for her – this woman so clearly, so happily, in love – with how furious she regularly made me feel in the middle of the night.

I even laughed when she played an elaborate game of peek-aboo with Lila across the table.

'She's so good with Lila, isn't she?' I said while Maggie was using the bathroom. Nick and Tim both smiled at me, the former glad to hear me talking Maggie up, the latter smug and eagerly lapping up praise for his beloved.

I sipped my coffee and went on. 'She keeps telling me how keen she is to have one of her own. In fact, she said she's moving in soon. Things have really sped up between you two!'

I pretended not to see Nick raise his eyebrows at me but felt a kick of triumph deep in my stomach when Tim seemed a little distant on Maggie's return.

3

Winnie

I played my part in it, but I was only sixteen too, remember. I didn't know any better, either.

I thought, after Jack, that I could end it. That I could end the friendship that had eaten away so much of my humanity over the years and left me saddled with this needy, neurotic woman who was always so desperate for my approval – and my forgiveness. It wasn't just that I couldn't bear to see her with her own baby, happy and complete, it was that I began to have dark thoughts about what I might be able to make happen.

Where would that baby go if an old crime were reported and Margot was taken in for questioning? Who would be a better person than the mother's oldest friend to help bring the child up if the old blackmail began to take its toll on her mental state once again? The possibility was so intoxicating I thought about it all day long as I sat in my rocking chair, looking out at the garden and enjoying the medicated numbness in which I now passed the time.

What did I owe Margot, after what she had done?

4

Maggie

Maggie was doing yoga on a lake when she saw Nick's number flash up on the screen of her phone, so she couldn't pick up right away.

She got several such invitations every day – yoga on a lake, dinner at the top of a skyscraper, private screenings of block-buster films that other people had to watch with the noisy masses – and she said yes to as many of them as possible, provided they didn't get in the way of seeing Tim. Maggie was all too aware that they'd dry up once she was out the door at *Haute*.

As the seasons changed, away from the harshness of winter and into the sociable warmer months, the anniversary of Maggie's first day approached and with it, the prospect of her last. Now she knew how a king feels, weary with the know-ledge that his heirs are waiting for him to die.

Maggie had grown used to living in the moment so that she didn't have to think about the future. That evening would be the first weather that was mild enough to sit outside and drink in; perhaps the girls from the office would be up for a few. It had been a while since she'd cemented her friendship with them.

The last time they'd gone out together – it must have been a month or so ago – a bottle of wine chilling in an ice bucket, coats thrown over the backs of their chairs, and the niggles of the office forgotten, they talked about the fact Maggie's time at *Haute* was in its final trimester. They'd laughingly appropriated the language of pregnancy last time they'd gone for drinks, not out of disrespect to Margot but simply because the security guard Clive always referred to Maggie as 'the maternity'. It was better than 'the new girl', she supposed, which she had been for the first six months.

'Where's this package for the maternity going?' he'd ask in broad Cockney to the girls even though Maggie was sitting there, right in front of him and his little trolley.

She'd been riled by it at first, seeing in it the projected conspiracy against her and in favour of Margot that had tainted much of her early time in the office thanks to her own paranoia. More recently Maggie had realised Clive was just a bit shy of her.

Holly and Amma were sad at the prospect of her leaving but too professional – or loyal – to say anything about Margot's return or whether Maggie might stay. Just as Margot and she felt too awkward to ever really acknowledge the delicate equilibrium between them, so the girls were faintly mortified by it, too. Maggie felt the humiliation most keenly, of course – that one day she'd be there and the next, finished with, like an old issue that had been read and discarded.

Unlike Holly and Amma, Maggie hadn't got drunk that night. No longer being single had worked wonders for her alcohol consumption, she had to say. She couldn't bear the idea of Tim seeing her stumble into his flat the way she used to claw her way through the door to hers and Cath's. In fact, she spent most of the evening counting down the moments until she could leave to go and see him.

Maggie had sometimes wondered whether she was keeping up her own social life purely for the superficial effect of appearing to have better things to do than spend all her time with Tim. But that was before Winnie.

When the two of them had met in the pub last week, they had had the sort of evening, the sort of chat, that only happens

at the very beginning of a friendship: one that darted all over
the place so quickly as they found common touchstones and
shared interests that they never really finished a sentence or
rounded off a topic properly.

Winnie was charming, funny, thoughtful, clever. She was
deeply magnetic without being overbearing. But there was
something *closed* about her. As quickly as conversation flowed,
Maggie was unable to get a question to her companion, who
deflected them like rain off a windscreen with yet more of her
own. Winnie might have been the life and soul of the wooden
booth they shared that night, but she refused to let Maggie
anywhere near either of hers.

When her alarm had gone off the next morning, head
throbbing and mouth dry from having drunk too much in her
excitement, Maggie hoped she hadn't prattled on about
herself for too long: she had a tendency to boast when she'd
had a few. She scarcely knew anything about Winnie's home
life, other than the fact she was married and on some sort of
sabbatical from her job in a gallery. She'd left with the feeling
that they had so much more to discuss.

Now, as she downward-dogged on a pontoon that bobbed
with every stretch on the murky water of the Serpentine (the
floating aspect was supposed to make for better energy flow),
Maggie wondered what it was Nick had to say to her. She
didn't really want to have a conversation with him about how
she thought his wife was going not-so-gently bonkers; she
wanted as little of it as possible to be traced back to her, if she
was honest. Maggie was rather concerned about its seeming
as though – in Margot's mind, anyway – her maternity cover
was the one wielding the knife, so to speak.

As it turned out, he just wanted to see whether Maggie was
available on Friday night.

'Please feel free to say no, but I'd really like to take Margot
out for dinner,' he explained when she called him back, his

usually mellow voice uncharacteristically spiky and forced. 'I think it'd be good for us to get out for the night, try to feel like ourselves again. And you're so great with Lila – it would be perfect if you could do it.'

Friday, Friday. She mentally scanned the blue-paged, gilt-edged, leather-bound diary she'd bought herself with her first month's pay from *Haute*. She'd already accepted an invitation from a big designer brand to go and see the new musical that everybody was raving about – not because she particularly enjoyed the genre, but because it was so impossible to get tickets to it that even an Instagram shot of the stubs was bound to inspire jealousy – and likes! – in most quarters.

Perhaps she could still post that picture and just not actually go. She'd be doing Nick a favour, and that would keep him on her side, make him more likely to persuade Margot she wasn't a threat at work, to tell Tim that she was the One. After another weekend spent at her boyfriend's flat and exploring the surrounding neighbourhood, Maggie was feeling with an ever sharper urgency that this was the place for her.

Being in Margot's house, alone, for the afternoon had given a covetous edge to her desire. Maggie had taken the opportunity, when she'd looked after Lila so Margot could go spinning, to acquaint herself further with Nick and Margot's home. Not so much interior decorating as identity decorating, she decided as she strolled from room to room, the baby perched on one arm, tibbling her silver necklace with chubby little fingers.

Everything was calibrated just so to speak of the status of its owners. The brass handles on the navy kitchen cupboards and trailing plants hanging from the ceiling in the sort of crocheted slings you only used to find in flats belonging to German grannies but that had been recently co-opted, just like their Birkenstocks, by the in-crowd. The blond herringbone floor-boards and cream Berber rug. Maggie had never even heard of these fancy wool carpets until recently and had leaped back from her work computer as if it had burned her when she saw how much they cost – £3,000! She noticed smugly that a puff from Lila's rice cakes had stuck to one of its outer loops.

Appraising the bare brick fireplace cut into an otherwise plain white wall, she thought of all the flowers and stiff invitations she'd proudly arrayed above theirs back at the flat. It had never crossed her mind that a mantelpiece could be summarily dispensed with.

She'd been in these rooms already, of course; it was upstairs that really exerted a pull. Although Maggie had been round several times already, she'd only eaten in the dining room, leaned on the kitchen workbench to chat, sat on the sofa with a glass of wine. Upstairs was Margot's inner sanctum. Maggie was desperate to barge her way in.

Climbing those steep stairs, she took in the exhibition posters that lined the sloping walls. Obscure photographers, Flemish primitives, fashion retrospectives – all from European galleries rather than the bog-standard London addresses. Maggie looked forward to the time when she and Tim could share culture together and then show off about it to their guests.

The master bedroom – bed tidily made with plain white linen sheets, bedside tables piled with books and baby gear – and Lila's were painted matching shades of terribly tasteful grey, accented with Scandi pine and white-lacquered wood. The bathroom was full of more hanging greenery to match the sage walls and post-ironic (or was that post-post?) avocado bathroom suite.

When Maggie saw all that self-consciously cool matching porcelain, she felt an ache of envy that related directly to the shitty bathroom where Cath and she showered under mould and constantly had to wipe down the walls to stop it from spreading any farther. There was no such thing as a nice rented bathroom. Forget a room of one's own; Maggie just wanted a loo that only her family and close friends had sat on.

She felt a familiar stab of self-loathing when she realised how it would sound to anybody else, her being jealous of Margot's toilet. Beyond pathetic. Envy might be one of the least attractive qualities a personality can contain, but Maggie's had a bathos all of its own. She closed the door in a huff with herself.

Was this how Margot felt, Maggie wondered, *when she saw the posts I put up?* Some days she almost willed her counterpart not to like them in a small show of spite that the replacement could take as a sign of having got to her. Why? Because Margot continued to get to her, even after all this time.

Margot always liked her posts: it would seem too pointed not to.

Did they also make her scratchy and dissatisfied with her lot, bitter at what she didn't have, irritated that it should have gone to someone else? The difference was, of course, that Maggie had gone poking around in Margot's house to feel this way. What she put on social media she did so in the knowledge that it would infiltrate the other woman's comfortable existence and impinge on her consciousness without her inviting it in. The realisation made Maggie feel even worse.

Thankfully, what lay behind the next door soothed her sore pride a little – a spare room bursting with boxes stacked high, untidy heaps of polythene bags bulging with what looked like old clothes, and books piled in teetering towers. *Not much of a scheme here,* she thought, smug that she'd found proof Margot was mortal, although she covetously noted a rather luxe 'I'm a creative' computer with the perfect midcentury chair neatly tucked under the desk it occupied.

Satisfied that Margot and Nick's junk room was evidence they were as fallible as everybody else, Maggie had carried Lila back downstairs and got her ready to go out.

It wouldn't exactly be a hardship to spend another evening in that house. Like going to a hotel for the night. She'd forgotten to nose in the bathroom cabinet last time, too.

'What do you think, Maggie?' Nick was saying. 'I'm so sorry to ask again, it's just that Lila knows you, and you've done it before. I know Margot would rather you than anyone else . . .'

What the hell.

'Of course I can!' she told him as she packed away her yoga stuff. Maggie was glad to be the means of getting them out of the house for a rare evening together. 'Let me know what time you want me.'

By the time he rang off, Nick's voice had lost that slightly desperate note and Maggie was pleased to be the reason for it. He was such a nice guy. He didn't deserve to be collateral damage in whatever it was Margot was going through.

She made her way back to the office then, invigorated by a morning's exercise and the prospect of being useful. The weather was definitely turning, the air less chilly and the sun's rays a warm glow on her face where they had sliced coolly into her skin only the week before.

The magazine's staffers were beavering away under the pressure of next week's print deadline when she got back from the lake to her and Margot's desk. A3 proofs of pages were being carried by section editors and their assistants between the subs and the fashion desk, smaller versions of them slotted and reslotted into the Wall, where editions lived in miniature until they were okayed and sent away to be turned into the copies that would eventually reach the readers' hands.

'Ah, Maggie, I'm glad you're finally here.' Moff didn't look up from the proof she was reading as she leaned on the filing cabinet to one end of the fashion team's pod of desks. Holly met Maggie's eyes with an almost invisible shrug of apology:

her late arrival had been noted and the stylist hadn't been able to fib for her.

'Come into my office a moment, will you?' Moff flicked her gaze up and over the half-moon lenses she used for reading, into Maggie's face. 'We need to discuss your future here at *Haute.*'

5

Margot

The next Monday morning – after more hours spent lying rigidly awake and atrophying in the dark, watching the ceiling and waiting for my daughter's cries and Nick's alarm clock – I began the daily ritual of clearing my mind of another night's worth of stressful and violent visions. I made a breakfast coffee for myself and mashed banana for Lila, who was already gesticulating eagerly for it from the seat of her ergonomic Danish high chair. Deep breaths and full concentration on the baby as she smacked her lips around the sticky spoon.

How will I get through today?

The same way I had got through everything for years: by simply not thinking about what I knew it was best not to. Starting as I meant to go on, I threw myself into delivering the pulpy banana into Lila's smeared chops so that my daughter cackled with delight between mouthfuls.

We went on this way until the orange plastic bowl was empty, the little chin wiped – no easy feat, given Lila's resistance to being cleaned up – and her nappy efficiently filled and then changed. *One in, one out.* At that point, my phone thrummed the sound of a message onto the coffee table, where I had left it facedown, while Lila and I built up bricks and knocked them down again.

Propping the baby against the nook in a pair of cushions, I reached for it and read the text on its screen. *Moff.*

'Hope it's all going well at home. Perhaps we could have a talk about your plans. I'm giving Maggie a column.'

My stomach plummeted so far I felt it land where I had stitches after making room for Lila to pass through. A curdling happened at the back of my tongue, where something acrid gathered in my throat.

I had thought my envy of Maggie had peaked as she stood in my kitchen, eyes bright, telling me about the £7,000 dress folded in yards of tissue at her feet. Telling a woman who hadn't so much as been to the loo by herself for months about the champagne reception and gala night at the gilt-domed museum in town she and Tim had lined up. I hadn't planned it, but when I realised the masala ladle in my hand was as good as a weapon and angled it over that expensive carrier bag, I felt a release as though I'd slapped her.

But that jealousy didn't come close to what I was feeling now. My every ligament was tensed with hatred, my pulse a scream in my ears while the heart that drove it cracked in half inside my chest.

A column. She'll be at the front of every issue; her face will be the first thing you see.

It was true. Columnists smiled out their pronouncements right at the beginning of the magazine for the reader to take in straightaway. They were chatty and glamorous, the people readers wanted to be; the ones I, Winnie, and Helen had always lingered over. The byline photos that ran with their words – shrugging, laughing, sometimes full-length and leaning against their own text – made them borderline celebrities, recognised in the street and booked for television appearances.

It was the spot every journalist lusted after. Having a column lifted you out of the bracket of working hacks – of which even fashion editors were a part – and into a much smaller pool that also included actual celebrities. Not only that, you had one deadline a week – or a month, if you were really lucky – and wrote at home, but were paid as though you were in the trenches every day from nine until five. The rest of the time you just swanned around working on your personal brand and picking up profile-building TV and radio spots.

Having a column meant you were the face of your publication, that your editor thought you encapsulated their vision.

Ten years I've worked there and Moff has never even mentioned a column.

Ten months and Maggie barely had to try.

It was a less-than-tacit acknowledgment that Maggie was more personable than me, more attractive. More charismatic. Not quite as insulting or aggressive as simply giving her my role outright, but all the more hurtful for the fact it elevated Maggie's status beyond mine and inevitably handed some of the profile I had built up over a decade to the woman who had covered my job for less than a year.

Maggie was fresh where I was stale; the readers wanted to hear more from her than they did from me. How would I be able to meet anyone's eye when I went back?

Helen's eyes. They had found mine as she dropped and looked right into me.

How would they treat me on the desk now? As the boss? Or as an irrelevance, a forgotten extra body that was larger than it used to be? PRs would bypass me with their pitches and their promotions because the person they'd been dealing with instead was still there. Younger, prettier, thinner. Easier and less awkward. More famous and more fabulous.

My world bottomed out. I had the same feeling I did in my dreams. Of being chased, of letting people down, of being mortified, of being guilty, of being the reason everything had all gone so very wrong.

Maggie, this is all your fault.

And yet—

No, it's mine. I got her in in the first place. I should have found someone crap, I should have left them with a dullard. Instead, I gave Moff a columnist.

I wondered when the war between us had started and remembered the misstep over my – our – name at Maggie's interview. Had that been the first of the many calculated underminings, the subtle belittling, that had taken place over the past year?

I still couldn't bring myself to hate Maggie outright: there was too much of myself in the woman currently occupying my desk – the same sense of humour, the shared tastes, such similar personality types it was as though we'd known each other for years. At first, I had thought of my replacement as a reflection in a fairground mirror, myself in antithesis: short where I was tall, dark where I was fair, pretty where I was severe, and outgoing where I was painfully shy. More recently though, I had felt in Maggie's company a rippling sensation, a stirring of memories and of familiarity surfacing as if from somewhere dark within me.

I didn't want to think of that day at school, so I pushed it all back down again, reread Moff's text, and typed out a reply. I sent it before I could change my mind.

'Great idea. She can write about her new boyfriend!'

I knew it was petty, but I also knew my boss would be annoyed – not only at Tim's existence but also at the fact Maggie had kept him a secret.

Moff's many jokes over the years about my being middle-aged before my time had been her way of joshing, but they'd also been rooted in an undeniable truth: that she believed successful women who settled down were cop-outs, which was why she herself had never done it, though plenty of boyfriends had begged her to. When I had told her a few years ago that Nick and I had got engaged over the Christmas break, Moff had looked almost sorry for me.

Throughout nursery rhymes at the local library that morning, coffee with Gemma, pushing Lila on the swings, and singing her to sleep for her afternoon nap, I spent the day festering with disappointment and envy. Lila lifted my heart, but the feeling crashed back every time I raised my thoughts beyond her.

As the hours passed, towards the time when Nick would return home, a different feeling crept in: regret. A sense of shame, and a further depressing feeling of having been defeated. Maggie would know it was I who told Moff she wasn't single anymore; I had broken my own rule about letting my replacement know that she had got to me.

Don't let her see this as a victory. She has to think you don't mind, she can't know she's beaten you.

Perhaps in another life we might have been friends, but I couldn't forgive my maternity cover for having made the leap from protégée to peer, and now to one rung above me.

6

Maggie

When Moff told Maggie she was giving her a column, *Haute*'s acting fashion editor almost shrieked with delight. She just about managed to hold it in, but the editor had given her an indulgent little half smile at the excitement that nevertheless managed to leak out from beneath what Maggie had hoped was a veneer of cool. As if.

A column. A page, a voice, her face. Maggie remembered reading magazine columnists as a teenager and envying their existences, their sleekness, their sense of humour, their wonderful lives that seemed to be conducted between glass-walled offices, kooky bijoux apartments, and brand-new restaurants with inscrutable foreign names that you only knew how to pronounce if you spent time around people who talked about them. Needless to say, there hadn't been many of them up in her adolescent bedroom.

This was her chance to be that person – the one she'd dreamed of being before real life intervened. With a column, her years in the wilderness, hustling for writing gigs here and there, were over. Next stop: TV, a book, film rights? But she was getting ahead of herself again.

'Of course, it's a fashion column, so Margot will still be your editor,' Moff carried on, slowly and silently drumming her fingers on her desk. 'I'll let her know about it. You start next issue – oh, and well done.'

Understatement didn't even begin to describe the way Moff did praise, a spectrum of microexpressions that ran all the way from a long blink of acceptance to a grudgingly appreciative eyebrow-raise. Those four final words practically added up to a eulogy.

As Maggie left her corner office, walking on air but also along the grey carpet tiles of the runway, hair bouncing and hips popping without her even needing to instruct them, she found the person she most wanted to share the achievement with was Margot. She alone among Maggie's friends would understand what it meant, how huge it was, an ambition ticked off, a life pinnacle reached. She'd gasp and laugh at Maggie's having got a positive review from Moff, maybe even high-five her, tell her it was amazing news.

There was no one else who'd get what a big deal it was, which was precisely why Maggie couldn't call her up to squeal about it: Margot would be devastated. It wasn't meant to end like this for her; Maggie was supposed to slink off when she came back, leaving her in line for the next promotion, the next column.

Had she let Margot down? Not stuck to her end of the bargain? Surely she wouldn't expect Maggie to turn the opportunity down for her sake.

Sitting at her desk, proofs to read and marks to make where sentences needed subtle altering and credits adding to the glossy images, the more Maggie thought about Margot, the more resentful she felt towards the other woman for indirectly making her feel guilty. Yes, she was grateful to Margot for having put her forward for the job, but should that override Maggie's own ambitions, her own happiness? When could she stop saying thank you?

Maggie was fairly certain Margot would rather she wasn't seeing Tim, increasingly positive she wouldn't want her to write this column. But life is an ongoing navigation of people who sometimes aren't as appreciative as you feel they should be, or who seem to think you owe them something in return. Isn't it?

Instead, she dialled Winnie's number and arranged to meet her again that evening.

7

Winnie

I wasn't planning to tell Maggie about Jack, not at the start. Once people know about him, they tend not to focus on much else – their voices change around me, from normal and brusque to a soft, gentle, churchlike whisper that makes me even angrier than usual. That makes me want to throw things at them just to show them how strong I still am.

No, I enjoyed the time Maggie and I spent together because it reminded me how good friendship is, how exciting the gradual knitting of two personalities can be, how gratifying to note where they converge, how they differ. I grudgingly admitted to myself that perhaps I had missed Margot these last few months, after all.

Most of all, I enjoyed laughing without feeling guilty for it. There isn't much humour in my and Charles's house.

So I was only too happy to celebrate with Maggie, when she dashed into the pub to meet me and blurted out her success at work. A column! I made all the right noises, knowing as I did what it would have meant to Margot to have been given one. And what it would mean to her that Maggie had got it instead.

I was pleased for Maggie, but my delight ran deeper than my feelings for her: I felt the thrill of cruel satisfaction. Margot had sailed along in life; she worked hard, but things came to her easily. Dream job, great man. She'd got pregnant without really even trying, where it had taken an increasingly fraught year for me and Charles, and then—

So when we drank to Maggie's success, our glasses in the air for ever more convoluted and silly, wine-blurred toasts, I was sticking a metaphorical finger in my oldest friend's eye as much as I was cheering on my newest one. Finally, something that would take the lustre off Margot's gilded existence, dull it almost to the cloudiness my own had taken on.

A couple of bottles down, I had sunk into my seat and into such torpor while Maggie was in the bathroom, thinking of Margot, and of Jack – always of Jack – that I had to ask her to repeat what she'd said as she slid back into the booth next to me.

'I said, I'm babysitting on Friday night,' she laughed. 'Wild, I know. Hey, what about keeping me company?'

Tears sprang to my eyes before I could stop them. The lead in my heart seemed even heavier than usual. The smell of caramel, and then ferrous, bloody rust, wafted into my nostrils, and I found I was telling Maggie about the little boy who had been wrenched away from me only an hour after I'd brought him into the world.

About his tiny fingers, their fleshy pads a row of pink peas in a pod. About the spiral of black hair on the very top of his head that we covered with a white cap. About the moment his death changed the world for me: from one I actively partici- pated in to one I stared down at from somewhere way above, like an astronaut seeing Earth from space, with a knowledge so terrible it was beyond most other people's comprehension.

'Oh my God, you poor thing,' Maggie said, laying one hand on my arm across the table, as I spoke.

Tears dripped down my nose and landed on her wrist, but my voice no longer wavered when I cried; my voice didn't crack with emotion anymore. I had become an expert in doing pretty much everything while crying these days: talking, watching TV, washing up, phoning the bank, going to the supermarket.

'I'm so sorry,' Maggie said earnestly. 'That's fucking terrible.'

I liked her even more for swearing. I had stopped going to the support groups and seeing the professionals who made euphemisms of what had happened to me, who told me Jack had 'passed' or 'moved on'. He'd fucking died, and it was fucking terrible.

'It isn't just that,' I continued. 'It's Charles. He won't talk about any of it. All I want – all we both want – is another baby . . . But, I don't know how . . . He doesn't want to dwell, says it isn't helpful. He shuts me down every time, says I need to move on.'

At this, my voice finally broke.

It was a truth I hadn't shared with anybody – who did I have to tell? Charles and I were like survivors of a bomb, staggering around opposite sides of the pit it had blown open in the centre of our marriage, our home, our hearts. I was picking my way through the wreckage and stumbling over the rubble, still reeling from the impact, while he was neatly trying to rebuild the walls.

My hope was that another baby would bring us back together; my fear was that we had been blasted too far apart already to manage it.

'Winnie, that's awful,' Maggie said soothingly. 'Can you talk to anybody about it? I'm sure time will help . . .'

I nodded and stared down at the wooden pub table, names scratched into it and sticky rings where earlier glasses than ours had stood. It had helped release some of the pressure, talking to Maggie; she knew the right things to say, even if she didn't have the answers.

'And obviously, no worries about Friday,' she continued. 'Babysitting is probably the last thing you want to do.'

How wrong she was there, though. I'd have given anything to take that little chick in my arms, to comfort her and sing her to sleep. To stroke the bridge of her nose to make her eyes close, something the books had told me and I'd never had a chance to try.

'Are you looking after that little blond poppet?' I tried to make my voice sound casual, as though I were making the connection for the first time.

'Lila,' she said, nodding. 'Yes. Her mum's actually the woman whose job I'm covering. I think she's having a bit of a tough time.'

This was the first time Maggie had mentioned Margot, and her presence was an electricity between us: I could feel a mirror image of resentments against the woman we had in common. This was my chance to tell her, to reveal the link, but I let the moment slide by, because anonymity was my passport into that house with Maggie on Friday night; it was the camouflage I'd use to get close to Lila. Just for a moment, I told myself. Just to sniff that sweet baby smell from the top of her head the way I had with Jack.

I'd wanted to meet the woman who was covering Margot's job for some time. I knew my oldest friend well enough to realise whoever had stepped into her shoes at *Haute* would make Margot feel compromised at best, completely discombobulated at worst. The reality sounded more serious than I had expected, and I wondered – briefly, distractedly – what role I might have played.

I thought wryly of the evenings Margot and I had spent together in pubs, at parties, in my old flat as she had whinged about the workload, the pay, the offhand injustices dealt to her by the entitled women she worked with, who looked down on her for being normal. Maggie seemed to have found the joy in that job; all I had ever heard from Margot was the anxiety. Perhaps that's just the pattern our friendship had taken, after what had happened at school: we had become a sounding board for each other's fears rather than our triumphs.

I'd been following Maggie on Instagram for months already, eager to see how she'd slot into the role I'd heard so much about over the years. This is how friendships form now: in scrolling rather than handshakes. They populate the sidebar of your own feed: 'you might also know . . .', like useful things to buy rather than real people that you might get on with. It's how dating apps work, after all, so why not friends too?

You know their faces as pixels before you've heard their voices. You've seen their wedding pictures, scrolled through their holiday snaps; you know their exes, how many children they have. You almost start talking about their kitchen extension before you've even been introduced, and then you realise you're not supposed to know. It's a performance, though – because everyone knows you've done it, looked, searched, pried. There is no mystique, no getting-to-know-yous; there are no secrets anymore – apart from mine and Margot's.

That was why, when I recognised first Lila and then Maggie in the café, I slipped the baby's water beaker out from the basket beneath the pushchair seat in order to have a reason to catch her up afterwards. I knew from her Instagram that she'd been to the bakery before, but it was pure luck we'd ended up there together the next day. I couldn't have planned it better.

'Poor woman,' I said thoughtfully. 'Do you know, perhaps I could join you for a little while. I'll have to face up to other babies eventually, and it'd be good to do it somewhere calm and quiet. And to have you by my side.'

Maggie clasped my hand tightly and her own damp eyes sparkled up into mine as she ducked to see into my face, bent over the table. I gave her my best wobbly but brave smile while, inside, I felt I was made of pure, shining, emotionless steel.

8

Margot

@HelenKnows: How come you didn't get the column @hautemargot?

My phone alerted me to the comment that had been left under Maggie's latest Instagram post just as I was about to tackle the problem of what on earth I could possibly wear out that night.

I was furious with Nick. How could he have arranged for Maggie to babysit without asking me first? He knew I hated surprises but had turned up after work one day with it all planned out and an expression so hopeful, so endearing, I didn't want to ruin it – again.

Instead, I swallowed my suspicions and let them continue to buzz and to drone on in my mind, because I knew how they would sound if I let them out of my head. *Paranoid. They would sound insane.*

And yet, here she was again: this troll who knew exactly the weakest spots in my emotional range.

Winnie.

It could have been some other former schoolmate targeting me, but it seemed unlikely given none of them had ever really noticed me enough to bear a grudge.

I just wished I knew what she wanted. I went about my daily tasks and looked after my daughter under a cloak of fear and anxiety.

That's what you want though, Winnie, isn't it?

It was true: the more scared I was, the safer Winnie had always felt.

I couldn't be angry with Maggie for posting about her news – and yet I was. She'd sent me a sweet message, saying thanks so much, she so valued the opportunity I'd given her to start at *Haute;* she knew I must have had a word in Moff's ear for such an amazing opportunity to have come up.

I felt like I'd eaten a lemon. My insides convulsed with shame at the memory of what I'd actually said to Moff. She hadn't even replied to the message, something I felt increasingly grateful for. I regretted trying to land Maggie in it with our boss – but then she put a saccharine selfie up on Instagram with some bullshit caption about how she'd 'grown as a writer' and was delighted to become *Haute*'s newest columnist, and I knew I'd eat a whole bag of lemons just to see her taken down a peg or two.

No sooner had I unlocked my phone and swiped through to read the comment – the @HelenKnows profile page remained blank – than it disappeared. Maggie must have deleted it, for appearance's sake. I had to admit that was kind of her – and then I felt angry at her charity.

'Urghhhhhhhh!' I tugged at the ends of my blond hair and pulled my tired face down in a gruesome but honest-feeling stretch, thoroughly sick of myself, before seeing Lila's worried expression reflected behind me in the mirror. I peekabooed back at her, and danced about on the spot, and she became a little emoji of joy, the clouds lifting from that round face of hers into a sunshine grin. I felt my heart relax, if only for a moment.

I propped Lila against the pillows on my and Nick's king-size bed and gave her the box of plastic eggs she loved so much to play with while I, a mother now but once someone else, tried to remember who I was – who I had been – enough, at least, to pass for a woman who went out for dinner on a Friday night.

I lost count of how many pairs of jeans wouldn't fasten, of the T-shirts that pulled across my stomach, of the shirts through which my breasts strained heavily. I marvelled at the distance between the two sides of a zip as though it were a fresh revelation. I knew I was bigger, but by this much? When? And how? I had lived in elastic waists since halfway through my pregnancy; I had lost track of who I had become.

I wondered whether people were talking about it behind my back – that feeling I knew all too well. *Thank God Moff hasn't seen.* Whether Maggie had noticed. *Of course she's fucking noticed, she's probably thrilled about it.* That wasn't fair – Maggie wasn't spiteful. Or was she? *The photo.*

Defeated, I yanked my maternity jeans back on and doubled the now-empty jersey panel where my bump had lived over at the low-rise waistband, which nevertheless bit tightly into the flesh around my hips. Over it, I pulled the petrol-blue metallic sweater I had last worn at our Christmas party. *The one Maggie bought in a different colour.*

I regulated the purple beneath my eyes and the pinkness in my cheeks with a few sponge dabs of foundation, and lined my eyelids with the liquid black I had applied six out of every seven days in the lifetime before Lila but not touched since. I had to crack the seal where the fluid had dried around the lid. It felt like delving into a memory.

Never mind that I was bigger than I used to be; Nick hadn't seen me with makeup on for months. He'd appreciate my making the effort. Although that effort felt like so much more of an exertion than it used to.

When Maggie arrived at the door, we circled each other like two boxers in the ring. Even when we tried to tiptoe around each other's feelings, we nevertheless managed to trample on them. Now that she was here, I couldn't bring myself to congratulate my rival. She was so excited, so fresh and ener-getic in comparison to the version of me I had cobbled

together in the past half an hour, that I found it almost physically painful to look at her.

Not now. I heard Winnie's voice in my ear, the old exhorta-
tion for calm, for peace, for me to allow myself some distance
from my own thoughts.

'Thanks again!' I trilled falsely as Maggie hung her coat up
in the hall. It was a beige gabardine mac of the sort I had once
found, many moons ago, in the debris of the fashion cupboard
– but hers was brand-new, spotless and crisp.

My every fibre screamed a protest against leaving my most
treasured possession in the company of the woman who had
spoiled the last thing this precious to me.

A flashback to a dream, where Lila was being handed past
me, above my head, on the interminable staircase. I shook it
from my head and plastered on a smile.

'She's in bed now, almost asleep I think.' I cocked my ear
from the bottom of the stairs towards the top, where a faint
chirruping could be heard: two notes, a high and a low,
repeated over again. 'She sings for a while before she drops
off.' My love for Lila made the breath catch in my throat.

Maggie placed the heel of her hand over her heart in solidarity. It was the one topic on which there was no jostling for
position: each of us adored the baby who was cooing to herself
above our heads, and rocking herself back and forth on the
little monitor screen I'd set up in the sitting room.

'Please don't answer the door to anybody,' I insisted in a
blurt. 'Don't let anyone—'

'We'll be fine,' Maggie purred, one hand on the front door
to close it as I stepped out onto the terracotta tiled porch.
'Now! Have a wonderful date night! Get really drunk! Snog
like teenagers!'

I never snogged as a teenager, I was too busy not cracking up.

9

Maggie

She'd had to almost physically push Margot out of the door. Maggie had never seen anybody look less excited to be going out. She could have been in deep space, in a convent, in a coma, and still her every cell would have known when it was a Friday night – she lived for them. Except, of course, when she spent them looking after someone else's baby.

Maggie put it down to a newfound maturity that the prospect of a Friday night in had become as appealing as one spent out and about, trying new food, new places, giggling with delight at the fun of it all. But it was more that she simply loved spending time in Margot's house. A Friday night chez Cath was a little lacking in allure by comparison.

Margot's house put her at ease – so calm and quiet, so cosy and well appointed. It was a grown-up's house. Everything about it was bountiful, from the plumpness of the cushions to the generous span of the artisanal ceramic plates to the vintage yellow-tone glow of the Edison lightbulbs she had all over the place. Maggie and Cath existed under mean strip lights and glaring halogen spots.

The first time she babysat for Margot, Maggie had briefly pretended that the house was hers and flounced around accordingly, picking things up and putting them down again. So no, she didn't mind a Friday night in at all. In fact, she even had a little lie-down on Margot and Nick's bed, just to test how comfortable it was. It felt like being prone on a marshmallow.

Margot had put a feather duvet on the mattress under the fitted sheet so lying on the bed made you feel like an ancient god reclining on a cloud. Maggie wondered whether Margot had learned the trick, as she, Maggie, had, from the smart boutique hotel they'd stayed in during fashion week in New York. Discovering that had been one of the new girl's more slack-jawed moments of the season.

Ever since, she'd found out so many little life hacks designed to make even the most privileged existence a bit more enjoyable that she'd started writing them down in her little notebook: scrambled eggs made with cream; botanical hand wash with little scratchy beads in it that gave you a mini massage as you soaped; satin pillowcases to stop your hair from going fuzzy overnight. The very act of writing them down was inherently uncool, Maggie realised, but it felt important to document the minutiae of the high life, in case she forgot them when she was no longer living it.

Maggie sighed. A column was all well and good, but it wouldn't stop Margot from coming back to claim the job from her.

10

Margot

As I quickly walked the ten-minute route to the high street, where I was meeting Nick for cocktails, I wondered that it had ever felt normal to go out alone. To be out without responsibility. To be out without knowing whether I'd go home that night or in the morning. To stay out, indefinitely, if I wanted.

I had done that once, spent a whole weekend in a warehouse illegally converted into a dusty dance floor. I had turned up on Winnie's doorstep at eight a.m. on the Sunday, covered in silt kicked up from the disused railway sidings I had spent two days marching on to a repetitive, thudding bass line. Winnie told me I looked like a scared rabbit and hustled me into the shower before talking me down, shifting her afternoon plans with Charles so that she might stay with me and reason away the saucer-eyed dread. Because Winnie knew my fears so well, she knew how to soothe them too.

No, I knew exactly where I would be at eight a.m. this Sunday: mashing more banana with the radio on. It was everything that dancing girl had resisted for so long, but the woman ten years her elder had never found the prospect more comforting as she turned the corner onto a pavement that bustled with angular twentysomethings sporting jarring hair dye and bleached denim.

The bar my husband had told me to find him in hadn't even existed the last time I'd had a night out; it was younger than Lila. That was what the places near us traded in and thrived on: newness and obscurity, lean and bare-bricked dens run by lean and knowing young men and women. The whitewashed shop fronts of brands long gone had been wiped clean by ectomorphs with piercings who felt passionate about coffee and spirits, the walls inside a froth of layers that revealed the building's previous identities.

The peel of paint and wallpaper beneath reminded me of my stretch marks. I wondered whether, if a hipster set up shop in my body, they'd be able to find the real me underneath all the incarnations of myself I had built up on top.

I know what you did.

The unbidden thought made me recoil and remove my hand from the door before I had pushed it.

Don't be so stupid. You're not some ancient crone. Until very recently, you were fashion editor of a glossy magazine. Now fucking go in.

Nick was waiting for me at the bar, two misty tumblers decorated with sprigs of rosemary in front of him. He knew I loved the smell; Lila had almost been a Rosemary. I laid a hand on his arm and he turned his face, careworn and apprehensive, to me and beamed.

'You're here.' He leaned in to kiss me, slipped an arm around my waist, then gestured around him: unencumbered people sipping beers and chatting. 'Remember this?'

I did – just. A sense memory, like a touch on skin felt long after contact, or music that can be summoned though it hasn't been played for years. Just as I knew all the songs on the tape Winnie had left for me without hearing them aloud.

I recognised the scene but had no sense of my own involvement in it. I dropped my bag onto the stool next to my husband and went to the loo, where I repeated to myself a mantra that I wouldn't spoil the evening.

When I returned, I blurted out what was uppermost in my mind and felt my eyes fill with warm water.

'Moff gave Maggie a column.' I sat and sipped from the cool glass. 'I'm gutted. I can't help it. I know I should be pleased for her, but I just feel sick.'

Nick put an arm around me. 'That's annoying,' he said, but he didn't sound annoyed. 'You'd be a great columnist. But Maggie will write this one thing every month – the rest of the time she'll be freelancing. You'll be there every day, 'Go, right in the thick of it. It's still your dream job, remember? Nothing's changed.'

'They think she's better at it than me,' I muttered. 'They like her more. She's prettier, nicer.'

'Margot, don't.' Nick was instantly cold. 'You have to stop this. It's bad for your health – Maggie is none of those things. She's just getting on with the job you are on leave from. When you go back, it'll be yours again, and hopefully all this resentment will go. It needs to go, because she's looking like a permanent feature now that it's going so well with Tim . . .'

He studied the sprig on the top of his drink, pulling it out from between the ice cubes and driving it back down again.

'I don't know where this obsession with Maggie has come from.' He paused. 'Actually, I can guess. Look, I wasn't going to mention this tonight but seeing as we're talking . . . I know about Winnie.'

I felt very cold and heard his voice as though he were much farther away from me than the barstool next to mine. I played with the brass hardware on my handbag.

'Charles told me he saw you at the house on Saturday.' Nick spread his hands, a taut gesture of bafflement. 'I thought you'd booked into a spin class. You seemed so excited about it. What were you doing round at theirs? Spying on them?'

I stopped breathing. My insides decontracted at what Nick thought he knew. For a moment, just a fraction of a second, I had thought Winnie had told him everything. Like she'd threatened to do so many times. Like the many evenings over the years she'd spent pretending she might until I cried and pleaded and bargained with her not to.

Yes, I had gone to Winnie's house on the weekend. I didn't want to speak to her, hadn't been planning on ringing the doorbell. I felt drawn to the house where the woman who occupied so much of my mind was, wanted to see from outside whether anything was different, whether it showed the scars of the grief within. Maybe to catch sight of its occupants and remind myself they were just ordinary people, rather than the angry, vindictive caricature that occupied my mind so relentlessly.

What Nick didn't know – *apart from all the rest* – was that it had taken all my willpower not to go round there every day since the moment Winnie's message had ended our friendship. Part of me wished I had: Saturday had been a stupid, pointless exercise that had failed to make me feel any better, and I'd wasted six months plucking up the courage to do it. I had stood in the drizzle, obscured (at least I thought) by the wheelie bins at the end of their drive for five minutes before realising that the drab house had no solace to offer, to either me or the couple trapped inside it.

'You're in touch with Charles?' I replied. The betrayal was piercing.

Why? When Winnie disappeared on me and you know how much it upset me? And why didn't you tell me?

'He just messaged me when he saw you round there – I think he was worried, to be honest. It's pretty weird behaviour. What were you hoping to achieve?'

I sighed and pulled out my phone. 'Nothing, I don't know. It was a stupid idea. Let's go to the restaurant, shall we? I'm just going to call Maggie and check everything's okay at home.'

But as my hands started to flick around the screen to locate Maggie's details, Nick reached out and stopped me, eyes earnest and loving once more.

'Everything's fine, 'Go. Stop fretting. Maggie will be eating crisps and watching TV.'

She would. The woman liked nothing more than throwing herself onto the fat cushions on our sofa and exclaiming at how much more comfortable it was than hers. She'd have the fringed organic wool cushion clutched over her tummy the way she'd done the other Sunday after brunch. I briefly felt something not far off affection for my replacement, before Nick's next sentence snuffed it out.

'Besides, she told me she had a friend who lives nearby who's going to come round and keep her company.'

II

Maggie

If anything, Margot's bed was too comfortable. Maggie opened her eyes to find the room had lost its daylight. She sat up on the bed and rubbed her temples. For some reason, she thought of Winnie. Did she wake up every day with Jack's death at the front of her mind?

Maggie had known grief and bereavement, but never of the magnitude that Winnie had been through. Maggie had lost grandparents, elderly relatives, her parents' lifelong friends. This was the natural order of things: a sadness, often an intense sense of loss, but one that was smoothed over by time passing and the hard logic of age and inevitability.

At university, a girl on her corridor had died in a car crash in their first term, a month after leaving the home she had spent eighteen safe years in. Lindsay Deeds: friendly but not someone Maggie had been close to. Had she lived, Maggie doubted whether she'd still recall her name or remember her in such startling detail, from side parting to straight, pearly teeth. This is how death out of sequence asserts itself on the brain, and it was the closest Maggie had come to the way life can cheat the young.

No wonder Winnie and her husband were finding it so hard to make sense of each other. She hoped they could find the next steps together; Maggie had seen on Winnie's face as she had spoken in the pub how much she relied on Charles. Maggie knew, from hard experience and years of loneliness spent looking over at couples at neighbouring tables, walking hand in hand, leaning their heads on each other's shoulders on the tube, that love like that doesn't come round very often – or at all, for some people.

She would help her new friend through it in whatever way she could.

Shivering in the cool evening air of the master bedroom, she hopped down from the firm mattress and poked her head around the door to Lila's room, where the baby lay snoring softly. Satisfied, she made to go downstairs, to make sure the monitor was on and in view of the settee, and wait for Winnie to arrive.

12

Margot

'A friend?' I repeated to Nick through the roar of blood in my head as the invisible band of pressure constricted around my temples again.

No no no.

Winnie.

The selfie she had sent of herself with Lila; the fact she and Maggie were now Facebook friends; the mixtape left outside our front door. They all pointed to one thing: Winnie was getting closer to home. My home.

Winnie, who had been there so many times, on so many happy occasions. Winnie, who had been in our house the day we collected the keys to it, drinking cheap fizz from a plastic cup in a room that was all moth-eaten old carpet and damp spots on the walls and nothing else. Who had been in our house when I had revealed I was pregnant too, hugging her oldest friend over the mound of her own burgeoning belly.

Winnie, who had been in our house and was now always in my head, because she had been there that day all those years ago and because each of us relied on the other to keep it a secret.

She had broken that bond, though, when Jack died, when she'd disappeared and resurfaced, hostile and hurt. I knew this Winnie – the one that lashed out, the one that loathed – and I was scared of her. Once I had feared for myself, but now all I could think of was Lila.

Lila, my Lila. At home with Maggie, who had laid me low at work already, and now invited Winnie to wreak whatever it was she had planned.

'I have to go back.' I stood up, shrugged my coat on, and set the bells above the door jangling discordantly as I yanked it open and stepped through.

The pavement was as busy as my mind, and I notched up my speed from a walk into a trot. It was the fastest I had moved since my first trimester, when nausea and breathlessness had stopped me going for the regular runs I took in the leaf-strewn park I now ambled through most days with Lila and the buggy. I cursed myself for not trying harder to get my fitness back.

You can't protect your child, because you didn't put the effort in.

I had to slow to a brisk walk again when the pace became too much, and felt that in trying to hurry my feet along I somehow tangled my legs into an even slower rhythm. As I went, I tapped at my phone repeatedly, in case Maggie had posted anything more on Facebook or Instagram since I had left home. *Nothing.*

I remembered how my phone had fostered the resentment I felt for my replacement in the early weeks of Lila's life and small hours of the night, memorising the web addresses of her various social feeds to offer up for scrutiny when I was feeling at my most weak and most absorbent.

I travelled as if in one of my dreams, sticky footed and unsure what I was heading into or what I expected to find there.

Winnie would never hurt Lila.

But I had thought Winnie would never hurt me either. And what had my life since Helen been but a sequence of threats and intimidation – gently, subtly, but nevertheless constantly – meted out by Winnie?

I had reached the corner by the pub now, where the road broadened into a village green and the swings I visited so regularly hung still and unoccupied in the dusk. Home was five minutes away.

The phone in my hand buzzed into life with Nick's number, and I saw in the digits the comfort of his face and the strength of his arms around me as though they were formed in lines of code.

'Margot, what the fuck are you doing?' he shouted at me when I picked up.

'It's Winnie!' I cried raggedly. 'Winnie is with Maggie! Maggie left the photo of . . . of Jack, dead. On the computer. Winnie asked her to. And now Winnie is in our house!'

There was a silence down the line. An in-breath, a false start – and then:

'Margot, that was me,' said Nick, eventually, in a voice that was cold, hard, and almost unrecognisable as his. 'I left that photo on the screen.'

13

Maggie

Maggie couldn't help putting her head round the door of that unlandscaped spare room one more time. She was drawn to the mess inside that showed Margot was human.

The carrier bags were still heaped in untidy piles, the floorboards beneath barely visible. On the imposing wooden desk, to one side of the giant screen, lay a stack of Nick's paperwork. The bulging folders and document wallets trailed handwritten notes and Post-its from between their covers.

Maggie closed the door and went downstairs to the kitchen.

On one of her previous visits, while searching out the crockery to lay the table, she had discovered a whole cupboard in Margot's kitchen that was given over to small, decorative bowls. Marbled, hand-shaped, some ridged and off-kilter, others finished with painted designs and gilt curlicues, they had become, in Maggie's mind, emblematic of the difference between the two women's lives. She and Cath ate their crisps straight out of the bag; Margot's snacks had a veritable wardrobe to choose from.

Maggie couldn't decide whether she'd rather break one or take one home with her.

She fished a chunky midsized glass vessel from the back of the cupboard, emptied some peanuts into it and carried it through to the sitting room, where she switched on the TV and settled herself on a sofa so well stacked with cushions she felt like a maharajah. The Sultan of Suburbia: that would make a good caption for a selfie. Scrap that – it would make a great column.

Maggie smiled to herself as she remembered her latest achievement.

Between the patter of the sitcom she was only half watching and the hypnotic pull of the various social feeds she dragged to refresh on her phone every five minutes, Maggie was only distantly aware of the noise of footsteps along the path outside the front door.

The peal of the doorbell drew her mind back into Margot's house, back to Lila asleep upstairs rolling over every so often on the grainy screen of the baby monitor, and she checked the time on her phone: just over an hour since Margot had left.

'Winnie!' Maggie exclaimed to the empty room.

14

Margot

I hadn't felt fear like it since school. Since Helen plunged.

Helen, with her insistence that things had to change. Her notion that we were boring before she arrived to take us out of ourselves, when actually what we had been was happy.

I had been happy with Nick too – but not recently, I realised with a jolt.

Now my mind played and replayed scenes between us, glitchily and from different angles. Nick comforting me after Jack's death; my trying and failing to find a way into the conversation between him, Maggie, and Tim that my tired mother-brain was struggling to follow; my husband's face, closed and exasperated, as I tried to explain to him how anxious I was.

There was a word people had started using, online and in the office, just before I left to have Lila. I had to Google it the other day when I came across it in an article I was reading because I couldn't remember what it meant. The old me would have known.

Gaslight (verb): to manipulate (someone; usually a spouse) by psychological means into doubting their own sanity; usage: 'in the first episode, she is being gaslighted by her husband.'

I remembered that word now, and my lip began to wobble, my jaw to tremble uncontrollably.

Nick had been the one to bring the parcel of smashed, rejected things from Winnie into the house – things I assumed she had broken in her rage at me, but he could just as easily have done it before I'd had a chance to see inside. Nick was in touch with Charles and hadn't told me. Nick had insisted on Tim and Maggie's coming round so often, even though he knew how it made me feel – he was usually the one that turned the talk to things I hadn't had a chance to catch up on, in fact. Most of all, Nick had watched me become more and more uneasy about my job and about the abuse I'd been receiving online – had that been him too?

Whenever I had gone to him, Nick had told me time and again that I was overreacting.

Was it all in my head? And had Nick put it there?

The notion made me cry out. There were tears on my face. My heart ached and my head spun.

'Margot, are you there?' Nick's voice was tinny from the phone I'd forgotten I was gripping. It was all I could do to croak my presence into the handset.

'Look,' he continued, exasperated, 'Charles emailed me a couple of weeks ago. It's nearly a year since . . . He asked me to design something with the photos they have of Jack. I must have left it on the screen without closing it down properly. I'm so sorry, I know how that photo made you feel.'

He paused. 'It was me,' Nick said, 'not Maggie. No great conspiracy, no secret plan.'

I stopped where I was, stock-still in the street. I had just mapped in my own head a complex itinerary of deceit master-minded by the man I was married to, the person I loved most in the world – bar Lila, who took pole position mainly because she was half Nick anyway.

You are going completely insane.

'Look, I'm coming now, just behind you.' Nick sounded cross but not furious, his voice sharpened by irritation and disappointment. 'Someone had to pay for those bloody drinks. Can't you wait for me?'

If not Nick, then . . .

'No!' I barked, breathless with the pace I'd set myself. 'I've got to get home!'

I dropped the phone from my ear and ran. I needed to get there. Get back to whatever was waiting for me, to whatever punishment Winnie had decided to exact.

Finally, after all these years of holding off.

As I hurried, I felt my phone buzz again – a text message, from a number not saved in my contacts:

'Enjoy your night out @hautemargot.'

She knows I'm not at home. She knows I'm not with Lila.

It could only be Winnie.

I spun around in the street, looking over my shoulder in each direction without really seeing anything – without expecting to – and ran the final block.

15

Winnie

The things people will do online that bear no correlation to their real-life behaviour; the things they will say virtually, when they don't have to see the expressions of those on the receiving end.

16

Margot

By the time I turned into our road, the sky was fully dark, with a wind whipping up between the branches of the handsome old trees that lined it. It wasn't until I neared the brick garden wall that I noticed our gate was wide open and swinging in the breeze.

Did I forget to latch it?

I almost missed it – the simple tortoiseshell hairpin on the front step.

I saw it sliding into a scrunch of auburn hair. I felt it, cool between my fingers as I twisted a ponytail into a chignon, remembered it clamped between my teeth as I perfected a French plait. I had used this sort of clip too many times to count, but I only knew one person whose coarse, unruly curls had ever needed them.

It was the sort of thing that had fallen out of style with mohair and blue eyeshadow, the preserve of frumps and bluestockings.

And Winnie.

She'd been here.

For the briefest of moments, I'm embarrassed to say, I was almost relieved. Relieved that Nick was wrong, that I hadn't conjured it all up in my head. Everything I had worried about for months now – the constant dread, the lingering sense of threat: none of it had ever sounded serious in the world beyond my own head. Emotion never did from women with babies. I was just another tired new mother with a clutch of out-of-control feelings.

Except I wasn't. I had been right.

I bent to pick up the barrette and, straightening, repressed a shudder as the gate banged shut behind me.

Winnie had finally come for me. And for my baby.

17

Winnie

Grief makes you crazy. The insistent prod of unrelenting misery, a drip-drip of pain – it's like a TV jingle that you can't tune out. Imagine singing the same lyrics inside your head for the rest of your life.

18

Margot

Winnie has been here. Where is Maggie?

I burst, shaking, into the silent hallway. The white globe ceiling lights blazed in the sitting room, and the articulated wooden standard lamps too. The television screen flickered with pictures – a woman lathering her hair in a shampoo ad – but its sound was muted.

Heart racing, I stepped quietly past the empty room and looked towards the kitchen, dark and vacant at the end of the corridor. The French doors onto the garden reflected only my own shadow looking back at itself.

'Maggie?'

No response.

I paused, my breath ragged, before calling again. 'Winnie?'

More silence. *Could Nick be right? Am I losing it?*

Then a snuffle. A whimper and a cry. I knew well the sounds of my daughter waking up. But too close, no longer in her bedroom. Up on the landing instead.

A shape detached itself from the shadows at the top of the stairs.

Please, no.

I knew what came next. Of course I did. I had been reliving it for almost twenty years.

19

Winnie

Faced with an evening in Margot's house, the buzz in my head suddenly fell silent for the first time since Jack died.

20

Margot

Winnie was standing there, behind the balustrade, just as Helen had stood above me, so many years before.

'Lila . . .' My voice sounded like I hadn't used it for decades. *The eyes, looking right into me.*

'Margot—' Winnie's voice was urgent and raw. As she stepped forward, I could see that she had one hand raised to stop me from approaching and that the fingers reaching out towards me were trembling. In the crook of her other elbow I could make out the dim lines of a small bundle, one that I knew – as well as I knew my own face – would be soft and warm and breathy in her arm.

I had seen that sense of wild purpose in Winnie before, at school, as the teachers and then the police had asked us their endless questions.

The scream as she fell. And the noise she made as she landed.

The landing seemed as high as that balcony from long ago. Even if I ran, there was no guarantee I could catch Lila once the woman who'd been my dearest friend dropped her over the side of it.

I took a step towards the bottom of the flight of stairs. 'My baby . . .'

'No, Margot,' Winnie said in a low voice, with a finality that turned the blood in my veins to solid ice.

'She isn't yours,' Winnie said. Her gaze flitted about, unable to focus on me. The wildness in her eyes, the twitching of her head: Winnie seemed to vibrate with nervous energy. With rage.

I knew how furious she was with me. That she could never forgive me for having a beautiful, living child, when she had lost hers. I stepped closer, carefully.

'No!' I held my hands up, craven and cowering, wanting only to placate her, to know that my daughter was okay. To hold Lila and shush her, to brush my lips over the button of her nose, to nuzzle into the soft down of her cheek, the sweet, hollow undercliff of her nape.

'You don't want this.' Chillingly, her voice had softened. 'We don't need this. We were okay, just the two of us. We don't need anyone else.'

I peered up through the gloom of the hallway at her as I had once falsely smiled up at Helen through the shafts of sunlight.

The eyes. The scream.

What I did to Helen had felt good for less than a heartbeat. Regret took hold and panic set in almost as soon as the new girl laid her hands on that spongy, rotten handrail. After that second, the one that stretched longer than I thought time ever could. When my heart started beating normally again, I'd become someone else. Someone who had done that.

It wasn't my fault.

When the police had gone, I thought everything would be okay again. My teenage mind hadn't realised that after something shatters, the lines where it has been glued together again are always visible – and vulnerable. What I wanted from Winnie was the same pleasure she'd taken in my company before Helen, and what I got was tight-lipped pity carried out with martyrish resignation. Duty. She tolerated me, because she felt guilty about what had happened. She tolerated me, because she had lied to protect me. And I tried to please her, because I was scared of her.

'What are you doing here, Winnie?' My voice was high in my own ears, unnatural and reedy, as I tried to sound ordinary, nonchalant even. *Just like Helen.*

'We have to put an end to this thing,' Winnie said. 'It's been eating us both up for too long now.'

I began to babble: 'I haven't heard from you in months, you've ignored me, sent me all that stuff . . .' I stepped forward, holding my arms out for my daughter, imploring Winnie to give her back to me.

'Stop!' she interrupted, her voice strangled high in her throat. 'Don't come any farther!'

'I know it was you on Twitter . . . Those threats . . . HelenKnows . . .'

I saw the toll that staying calm was taking on her in her wild eyes, her terrible pallor.

'Please, Margot, I'm so sorry,' Winnie said. She sounded pathetic, yet I was terrified of her.

Terrified of what she might do.

'It isn't me you need to be afraid of,' Winnie said carefully.

I saw that she was frightened, too.

A movement then, and I made out another shape up there in the shadows behind her.

'Let me help you, Win,' a voice said in the dark. 'You don't need to hurt anymore.'

21

Maggie

Maggie had untucked her legs so suddenly to answer the doorbell that the bowl of peanuts beside her tipped over and the nuts rolled everywhere, into the plump sofa's many crevices and onto the floor.

'Hiya,' she called as she swung the door open. 'You're just in time to save me from disappearing down an Instagram hole.'

But it wasn't Winnie. Or Margot or Nick. Instead, a dark-haired man with a nervous smile stood on the front step.

This was how seventies porn films started, wasn't it, with a mistaken identity and a lonely housewife? It was either that or a horror film, Maggie thought, and immediately cursed her overactive imagination.

The man nodded and clasped his hands one in the other as if to warm them, then plunged them into the front pockets of his black zipped hoodie. With it, he was wearing a pair of dark navy jogging trousers. He looked as though he hadn't shaved for days.

'And you are . . . ?'

22

Margot

'Let me help, Win.' The voice came again.

Charles, gentle Charles. *Oh, thank God.*

'I've come to help you,' he said to his wife. 'To make things better.'

My heart soared to hear Charles up there. He would know how to calm Winnie, how to stop her. How to take my tiny, innocent daughter out of his wife's arms. Charles had been so kind throughout, and so patient. I saw Winnie shift her stance slightly, as though his words were weakening her resolve. Some of the terror I was feeling began to dissipate.

My fingers itched to hold my baby, whose whimpers I could hear above me.

'It's not right, Charlie.' Winnie shook her head mournfully. 'It won't work.'

But as she turned her body towards her husband, a sliver of moonlight from the window on the landing illuminated her arms. She was holding one of the teddy bears we had been given after Lila was born.

Lila wasn't there.

23

Maggie

'Hi,' said the man in a slow drawl. 'I'm a friend of Nick's. I've just come to collect something from him.'

He smiled, as if slightly dazed, and Maggie wondered whether he was a bit stoned. She had met these hip design types before.

She smiled and stood back from the doorway. 'Oh, sure! What is it? Would Nick have left it out for you?'

As Maggie looked at the hall stand behind her for a likely package, the man walked in and closed the door behind him.

'Nick's been doing some graphics stuff for me,' he said. 'I need my pictures back, they were in an envelope. Mind if I just . . . ?'

He took one hand out of the front pouch of his hoodie and motioned up the stairs, towards the landing. The end of his question hung in the air.

The folders. 'Oh, of course,' she said. 'I've seen it. Let me get them for you.'

But Nick's friend had already moved towards the bottom step. 'I'll do it – need to check they're all in there.'

Maggie wavered: it would be rude to say no, but surely she shouldn't just let this guy rummage about in their rooms up there? She put it from her mind that she had been doing much the same less than an hour ago.

He had climbed the first few stairs before she could think of a reply. The man's back disappeared as he quickly mounted the steep treads and turned the corner towards the study.

Maggie couldn't deny it felt a bit weird. She cocked an ear upstairs and could hear nothing. He had only been up there thirty seconds.

After thirty more, a thought came to her – just at the moment the small screen on the table flicked on in grainy black and white as it picked up movement in Lila's room.

Margot had told her not to open the door to anyone. Margot had also asked her not to let anybody in.

On the screen, Maggie saw an arm reaching into the cot.

It seemed too ludicrously melodramatic to be true; there would no doubt be some logical explanation as to why this man was in Lila's room, but Maggie had hurled herself up the stairs after him before she had really thought about what she was doing. She rounded the doorway of the nursery to see a dark shape bent over the crib.

When she spoke, it was as close to a shout as a whisper could get, and her first thought – so British! – was whether she might seem rude.

'Careful, don't wake her! Did you find what you needed?'

But as she whispered, she could hear him crooning down at Lila. A lullaby, Maggie thought at first, but not one she knew.

'Baby, baby,' he sang softly. Maggie held her breath and wondered what to do.

'Winnie will love you so much,' he lilted.

Winnie? Why her? Maggie's mind whirred as she tried simultaneously to check on Lila, in the shadow of whoever this man was, without disturbing either the baby or him.

This man, this friend of Nick's . . . If he knew Winnie, then Winnie must have known Margot.

Why hadn't Winnie said anything to Maggie when she told her about covering the job at *Haute*? When she'd given Winnie the address where she'd be babysitting? Winnie would have recognised it immediately if she and Margot knew each other.

And where was Winnie? Why hadn't she arrived yet?

Amid the scrambling of her neurons, another thought arrived that stilled the others: was this . . . Charles?

The man straightened and Maggie was relieved to see that he had left Lila to sleep. She would ask him all these questions downstairs. *He must just be a bit weird,* she decided. That must have been what Winnie had meant in the pub – that the tragedy of their baby's death had affected Charles even more than it had her. Maggie felt a rush of pity for this bereaved father.

Charles turned and stared at her, then went to leave the little nursery. Was he beckoning Maggie to follow? She nodded encouragingly towards the landing, where light from the hallway below bled up the stairs.

Without moving through the doorway, Charles brought his hand to her face, gripped her chin, and smartly rapped her head hard against the grey plaster wall behind – once, and then twice – as easily as if he were cracking an egg against the side of a bowl.

24

Margot

My breath caught in my throat when I finally saw my baby in his arms. But as the moonlight shone onto her little face, crumpled and confused, it threw relief onto Charles's too, and I knew something was terribly wrong.

His usually clean-shaven face was covered in a few days' worth of stubble, his eyes red and swollen.

'Look what I've got for you, Win.' Charles's voice was high and tight with tears. His words were slurred, catching on his tongue as though he were chewing stones.

'Isn't she sweet?' Winnie answered lightly. Breathily. 'Will you pass her to me, darling, so I can have a cuddle?'

'I've got her for you,' Charles said again. 'To make things better.'

As he stepped towards his wife, holding out his arms, I saw my precious little bundle, squirming with the attention, wondering what on earth she was doing out of her cot. Looking for me.

'Charles . . .' Winnie took a slow step towards him. He stared at her, as if he were struggling to remember why he was there.

Winnie stopped moving. I heard her soft intake of breath. 'I'm okay, Charlie. I'm getting better. Come here, darling. Let's give Lila back to her mum.'

Charles stayed where he was, a dark shape against the even darker landing behind him. 'I just want you to be happy again, Win. I just – I just—'

'I know you do,' Winnie said quietly and firmly. 'And we will be, darling. But Lila isn't ours, Charlie. She's Margot's baby. You have to give her back now.' She stretched out her arms.

I knew the voice with which she spoke to him. It was the soft, gentle voice that had lied to protect me. The very same that had breathed terror into me for almost as long, in case she betrayed me. I heard in it now Lila's salvation and my own – maybe even Winnie's, too – but it was undercut with steel tones of worry that she could not hide from me. I knew her too well.

During my time off with Lila, I had come to realise that caring for a newborn was as much pagan intuition as it was medicine and textbooks. When Lila was upset and needed soothing, I had learned to listen to what my blood was telling me. It told me now to listen to Winnie.

From where I stood, rooted to the spot, every muscle flexed to stop me from screaming and throwing myself at him, I saw Charles's ravaged face. He was sobbing now. Spiffy, precise Charles with his prestigious job designing luxury flats, now so far from his professional persona that he put me in mind of a new mother, bedraggled, unwashed, and with tears trickling down his cheeks.

I had been just like that in the early days. Afraid to ever let go of this marvellous, unexpected gift, this new girl, who had suddenly made me whole even though I'd never noticed anything missing before. The discovery that if I put her down, even for a minute, I was bereft.

It changes you, having a child; you'll never feel the same again. I remembered the unasked-for opinions offered throughout my pregnancy with a wry bleakness.

Did I feel sorry for him? No. Not while he had my baby in his arms.

Winnie took another step, and as she did so, the door burst open behind me, catapulting Nick into the hall.

'Margot, what the fuck—' he started, and then his eyes alighted on Charles. 'Hang on, mate. What are you doing with her?'

Shut up shut up shut up, Nick—

Charles's head snapped up at the male voice, and the despair on his features rearranged itself into anger. All the hatred, the resentment, and the envy I had imagined coming off Winnie in waves towards me throughout my maternity leave I saw broadcast in her husband's face, and I knew once and for all who had sent me all those messages, who had left the mixtape for me to find.

'Mate,' Charles spat. 'You haven't got a fucking clue, have you? You've hardly been here. You've done the bare minimum. Three weeks! Three weeks and then back to work! You don't even know her, do you?'

If he hadn't still been holding my child, I might have applauded. Nick looked like he'd been slapped, and I felt like I had been: until that moment, I hadn't realised how much I had resented him and for how long.

'Charles—' Winnie spoke in the low notes I recognised from the many times she had had to talk me down from spiralling panic. 'Charlie, darling, let's go home, shall we?'

He moved closer to the top step and to the wooden banister where the landing overlooked the hall. I noticed Winnie take a few more steps towards him as he did.

'Look at her!' Charles sobbed. 'Look at what she's been through!'

He gestured towards Winnie, moving Lila in a wide arcing swing over the edge of the railing that made my stomach jump to my throat and force out a guttural shriek from between my lips. It served to focus his attention on me once again.

'You! After what you did! You don't fucking deserve this, either of you. You don't deserve her!'

And he held the baby – my daughter, my precious girl – out over the railing into the empty space above our heads. Lila was a placid baby, trusting and secure; Nick and I were grateful to her for her forbearance with us several times a day. But now – held aloft like that by someone she had never met – she finally sensed something amiss. She began to wriggle, then cry.

Not again. Not Lila. Please. Anything but that.

25

Winnie

I had just come home after a few hours in my safety zone, watching office workers clock out for the weekend, drunk in anticipation of the pints they'd neck and the Sancerre they'd swig before they'd even reached the polished bars of the watering holes with faux-Dickensian names that occupy every corner in that part of town.

I realised I couldn't go round to Margot's house any more than I could shop my oldest friend to the police. I was disgusted with myself, and exhausted.

We needed to get on with our future, Charles and I. We would move away, leave the house that Jack had never come home to, in which the nursery was still as we'd left it the day I went into labour, sealed up as clinically as a crime scene. We would move. It had worked for Helen, after all, although broken bones heal faster than broken hearts.

When I got home, I discovered him sobbing in front of the computer in our study, his head bent against the grained wood of the old policeman's desk we'd found in a flea market when we'd first moved in together ten years ago. His tears had soaked into the varnish and turned the surface different shades of salty blotches.

There was no need to ask what. Just as he knows exactly what is going through my mind when he finds me in my rocking chair, silent and white faced, staring at the walls, so I knew he had been overwhelmed by it afresh. Sometimes it just hits you, as if it's happened all over again; as if you hadn't already spent the best part of a year trying to live with it.

What I wanted to ask, though, was why. Why had he spent so much time sitting at this screen lashing out at people he didn't know and had never met? Had it hit the spot? Had frightening Margot made him feel any better about things?

No, Charles admitted through the tears. It had just made him hate himself even more.

I could hardly bear to look at him.

I had forced myself to be constructive after it happened: to come back to life, get fit, and sort my head out. He had shut himself away, shut me out and retreated behind that screen to spread his misery online. To make people who had nothing to do with it feel that little bit worse, as if he could parcel up his pain into little nuggets of bile and hand it out in portions to other people, like cake at a wedding, until he himself had none of it left.

Perhaps I had done something similar with Margot.

I didn't notice right away that her name was among the list of wretched one-sided sallies Charles had been throwing out into the digital shitstorm, but when I did, I made him give me his passwords and sent him to bed with a couple of the tranquillisers we both had prescriptions for. Just one more thing, packed in the overnight bag next to the little suits along with the funeral literature, that I hadn't expected to leave the hospital with after the birth of my first child.

'Why should fucking Margot be fucking happy?' he wailed before I managed to calm him. 'Why should it work out for her? What's she ever done to deserve it? It could just as easily have been her!'

Throughout my grief, I had never liked thinking that way – although, of course, the thought had crossed my mind more than once. But I wouldn't wish what happened to us on my worst enemy – let alone my supposed best friend.

I saw the comments Charles had made to her on Twitter. They were petty things, stuff about her weight, her looks, how Maggie was doing so well in her role at the magazine, but I couldn't deny they were aimed well. Charles had picked just the right things to worry at. They would have hit the spot all right.

I marvelled that grief had given Charles the imagination to be as cruel as a teenage girl and wondered whether adolescents treated one another so badly because they were all actually in a state of mourning – for their childhood, their innocence, the security of their tender years.

I wondered whether she thought I had sent them, if when she saw HelenKnows's stupid oversized sunglasses pop up on her phone screen she thought instead of my red hair. I could see why she might. I imagined her doing a patronising pity-nod and shrug, and telling people 'Winnie's been through a lot,' as if to explain it away, and I felt suddenly furious at where my life had gone.

I had to apologise to Margot for what Charles had done and for the way I had been with her. Then we could part ways forever, closure finally attained on a friendship that would have politely faded out but for drinks during university holidays or if we both happened to be up north for Christmas. Until we had babies, at least, by which point perhaps we'd have left each other a quick message of congratulations on Facebook before carrying on with our lives.

It struck me with blackest humour that Helen had ended up prolonging the friendship she had tried her best to put a stop to for another twenty years.

I shut down each of the tabs on Charles's computer one by one and winced every time I saw the pointless cruelty of his words. They jarred with the abiding memory I had of our little boy as something that had been purely good, untouched and untainted by the world and what it does to people.

I noticed as I scrolled back through the Twitter account, my eyes glazed after a while so I didn't have to take in the hate and the venom that the man I most cared for had been spouting, that it went back far beyond Jack's death. Silly little jibes at the women who read the news; fights picked with men who voted differently. Charles was such a mild and kind man, thoughtful to a fault. I had had no idea of the secret, screen-lit life of bitterness he had been leading.

I would think about how best to talk to him about it later on. One thing at a time.

I dug around in the desk's sturdy central drawer for what I would need to take to Margot's with me in the morning: the spare set of house keys she had given me when they moved in down the road. In case of emergency, she had said back then, without a beat. As if our friendship weren't built on a case of emergency. As if that weren't what had tethered us to each other for years.

I could have sent those keys back with the gifts I'd returned to her. But I hadn't. I didn't want to ask myself why.

I dropped them into the ceramic dish on the table by the front door and rubbed at my face. My temples felt thick; my head was like a radiator that needed bleeding. I'd have a shower and change into some comfy clothes. Then I'd sit and let television dross wash over me as though it were any Friday night and I were any woman in her thirties at home on her own, with a baby asleep upstairs instead of a husband sedated for his own safety.

As I lathered and rinsed under the warm water, I thought about how different my life would be without Margot. I hadn't seen her for ten months already, but I felt none the lighter for it. She had been on my mind a lot – when Jack hadn't been, of course.

We had meant so much to each other, and then – what? I'd had my head turned: metaphorically, by Helen, but also literally, when Margot had most needed me in that dingy club. I had never forgiven myself for it, I realised, but more than that, I had never forgiven her for it. And it had hardly been her fault. If Helen and I hadn't left her outside; if we'd all gone home together and resolved to try again another night; if we'd sat and watched films the way we'd told our parents we were going to – what would have happened to those three girls?

I mentally added another apology to the ones I owed Margot in the morning, one that was long overdue and necessary if I ever wanted to move on: I was sorry for having left her all those years ago and for not having been there to protect her. I was sorry for making her feel that what we hadn't told Helen in time had been her fault alone, her sin of omission.

I had stayed silent too, all those years ago.

I stopped the water and reached for a towel from the rack. As I did so, I heard a clunk from downstairs and started, but then remembered that the washing machine was chuntering with a load of what I realised I now thought of as Charles's troll clothes: the jogging bottoms and hoodies he'd put on before sequestering himself in the study.

I had thought he was keeping busy with his architecture journals in the months he'd been away from the practice and remembered with fondness that he'd worn smart shirts and chinos even on the days when he used to work from home, he was so fastidious. I had loved how careful he always was with his appearance in the early days; a habitual scruff myself, I had always thought of him as dragging me towards being presentable.

I had been so preoccupied with what I had lost, with being a mother without a child, that I had failed to notice that Charles had changed too. I was glad he was asleep now, recharging. I would do my best by us both from now on, would pay attention to what was going on in front of me rather than the shadows cast by a moment long ago that I had no control over anymore.

I dried and moisturised, and dabbed lavender oil on my pulse points to help with anxiety and insomnia. Then I stepped into a pair of fresh pyjama bottoms, twisted my hair into the usual barrette, pulled a T-shirt on and went to retrieve my cardigan from the end of my and Charles's bed, expecting to have to tiptoe past his inert form.

There was no need: the covers were thrown back, the mattress empty but for the imprint of him.

I emerged onto the landing again.

'Charles?' I called, and was answered only with silence; I couldn't even hear the washing machine anymore.

It was only as I was halfway down the stairs that I realised the laundry I had put on this morning would have finished hours ago. The clunk I had heard from the bathroom had been the front door.

At first I didn't think about where he might have gone, but rather how. My stomach lurched at the notion of Charles's going anywhere in what I knew would be a pilled-up stupor after the dose I had given him, but my blood ran cold at the prospect of his having taken the car in that state. If he had an accident . . . My worn-out heart and tear-abraded cheeks couldn't handle any more loss.

As I ran to the dish of keys on the table, I saw with relief that the chunky electric fob to our beaten-up old hatchback was still lying there. Next to them: Margot's house keys – labelled as such and tied with a navy grosgrain ribbon from some fancy designer carrier bag. My entire core went cold.

Now I knew where Charles was going, I couldn't bear to think what impulse had taken him there.

26

Margot

I was rooted where I stood, petrified as though in one of my dreams, as my baby veered closer and closer to the long drop above my head. My eyes were fixed on Charles on the landing just as they had been on Helen, up on the balcony long before.

Please.

Then – a movement in the dark behind him, and Charles, unsteady with his arms outstretched, staggered sideways as something collided into him. In the gloom of the landing, I made out bleach-blond hair, a short figure that had come from the direction of the nursery.

Maggie.

As he buckled with the impact, Charles's arms began to tip Lila from them, as one might a bundle of washing into a laundry basket. I saw Winnie lunge the final few feet towards him.

I thought of another girl, a lifetime ago, in the arms of a man with no say over what was happening to her.

Winnie had rescued that girl, too.

I didn't like to think about what might have happened if Winnie hadn't barged into that back room all those years ago. She had courage in her blood, my oldest friend, and a loyal heart pumping it steadily around that spare frame of hers. I noticed then how rangy she had become, how grief had taken some of her sturdiness from her, and my own heart ached, even though it was preoccupied with Lila. There would always be space for Winnie in it, too.

The baby – my baby – was airborne for a few seconds, before landing in my oldest friend's hands. Those same strong, trusty arms that had clapped me to her so many times over the years despite everything.

I remembered how it had been with Winnie all that time ago. Before Helen, and before Jack. What a perfect fit we were, how joyfully we spent our days, how true we were to each other.

Winnie came to save Lila, not hurt her. She was talking to Charles as well as to me.

She had lost sight of me once, but now Winnie's attention was focused squarely on the little face gazing up into hers, learning the features it would – I knew then – in years to come recognise as well as it did my own.

Charles was trying to right himself, his arms flailing around in confusion. I realised then why his voice had sounded so strange – he was on something. Whatever it was had dulled his senses and slowed his limbs and, with it, his instinct for balance.

I recognised those movements, the ducking and the wobbling, as the ones that come before a fall. But it wasn't Charles who fell. With a dull thump, his left arm connected with Maggie, who was trying to disentangle herself from where she had thrown herself into him seconds before, and it was she who was knocked off kilter – and out, away from the top step and towards the bottom. Towards me.

She hit the stairs several times before she stopped moving, a bumpy slither that led with her head and followed with her shoulder, her knees, and her shins, fump-a-dumping down the flight towards where Nick and I stood on the wooden boards at the bottom, which her forehead hit with a loud crack.

In the second before I hurled myself into a crouch at her side, shouting her name, I felt a familiar sensation of looking from a height at the future as it slid out of my hands. Of the years ahead being unpicked from the pattern they had begun to form in and starting to knit another way.

I had spent so long dwelling on what I thought Maggie had taken from me, I hadn't even noticed how much she had given in return.

27

Winnie

The little fingers curled around mine, just like Jack's had done.
In the dark of the landing, Lila's big blue eyes stared up at me.
His had been brown.
I lost him all over again.

28

Maggie

She was lying on the floor in front of them all, a small puddle of black ink blooming next to her head.

This was not how she thought she'd spend her Friday night.

Shoes began to arrange themselves around her, but instead of a shocked hush, there were words. Gentle words spoken by quiet female voices whose strength came through in their calm authority.

Above her were two young women, one holding a baby and the other kneeling at her side. Maggie found she could not turn to look at Margot's face and when she tried, the sweet, soft voice above them told her not to.

'Lila . . .' she croaked, and felt a bubble burst in her throat.

'She's here, she's fine,' Margot said. Then a movement from dark to light, and Maggie heard a tiny mewling nearby. 'Maggie, what you did . . . How can I ever—'

A rumbling pain began in her legs. Like a plane about to take off, it threatened to get louder and louder.

Maggie heard tears. Men's tears. Grief, and ignorance.

'I'm so sorry, Margot.' Nick's words were ragged, like his breath.

'There's no time for that.' Margot sounded sharper now. 'Get Charles into the kitchen, and keep him there.'

'There's an ambulance coming,' the other voice – Winnie's – said with a waver, the first throughout all this composed efficiency. The women above Maggie looked into each other's eyes.

Nobody asked the question, because none of them knew how to answer it.

But Maggie knew. She knew what it was to want something that wasn't yours so much it made your heart hurt and your vision mist over with envy. She knew how cold life could be without somebody to share in it.

But she also knew – had learned from borrowing someone else's identity for a year – that life was so many tectonic plates, constantly butting into one another. That they overlapped in joy and sometimes in pain. That unless there was some give between them, they ruptured – often brutally, often irreconcilably – and that only made each little existence smaller and more fragile.

'I fell,' whispered Maggie, and she closed her eyes. All she could see was colour. 'Say I fell.'

29

Margot

As I stepped from the shower and reached for my towel, I felt a familiar throb in my stomach. A momentary pummelling from deep within, and I shivered.

I had laid out my clothes on the bed. A pair of black trousers and navy silk shirt, low block-heeled leather boots and a light, gray, unstructured jacket: a sombre outfit for a difficult day. Take me seriously, it said, listen to me. *Trust me.*

I could hear Lila downstairs having her breakfast with Nick. They had developed a routine together in recent weeks. He'd scramble her an egg – a single egg! We joked about its being pathetic, when really it was our lame parental heartstrings that that solitary yolk tugged on – while he brewed his expensive coffee in a silver stovetop coffeepot. Then he'd sit and post the yellow curds into her mouth on the end of a plastic spoon, while he sipped his espresso and chatted to her about the day he was about to embark on.

'Very busy today, actually, Lila,' I could hear him telling the fluffy, slightly eggy blond head in the high chair in front of him. 'A nine o'clock, a ten o'clock, *and* an eleven o'clock!'

I smiled as I dried myself and rubbed in the moisturiser, the same one I had used throughout my pregnancy. *Keep your skin hydrated and you won't get stretch marks.*

I had a tigering of wispy silver lines across my stomach, ones you could only see in certain lights and from a specific angle. There would be more, I knew, that would rise as these had, as if from the depths, as the arrow on the bathroom scales travelled – agonisingly slowly – back down towards where it used to point. The slight doming would never go – the realisation had been liberating – but that was okay: it had housed somebody once. The property was empty at present, but there might be another tenant in the future.

The throb came again: right now, it was a repository for nerves.

No, I thought as I dabbed foundation onto my skin, brushed over a little bronzer, and finished with mascara and a slick of black eyeliner across my upper lids. It was more than I used to wear, but things had changed, I was different: sometimes I needed help and that was okay, too.

Perhaps that fizzy feeling in there was closer to excitement.

'We need you, Margot,' Moff had declared when she found out, and my heart had lifted at the prospect of being in demand for something other than changing nappies, shovelling food, singing songs. It came thudding back down again when I remembered why I was suddenly necessary again.

Maggie.

My replacement had given me the space, I now realised, to relax into becoming a different woman – a woman with a baby – while offering me a link to the person I had been before. I had a line into the office via her. Most women on maternity leave are shut out of that life completely – most barely know the person who takes their seat – but I had been given a window to peer through, if I wanted to.

Instead, I had fogged it with my hot, resentful breath and clouded up the panes, until all I could see was a smeared distortion of my own making. I had tallied up Maggie's achievements and set them against my own in the past year without realising we weren't doing the same job. I had had a baby; of course I wasn't writing the cover story.

The fact I had managed to hammer one out at the desk upstairs in the week after the accident had shown me that other person was still in there, just waiting to be given a dead-line. If only I'd had the confidence in myself to realise earlier that I could do that *and* keep a little person alive, perhaps I could have settled more happily into just doing the latter.

Although actually it was Maggie who'd kept Lila alive. Maggie and Winnie. The two women I'd been most scared of, most wounded by, most preoccupied with, during the months I should have spent cuddling with my baby. It's a cruel fact of maternity leave – and yes, of illness and grief, too – that the mind is most busy when the body is not.

When I knew that Lila was safe that night, the tears started falling uncontrollably. They rolled down my face like rain-drops to a sill, and when I looked up at Winnie, I saw them sparkling on her cheeks as she returned my gaze. A girl caught in a moment had freed two women stuck in one for decades. A boy whose life hadn't started would be remembered in the one that had been saved.

Standing now, in the bright slats of sunlight filtering through the shutters, I shook my head from the daydream and checked my reflection once more. I looked older than I used to in these clothes – more experienced, more approachable, homelier, and less taut. Perhaps it was because the tension of a lifetime had dissipated in those moments after Maggie had given us her permission to lie – it had been for Charles's sake, but for Winnie's mainly. Maggie had just understood.

Like she had so many things.

Once the ambulance arrived, its yellow-jacketed men and women immediately wanted to know what had happened.

'She was just coming down the stairs when we opened the front door,' I said smoothly, gesturing to the coat I was still wearing. 'My husband and I weren't supposed to be back for hours, but we bumped into some friends on the way to the pub and decided to make it a house party instead – I think she must have got a shock, and slipped . . .'

They looked around at us, Winnie and me, and through into the sitting room where peanuts were scattered across the sofa and the floor, and a large wine glass stood on the coffee table, empty.

Does it look like there was a struggle? Was there?

They rolled their eyes and addressed Maggie.

'One too many, was it?' one of them said.

'Something like that,' she agreed, then fainted.

She'd broken her leg, they told us before they left with her; quite badly from the looks of it, but nothing a cast couldn't fix. That and a concussion, a couple of bumps on the back of the head. The blood, though it looked ghoulish as it spread across the floorboards, was from a small gash on her temple, where her head had caught the edge of a stair.

'Who's coming with her then?' the female paramedic asked.

'Me,' I said immediately, leaving Winnie to look after Charles and Nick holding the baby.

He'd been holding her ever since. As I came downstairs, I looked in on them, taking care to place my feet solidly on each step. My stiff designer boots had slippy Italian leather soles.

'Lots on the agenda today?' I asked as I put my jacket on and checked that my handbag contained everything I would need. I felt another throb of anticipation.

'Always,' Nick said, smiling, his eyes crinkling just like Lila's did whenever she smiled. 'We've got rhyme time first thing, then a meeting at the park, and a high-pressure business lunch at the café by the duck pond.'

Nick had suggested he take some time off work the minute I got back through the door from the hospital with Maggie. I'd left her side only when Tim arrived on the ward, flustered and worried looking, telling me how grateful he was that we'd all been there. *If only you knew.*

I hoped she would tell him the truth. I knew how difficult it was to maintain a version of something you never stopped thinking about. I had thought about it less since I'd told Nick everything. There was none of the disappointment or judgment I had expected from him – only sympathy. He had held both my hands, kissed them, and apologised for not having listened, for not having been there.

He was the first person to tell me it wasn't really my fault.

Now I saw him with Lila, enjoying her every day the way I did – a pure and heart-squeezing enjoyment that was tinged with exhaustion and the frustrating monotony of hours spent with a young child – and I knew we understood each other better than we had done in years. We irritated each other too, but that was another thing that was okay.

I had last seen Winnie at Tim's flat on Saturday night, six weeks after the accident. Maggie was staying there, ostensibly to recuperate, but we knew she'd effectively moved in. I went round there when Tim arrived at our front door to watch the football with Nick, and the pair of us swapped over like sentries.

Winnie opened his door to me and scooped me into a hug, then ushered me down the hallway – full of bikes and the rarefied sporting equipment men like to own so much of – to the sitting room, where Maggie lay on the sofa, her plaster cast resting on a stack of cushions.

We had come to terms with one another in this room, the three of us – four if you counted Lila, who had patiently sat on the floor in the middle of us playing with her blocks, her skittles, her little eggs. We had reconciled and reminisced, revealed and remembered. Maggie had joked that the best thing for a broken leg was talking therapy, but as her bones knitted together again, so did the three of us. No secrets, no wonky alliances this time. No Helen: we had exorcised her.

I didn't know what my and Winnie's friendship held for us now. It would never be the same again – and so much the better for it.

'Have you two been having fun without me?' I said, taking in a scene that involved several open bags of crisps, some dips, a pot of tea, and Maggie's latest favourite TV drama paused on Tim's pride-and-joy flat-screen.

'We were just saying how we couldn't wait for you to arrive, actually,' Maggie said. 'You have brought the wine, haven't you?'

I held my carrier bag up in answer and brought over three glasses from the drinks cabinet against the wall.

'Oh – er, none for me,' Winnie said, and then blushed.

It had happened before that night at my house, she told us, but she hadn't known. Winnie had asked us all to meet that evening after visiting hours were over at the clinic where Charles was staying, where she had told him the news. That he had something to get better for now.

She said Charles was calmer these days. His admittance to Upworth Park, and his treatment there, was a condition of our all maintaining the fiction that would keep him out of prison. It had been a bargain thrashed out in the small hours of that night – the one I could hardly bear to think about – not only between me and Winnie, but between her and Charles. He needed proper help before they could start their little family again, she had told him, and he had, tearfully, agreed.

When we heard her news, Maggie, Winnie, and I held one another's gaze for a beat longer than necessary and let the joy and the relief well in our eyes momentarily as glossy, unshed tears. We understood one another so well these days it was almost like telepathy.

As I poured the wine into two glasses, a cosy silence settled. The two women who had defined so much of the past year for me would be at my side in the future too, although on what terms I didn't yet know.

Maggie would be a colleague, a great ally in the office and the sort I could always rely on for smiles and support. And Winnie would be . . . a new mother.

When I thought about how having Lila had changed me, I found I looked back on myself as though one life had stopped and another started up after the birth. The same person tread-ing a different story. I knew Winnie would go through some-thing similar: our friendship had changed so much already that I felt optimistic about who she might be at the end – and the beginning – of her own story. It was enough for both of us right now to wait and see.

'Tell Moff that I've had some really interesting thoughts on hospital gowns for my next column, will you?' Maggie said. She gesticulated with her glass in the same way our editor did when she got excited.

'She'll love that,' I said, smiling. 'Very glam.'

'Seriously though.' Maggie reached for the hummus. 'She'll be so glad to see you. She was good to me, but she's been really looking forward to having you back.' She held up her glass to me in a salute.

'Not that she'd ever tell you that,' Winnie teased, one eyebrow raised, and we laughed. We had laughed all night, in fact.

Now my phone buzzed, with a message from Maggie.

'Break a leg!' she'd written, and then – *typing* – a photo of her plaster cast.

I'd forgotten how good friendship could feel.

As Nick cleared the remnants of Lila's egg and toast away – from her high chair, off the table, off the floor, even off the wall – I picked her up for a cuddle and pushed my face into hers to nuzzle her cool, soft cheek. She rested her head against mine for a few seconds, one navy blue iris staring in close-up right into mine, and I felt the juddering of her jaw as she sucked on her thumb.

Then I handed her back to Nick and went through the hall-way towards the front door.

'You'll be great,' he said, and kissed me on the cheek. He was holding Lila so she could watch me as I fiddled with the latch. He raised her left hand and shook it in a wave.

'Good luck!' he called, and I laughed. I could feel the excitement in my stomach building to a giddiness.

'Bye, darling,' I called to my little girl. 'See you later!' I shouted to my husband as I stepped through the door.

My arms missed Lila's precious weight already, but as I walked through our gate and onto the pavement, I spread them wide and greeted the warm, slightly hazy morning rush-hour air like an old friend.

When I arrived in the world of glass plate and revolving doors a jittery forty minutes later, there was a new face at the desk in reception, one I didn't recognise. With dark curly hair and wary eyes, she asked me my details for a new security pass as though I'd only just started myself.

'My name is Margot Jones; I'm the fashion editor at *Haute* magazine and I had a baby last year,' I told her, holding up my phone to show her the picture of Lila on it, fuzzy haired in her yolk-yellow cardigan.

It buzzed in my hand as I did so and I turned it over to look at the screen. The message was from Winnie:

'Enjoy your first day back in the office!'

I already knew that I would.

Acknowledgments

To the many people who helped bring *The New Girl* into the world, thank you – but particularly to my brilliant agent, Laura Macdougall, who had faith from the beginning, and Kate Miciak, who gave me the chance to write a book – and then taught me how to do it. To Kara Welsh, Hilary Teeman, Denise Cronin, and everyone at Penguin Random House in New York for their hard work and long hours, and to Kim Atkins at Hodder in London. To Alex, for providing all the encouragement, endless patience, and childcare necessary to sit down and type. To Freda, for sleeping well and smiling so much. To my parents: earliest readers and number-one fans – you gave me all these words and they still aren't enough to tell you how important you are. To my sisters, for being excited. To Jo Samuel for the contacts. To Anna for the wisdom and the wisecracks; to Nicola for taking the time to improve me; and of course, to Hattie for being the best maternity cover and a wonderful friend – you gave me the space to enjoy my baby and the peace of mind to indulge my worst fears.

About the Author

Harriet Walker is fashion editor of *The Times*. She has been a broadsheet journalist for more than a decade, and has also written for *Vogue,* the *Financial Times,* and the *Guardian*. She studied English at Trinity College Cambridge and lives in South East London with her husband and daughter.